WORDS MADE FLESH

Anthony spun Dean around and bent him over the edge of the bar. Dean rested his elbows on the surface as the other man manipulated him from behind – shoving a knee between Dean's thighs, spreading his legs. Dean was exposed and vulnerable, every inch of his body unveiled to his friends. Then, Anthony grabbed Dean's arse and spread his chunky globes, revealing his honey-brown hole and the tuft of light-brown hair that surrounded it. Dean burned with humiliation and pleasure. 'Oh fuck,' he moaned.

'That's right,' Anthony said. 'You're going to get fucked right here. In front of all your friends. In front of your boyfriend, too.'

WORDS MADE FLESH

Thom Wolf

First published in Great Britain in 2000 by
Idol
20 Vauxhall Bridge Road
London
SW1V 2SA

ISBN 9780753541050

Typeset by SetSystems Ltd, Saffron Walden, Essex

The Random House Group Limited supports The Forest Stewardship
Council (FSC®), the leading international forest certification organisation.
Our books carrying the FSC label are printed on FSC® certified paper.
FSC is the only forest certification scheme endorsed by the leading
environmental organisations, including Greenpeace. Our
paper procurement policy can be found at
www.randomhouse.co.uk/environment

Printed and bound in Great Britain by Clays Ltd, St Ives PLC

For Liam
for his love, patience and support

SAFER SEX GUIDELINES

We include safer sex guidelines in every Idol book. However, while our policy is always to show safer sex in contemporary stories, we don't insist on safer sex practices in stories with historical settings – as this would be anachronistic. These books are sexual fantasies – in real life, everyone needs to think about safe sex.

While there have been major advances in the drug treatments for people with HIV and AIDS, there is still no cure for AIDS or a vaccine against HIV. Safe sex is still the only way of being sure of avoiding HIV sexually.

HIV can only be transmitted through blood, come and vaginal fluids (but no other body fluids) passing from one person (with HIV) into another person's bloodstream. It cannot get through healthy, undamaged skin. The only real risk of HIV is through anal sex without a condom – this accounts for almost all HIV transmissions between men.

Being safe

Even if you don't come inside someone, there is still a risk to both partners from blood (tiny cuts in the arse) and pre-come. Using strong condoms and water-based lubricant greatly reduces the risk of HIV. However, condoms can break or slip off, so:
* Make sure that condoms are stored away from hot or damp places.
* Check the expiry date – condoms have a limited life.
* Gently squeeze the air out of the tip.
* Check the condom is put on the right way up and unroll it down the erect cock.
* Use plenty of water-based lubricant (lube), up the arse and on the condom.
* While fucking, check occasionally to see the condom is still in one piece (you could also add more lube).

* When you withdraw, hold the condom tight to your cock as you pull out.
* Never re-use a condom or use the same condom with more than one person.
* If you're not used to condoms you might practise putting them on.
* Sex toys like dildos and plugs are safe. But if you're sharing them use a new condom each time or wash the toys well.

For the safest sex, make sure you use the strongest condoms, such as Durex Ultra Strong, Mates Super Strong, HT Specials and Rubberstuffers packs. Condoms are free in many STD (Sexually Transmitted Disease) clinics (sometimes called GUM clinics) and from many gay bars. It's also essential to use lots of water-based lube such as KY, Wet Stuff, Slik or Liquid Silk. Never use come as a lubricant.

Oral sex
Compared with fucking, sucking someone's cock is far safer. Swallowing come does not necessarily mean that HIV gets absorbed into the bloodstream. While a tiny fraction of cases of HIV infection have been linked to sucking, we know the risk is minimal. But certain factors increase the risk:
* Letting someone come in your mouth
* Throat infections such as gonorrhoea
* If you have cuts, sores or infections in your mouth and throat

So what is safe?
There are so many things you can do which are absolutely safe: wanking each other; rubbing your cocks against one another; kissing, sucking and licking all over the body; rimming – to name but a few.

If you're finding safe sex difficult, call a helpline or speak to someone you feel you can trust for support. The Terrence Higgins Trust Helpline, which is open from noon to 10pm every day, can be reached on 020 7242 1010.

Or, if you're in the United States, you can ring the Center for Disease Control toll free on 1 800 458 5231.

One

Chilling Out

Joe Hart wrenched the cork out of the neck of the wine bottle. The sound that it made was deep and full-blooded, like the slap of an open palm cracking down hard on a bare upturned arse. Joe's handsome brown face flushed red beneath his crisp tan. The effort it had taken to release the obstinate plug was clear in his features.

'Stubborn little bugger,' he exclaimed, untwisting the cork from the steel coil. He tossed it over his shoulder into the bin.

Glenn smiled at him. 'Just pour it, will you.'

The goblets that they were using were large. The entire volume of the bottle was shared evenly between the two generous glasses.

'We should really give it a chance to breathe,' Joe said, putting the empty bottle in the tiny basket beside the bed. He would take it to the recycling bin in the morning along with the other dozen or so empties down in the kitchen.

'Who cares?' said Glenn, accepting the brimming goblet from him. 'We're pissed already so what does it matter?' He raised the glass to his lips and drank deeply from it.

Glenn sat with one buttock perched on the edge of Joe's dressing table. The overhead lights were turned off and the effulgence of a dozen candles warmed the room with their soft yellow flames, casting long shadows of the two men on the green bedroom walls.

There was a distinct and underlying scent to the hippyish chamber. Glenn suspected that the odour was a blend of vanilla and marijuana. Maybe one fragrance burned to disguise the other.

Joe smiled quietly at him. The long look that they exchanged was a knowing one. He moved across to his stereo. The four enormous speakers dominated the corners of the room. Joe may have designed his bedroom to resemble a spiritual sanctum but his style of living was far from frugal. He enjoyed his comforts. Another month or so would see an expensive transformation of the bedroom decor. He had already grown tired of this image.

He waved his hand over a pile of compact discs. The collection had long since outgrown the capacity of his bedroom shelves. The overspill was stacked on the floor, where it continued to multiply and grow. The pile was dangerously out of control and threatened to topple over at any time.

'Any preferences?'

Glenn shook his head. 'Just keep it mellow. I'm not in the mood for anything too demanding.'

After a moment of contemplation Joe made his selection, grabbing a CD from the second shelf from the top. Glenn doubted that the discs were arranged in any particular order. Joe wasn't the kind of man to waste his time sorting CDs. He dropped his choice into the mouth of the CD player. The music was a compilation album of light trance tracks – the Aloof's 'One Night Stand' began to pump like lazy sex from the grade-A sound system.

Glenn approved of Joe's choice. The base of the track was hypnotic and seductive. Just listening to it turned him on. He took another long draught from his wine. He was already loose and heady and it didn't take long for the alcohol to affect him.

'I shouldn't really be drinking this on top of everything else tonight. I've had a skinful and I need to have a clear head in the morning.'

Joe knocked back half of his own drink. 'Don't spoil what little is left of tonight by worrying about tomorrow.'

Glenn didn't need much persuasion. In the soft light of the candles, Joe looked incredibly hot. He had a sexy look of dishevelment about him that was the result of a blinding night out. His short black hair, which he had styled so perfectly going out, was now a damp and unruly tangle. It clung in thick patches to his broad, sweat-soaked brow. His dark eyes shone brightly with alcohol and excitement. His expensive designer clothes were as disordered as the rest of him. The heavy silk shirt that he wore hung loosely on his body like a reject from a jumble sale. Half of the buttons were already undone and the shirt tails dangled lifelessly from the front of his black jeans. He looked a mess.

A lascivious, irresistible mess.

Glenn had a hard-on – it lay long and hot along the front of his pelvis, his snug shorts pressing it tight against his body. His crown was leaking and he could feel its dampness in his pubic hair.

'Fancy a spliff?' Joe asked.

Glenn considered it for a moment. He was tempted but shook his head. 'No. I don't think I should. Not on top of everything else tonight.'

Joe nodded. 'I suppose you're right. I wish I had your resolve.'

They both yawned simultaneously and then laughed. It had been a long night.

'It's been good, hasn't it?' said Joe.

'I've enjoyed myself.'

'So have I. And yet . . .' Joe's lips broke into a broad, infectious grin. 'It somehow feels incomplete. I can't think why.'

Glenn laughed at the clumsy hint. But what the hell! He was drunk enough and certainly horny enough to go for it. 'I can think of a good way to finish it off.'

'Yeah? What's that, then?'

Glenn put down his glass and gazed directly into Joe's dark eyes. 'Come here and I'll show you. You can start by giving me a kiss.'

Joe covered the distance between them in two effortless strides. Glenn opened his arms and wrapped them around Joe's back, drawing their two bodies tight together. Joe leaned into Glenn's receptive embrace and his lips closed over his mouth. There was a potent flavour to Joe's kiss: he tasted of smoke and alcohol and sex. The taste of his lips aroused Glenn further. He responded with a feverish passion, shoving his tongue in Joe's mouth and returning the urgency of his kisses. Their tongues pressed together and rolled around one another, moist and strong, exchanging a savoury flow of saliva between their compressed lips. They sucked and murmured and devoured.

Glenn closed his eyes. Like vodka drunk neat from the bottle, Joe's kisses were intoxicating. His head was spinning in a careless, sensual void. His whole world revolved around this one man and his kiss. Glenn was drifting. He was pissed. He knew it.

He parted his thighs, drawing Joe deeper into his open embrace. He wrapped his legs around Joe's waist and held him near. They were both breathing heavily. Glenn felt as though his cock was going to burst inside his jeans. It was almost painfully swollen and throbbed hard within the limitations of his pants. He would have reached down to readjust himself but his hands would not let go of Joe's body. He reached underneath the tails of Joe's shirt and tugged it halfway up his back. He clung to Joe's broad shoulders, savouring the rippling muscle beneath his fingers. He pressed his fingertips into the taut flesh.

Their lips separated, searching for new pleasures. Glenn pressed his face into Joe's neck and kissed his hot skin. The dense extracts of salt and sweat caused his lips to tingle. He licked the moisture from Joe's skin while he shivered at the touch of the man's lips on his own body, malleable and moist. Joe's warm kiss sent a delicious shudder down his spine.

Glenn wanted to feel Joe with every part of his body, to live him and breathe him. There was a hunger in his mouth, on his tongue, his hands, his cock, his arsehole. They were sweating profusely. The heat and slick of their two bodies made him burn even further. His breath was shallow and short, his need for air secondary to his desire for cock.

Glenn felt the hardness of Joe's dick pressing against his own. The organ was hard and resistant, throbbing conspicuously through the layers of clothing that separated them. They rubbed against each other, grinding their hips together. Glenn could feel the dampness in his pants as his cock enthusiastically oozed its sap. It was trapped against his skin, burning, aching for release. He wanted to burst.

Joe began to undress him. His fingers undid the buttons of his shirt slowly. There was no hurry. Nothing could deter them at this passionate stage. Best to savour and enjoy the moment. As the last button was undone, Glenn's shirt parted. Joe opened the curtain across his flesh, slowly parting the folds of material. He explored Glenn's chest with his hands, caressing the firm contours.

His body trembled at Joe's persistent touch. He caressed Glenn's flesh with open palms, examining his lean belly and smooth hairless chest. Glenn felt his inhibitions thaw; his body melted into warm liquid at Joe's touch. Willing hands stroked and lingered over his sleek golden skin.

Joe snatched a nipple between his thumb and index fingers and twisted the hard stub. The sensation was sharp and sudden. Glenn's breath hissed between clenched teeth. He leaned his body into Joe's grip as he squeezed and twisted his tit further. The pain was not really pain at all: the intense sensation sent a rush of pure ecstasy to Glenn's brain. His head was reeling.

Joe eased him off the edge of the dresser and they stood up, their arms still fixed around each other. Glenn pushed Joe's shirt over his shoulders and let it fall in a neglected heap to the floor. His nipple was red and swollen where Joe had been playing with it. Glenn closed his eyes and surrendered to the sensation as Joe bowed his head and covered his grand swollen nipple with his mouth. He bit down on the distended bud. Another rush of adrenalin went straight to Glenn's head and suddenly he was experiencing the pleasure with every part of his body: it tingled in his nipple, his cock, his arsehole. It was everywhere.

He threw his head to the ceiling and gasped. Joe's teeth were sharp and his mouth was hot and moist against the surrounding flesh of his tit. Glenn murmured. The booze and the music and the pleasure diffused through his mind with the cogent effect of a psychedelic drug. His whole universe was spinning in an intense vortex of heightened sensations.

He was losing it.

Glenn gazed down through half-lidded eyes as Joe sank to the floor and started to work on the fastening of his jeans. The heavy leather belt was undone in a second and deft fingers were at work on the buttons. Joe rived the fly apart and hitched down the front of his white shorts. Glenn's cock bounced against his stomach, finally free of its confinement. Joe curled his hand around the thick base.

Glenn saw that his glans was straining to escape from his stretched foreskin. Half of the head was visible – wet and shiny through the taut skin. A clear drop of seminal fluid glistened on its tiny open lips. Blood raged along its length, the thick veins protruding.

He felt the warm whisper of Joe's breath on his organ a second before his mouth enveloped the head. The moist void encompassed him. Hot, tight and wet. He slid deep into the recess of Joe's throat. Joe was an expert cocksucker and he devoured the full length without any difficulty. His jaw was stretched wide around the shaft and his cheeks bulged with its thickness.

Glenn exhaled slowly. His breath exited his throat in a low, significant groan.

Joe pushed Glenn's trousers down to his knees. With his free hand he took hold of Glenn's balls and rolled them lazily over in their sac, squeezing, caressing the juicy orbs of flesh. The skin of his scrotum was loose and his balls hung down low and heavy.

Joe moved his lips gradually along the length of his cock. Glenn felt the heat of Joe's mouth seeping through the finely veined skin of his organ. Time seemed to be unfolding in slow motion; each stroke of Joe's mouth on his cock seemed to last an eternity. The back of Joe's throat was tight as the blunt head probed deep inside its chasm.

Glenn guided Joe's head off the edge of his dick. A lazy trail of saliva was suspended like a thin silver bridge between his lover's chin and the tip of his cock. Joe looked up at him with wide eyes that questioned why he had stopped.

Glenn eased him to his feet.

'Let's go to bed,' he whispered.

Joe undressed himself quickly, while Glenn stamped off his shoes and pulled his half-mast jeans down the remainder of the way. He lay down on the bed and waited for Joe to get naked.

In keeping with the eclectic style of the room, the bed was a Japanese futon rolled out on the floor. Glenn lay on his back and looked up as Joe struggled out of his clothes.

His body was long and lean, defined by lengthy, athletic muscle on his limbs and stomach. His skin was coloured a rich brown –

the shading would have been all-inclusive if it wasn't for the band of smooth white flesh beneath his waist, which had been shielded from the summer sun by his brief trunks. He had a fine dusting of dark hair over his chest and stomach. The hair grew thicker as it descended lower; it branched outwards into a concentrated bush around his long cock. His erection stood out rigid from his body like a long medieval lance. The skin of his scrotum and cock was a darker shade than that of the rest of his body. Viewed from below, with its dense surround of hair, his ball sac resembled a swollen black purse.

Joe lay down next to Glenn and they pressed their naked bodies tight against one another. Joe's skin was hot against Glenn's own and they slid easily against each other with the fine slick of sweat that saturated both of their torsos. They kissed again. Glenn wrapped his body around Joe like a bone-crushing reptile. He enfolded his arms and legs about Joe's long body and gripped him tight.

Both of their bellies were wet with the sticky produce of their cocks. Glenn oozed a copious volume of pre-come from the tip of his dick. His foreskin slipped back and forth easily with its natural lubrication. His sensitive glans rubbed against Joe's stomach, his fine body hair matted with its juice. They rolled over and over, back and forth across the surface of the futon. Fumbling, grasping, caressing. Their hands were never still: exploring crevices of flesh, muscle, arse and cock. Glenn slid his fingers into the cleft of Joe's buttocks and slowly fingered his hole. The precious bud shuddered beneath his gentle touch.

The two men were both familiar with one another. Each knew the secrets of the other's body intimately and yet they acted like strangers. Discovering the mystery of each other's flesh for the very first time. Glenn held Joe's buttocks in his hands, squeezed them and parted them as if their beauty and texture were all new.

He kissed his lips with all the hunger and urgent passion of a one-night stand. It was like the first time and the last time that they would ever be together in this intimate way. He wanted to experience all that Joe had to offer him and carry the memory and the fantasy with him forever.

They rolled over so that they were head to toe and their faces were in line with each other's cock. Glenn lay on his back while Joe stretched out above him on his hands and knees. He reached for Joe's cock with his lips and let it coast into his mouth. The organ was long and thin, but its glans was massive. Glenn extended his jaw to take its full girth inside. The cock head was wet and sticky. He licked the salty dew from its source. Joe throbbed even harder as he tenderly explored the tiny lips with his tongue. The cock continued to pulsate and weep its gooey fluid as Glenn worked it with his mouth.

He stretched the foreskin back with his lips, guiding it into place behind the crescent ridge. He rolled his tongue around the smooth surface of his head. As Joe murmured a soft sigh of pleasure, Glenn concentrated on the sensitive underside of his cock, gently flicking the thick seam with his tongue. The shaft thickened with each stroke.

Glenn's own cock was once again enveloped by the moist caress of Joe's mouth. Joe went all the way down until his nose was pressed into the folds of Glenn's ball sac.

Glenn wanted to cry out in his pleasure but no sound could escape his stuffed mouth. Joe's own testicles rested heavily on his nose, the sac hanging loose either side of his face. He inhaled the manly essence of ball sweat.

Joe's cock slid out of his mouth and Glenn slipped his tongue further back. Joe's body shuddered above him as he followed the seam of skin with his tongue, tracing a wet path along the sensitive passage behind his balls. He licked the concentration of salt from his skin, working his way further back.

He grasped his arse in both hands and spread his buttocks wide, opening up the crack. There was a delicate dusting of dark hair in the cleft between his firm cheeks. In the centre, surrounded by a moist cluster of black curls, his arsehole was small and tightly drawn. The puckered flesh was a warm honey-brown hue, surrounded by a lighter tone of golden skin. Glenn raised his head from the bed and buried his face in the crevice of flesh. He worked gradually into the crack, deliberately holding back and avoiding the hole until the end. He skimmed all around its circumference, deliberately teasing his lover, tasting the most intimate zone of his body. He circled the tight opening languidly with the tip of his tongue, growing a fraction closer to the jewel with every passing.

Joe was sucking on his cock with an even greater devotion. He drew the organ to the depths of his throat and manipulated the root with his hands. Glenn moved his hips slowly up and down, fucking Joe's face at a leisurely pace.

He pressed the tip of his tongue to Joe's arsehole. The orifice quivered at his wet velvet touch. He held Joe's arse with both hands and closed his entire mouth over the hole. He slid his tongue inside. The sphincter melted like warm chocolate and allowed him to penetrate.

Joe had reached a peak of excitement. He bowed his head on Glenn's cock with increased fever and ground his arse back into his face. Glenn shoved his tongue up into his rectum as far as he could. The flesh fluctuated around him, gripping his tongue as if it was a cock.

He felt the final jolt of Joe's body and then the liquid warmth of his orgasm as it spread out in a sputtering pool across his chest. His come spurted across Glenn's skin in thick, pulsating waves. Glenn thrust his hips up from the bed. He had been holding back on his own climax and now was the time to let go. He followed his senses to the highest peak and when he at last reached that height, he hurled himself over the edge.

Ecstasy flooded his body and his orgasm was one long, drawn-out rapture. It burst from the hot depths of his balls and flooded Joe's throat with a torrent of thick, salty spunk. His body trembled and he clung to the man above him for support. It was a long, spurting, free-falling descent. One prolonged burst followed another until, at last, the intensity began to subside.

They did not speak for a long time afterwards. Joe rolled around so that he was face to face with Glenn and they lay together in voiceless contentment. Joe gently ran his fingers through Glenn's soft brown hair and massaged his damp scalp. Glenn's cock lay against his belly. It had softened to a flaccid state but continued to leak clear fluid long after his orgasm had subsided. A small pool had formed in the cleft of his navel.

The CD came to the end of its play and two of the candles had flickered and died.

Glenn glanced at the clock on the wall and then compared it with the time on his watch. It was very late. He turned and placed a quiet kiss on Joe's clammy brow.

'I should really go home now.'

Joe caressed his arse. 'No. Don't go. Stay with me.'

'I'd like to, but I'd better not. I've got an early start in the morning and I need to leave from home.'

Joe sighed. 'OK, then. Just use me and leave me.'

Glenn kissed his lips. 'Never.'

He swung his legs over the edge of the bed and stretched. His clothes were strewn all over the floor. He reached up for the half-empty wineglass on the dresser and downed what was left. He stood up.

Joe wolf whistled. 'You get an amazing view from down here on the floor.'

'Yeah, but you've seen it all before.'

Glenn walked down to the bathroom at the end of the landing. His eyes reacted badly when he switched on the harsh overhead light. He shielded his gaze with his hand until he became accustomed to the bright glare. He glanced at his dishevelled reflection in the mirror.

Urgh. Can't deal with that at this time of night!

He filled the sink with warm water and slowly washed his face and cock. He cleaned away the sticky patch of dried come from his stomach, his fingers lingering over his flesh, and then splashed water over his hair and flattened it back down into place.

Now things didn't look so bad.

When he returned to the bedroom, Joe had pulled on a pair of boxer shorts and was sitting on the futon rolling a joint.

'I've called you a taxi. It should be here in about fifteen minutes.'

'Thank you. Can I pinch a squirt of deodorant? I stink.'

'Help yourself, smelly. It's over there.'

Joe's eyes followed him as he sprayed his underarms and started to retrieve his clothes from the floor. Glenn preferred roll-ons.

'So what's the great urgency in the morning? I thought you were your own boss. Got up when you wanted to, did as much work as you wanted to.'

'I wish. My time's not my own at the minute.' Glenn had found his socks and underpants and put them on. He hunted round for his jeans next.

Joe sealed the skin of the joint and reached across the dresser for his lighter. He sat on the bed with an ashtray rested between his crossed legs and lit the spliff. He brought it to his lips and inhaled slowly, holding the smoke deep in his lungs. He exhaled with a long subdued sigh.

Glenn fastened his jeans and put on his shirt. It hung loose over his chest, the buttons still undone. He reached down and took the joint from Joe's hand, drawing deeply on it himself. He passed it back.

'I thought you didn't want any.'

'I don't. My problem is that, when something's put out in front of me, I can't say no. All my good intentions go to the wind. You're a bad influence.'

'Yeah, right.' Joe inhaled once more. 'So what's happening tomorrow, then? Anything interesting?'

'Possibly. I'm being interviewed for a magazine. I have to meet the reporter in Durham at eleven o'clock. I don't want to roll straight out of bed and hurry there looking like shit.'

Joe raised an interested eyebrow. 'What's it for?'

There was a slight hesitation before Glenn answered. '*GAYZ.*'

Joe threw back his head and snorted. 'That sad rag. What the hell for?'

Glenn shrugged and continued to dress. Despite trying to raise an ounce of enthusiasm within himself, he shared his friend's view of the magazine. It was a derivative, sensationalist publication. He avoided reading it. 'My publishers arranged it. I have the interview tomorrow and then they take photos on Wednesday. They're gonna put me on the cover.'

'All the more reason not to do it. You don't want your face splashed all over the front of that crap. You'll never be able to live it down.'

Glenn grimaced. 'I'll get over it. Besides the photographer's pretty cool. I'm looking forward to meeting him. It gets worse, though. Next month I have to go to London to do more interviews and signings and then there's a tour.'

'What a strange little life it is that you lead, Mr Holden!'

'Yeah. Not through personal choice, I can tell you.'

Glenn was fully dressed. He checked his appearance in the full-length wardrobe mirror and smoothed out some of the creases from his clothes. He looked rough, but not yet a member of the walking dead.

'I'll wait outside for the taxi. It shouldn't be too long now.'

Joe blew a lethargic cloud of smoke up to the ceiling. 'I'll give you a ring later in the week to see how it goes with *GAYZ*.'

'Are you going to the party at Dean and Gary's on Saturday?'

Joe nodded. 'I thought I'd turn up later on.'

'All right, then. I'll see you there.'

Joe wished him luck for the interview in the morning and, after kissing goodnight, Glenn let himself out of the house.

Outside on the street, the night was quiet. The dark sky was clear and there was an inert chill to the air. A thin wraith of mist twisted its way along the empty pavement.

Glenn gratefully inhaled the clean breeze.

His relationship with Joe was not a conventional one: neither of them considered themselves to be lovers. They slept with each other regularly but they were not partners or boyfriends. Just friends.

'We're mates who fuck each other,' Joe would often say after too much to drink. 'In America we would be called fuck-buddies!'

They had been friends for years, ever since Glenn first discovered the local gay scene. They had both had other partners in their time together and, if ever those relationships became serious, they stopped sleeping with each other for that period. But as neither of them had formed any lasting dependency on other men, they always ended up back in each other's bed. They were happy with things the way that they were.

The sex was always good, fresh; it remained exciting in a way that none of Glenn's personal relationships ever had.

'We'll end up two lonely old men with nobody else but each other,' Joe had once commented as they concluded another evening in bed together.

Neither of them was overly concerned.

The taxi arrived after a couple of minutes. Glenn was enjoying the purity and solitude of the night. He enjoyed being on his own and hadn't noticed the passing time.

The driver was pleasant enough. He smiled as Glenn climbed into the passenger seat beside him. He was called James and was somewhere in his late thirties. He was listening to some awful cassette of mid-eighties soft rock. Glenn hated the taste in music but decided that if the circumstances were right, in another place and time, he would fuck James given the chance. He asked James to turn down the volume.

James was uncertain of the destination Joe had given him on the phone and needed further directions. Glenn set him straight.

'Where have you been to tonight then?' the driver asked once he knew where he was going.

'Just out in the town centre. We went to a couple of bars and then on to Idols for a couple of hours.'

Idols was a cheap nightclub that was very popular with students midweek. Both in their late twenties, Glenn and Joe had felt over the hill among the crowd of teenagers, though it had not spoiled their enjoyment. The decor of the club was basic, with bare wood-boards on the floor. And there were no draught drinks, only bottles. It was the best club in the area without travelling to Newcastle or Middlesbrough.

'Did you have a good time?'

'Yeah.' Glenn smiled. 'We did.'

He was tired and not in the right frame of mind for vacuous chitchat – it was too much effort.

The interview the next morning was playing on his mind. He had encountered the interviewer, Freddie Brooks, before. The two of them hated each other on sight. Brooks was shrewd and underhand: if he did not get the story that he wanted, he would type up his own version anyway. Glenn did not relish the prospect of meeting him on what was now shaping up to be less than six hours' sleep.

The taxi ride was blessedly short and it was not long before the car pulled up in front of Glenn's three-bedroom house. He lived on a small estate of predominantly new property. All of the houses were detached and ranged from two- to five-bedroom properties.

He stepped out of the taxi and paid the driver in cash. Once more he was thankful to breathe in the untarnished night air. He inhaled the cool breeze and held it deep in his lungs. The estate was quiet. Only a handful of lights burned in the houses around him. He turned towards his own house, shrouded in darkness.

He noticed the man standing across the road from him. The distance between them and the consistency of the night made it impossible for him to clearly make out the features of the stranger. He stood on the corner, in the shadows of the wall.

He was staring directly across at Glenn as though he had been waiting for him.

Glenn squinted in the darkness, trying to make out the man's face.

He looked to be somewhere in his twenties. He was dark with closely cropped hair. He was of medium height with a broad-shouldered, stocky build.

Glenn should have been afraid, but he was not.

There was a vague familiarity about the man. Glenn was sure from the way that he stared that he must know who he was, and yet he could not place the stranger's shadowy face. Was he a friend or a half-forgotten lover?

They looked across at each other for what seemed like minutes. Neither spoke, neither approached. Eventually the man turned away and walked slowly down the road. Glenn stared after him, following the sight of his broad shoulders until he reached the end of the street and turned away out of sight.

The behaviour was out of place. What had he been doing just waiting around on the street in the middle of the night? Glenn was too tired to surmise.

He turned up the drive and let himself into the house, locking the door securely behind him.

Two

Bad Vibes

The morning dawned more quickly than Glenn had anticipated. He had slept through the eight o'clock alarm. It was no surprise to wake up with a bad head.

He lay in bed with his eyes closed, reluctant to move. His head was in a very fragile state and his muscles ached from too much dancing the night before. He was also tired. Dead tired.

Why had he inflicted this upon himself?

He wanted to drag the covers back over his head and withdraw into unconsciousness. He would sleep until midday at the earliest and consider getting out of bed for the afternoon. *Bloody Joe.* He always ended up hung over and deprived of sleep following one of their nights out.

His bladder was also torturously full and causing him even greater agony – he would never be able to sleep through the discomfort.

He forced apart one hesitant eye. It took him a moment to focus on the clock at the side of his bed. The insistent hands swam slowly into view. He opened both eyes and stared in disbelief, his memory returning to deliver a sobering slap across the face.

Oh shit. Not today of all days.

He pushed the bed covers back from his naked body and hauled himself over the edge into a sitting position. He tried to ignore the pain that pierced his skull when he tried to stand up. He struggled into the dressing gown that hung on the back of the door.

He had less than an hour to get dressed and make his way into the centre of Durham for his meeting with that execrable reporter. Freddie Brooks would rip him to pieces and spit out the unwanted bones.

You bastard, Joe. Why did you let me drink so much last night?

He went downstairs and switched off the burglar alarm. He collected a mammoth pile of post from the doormat and deposited it unopened on the kitchen table. It could all wait. He ran the cold tap and drank down a full pint of icy water. It sloshed uncomfortably on his delicate stomach. After filling the kettle, he switched it on to boil and ran back upstairs to the bathroom.

He stepped under the scorching rain of the shower head, flinching at the temperature. He liked to have a bath in the morning, to ease himself into the day at a moderate pace. Showering was too hurried, too unsatisfying. He quickly lathered up his body and rinsed off the soap. There was no time to wash his hair, though he could smell its heavy odour of stale sweat and cigarettes. After towelling himself dry and shaving off the craggy growth of stubble, he began to feel human, at least in some small part. His mind had yet to start functioning on a rational plain.

Freddie Brooks wasn't all that scary.

If he reassured himself enough, he might just start to believe it.

Glenn always got nervous when he had to do interviews. He hated them. Four years ago this kind of publicity had been unheard of for him. All he had to do was write his books, sign a few copies and then research and write the next. They sold reasonably well and he didn't have to worry about the mortgage too much. Now he had to take part in the whole grotesque media circus.

The publication of a new novel by Glenn Holden was now considered to be an 'event'.

And it was all starting up again. He was powerless to do anything other than play the game. To do as they told him and play his part in the freak show. His agent threw a bone and, like a puppy on the beach, he obediently performed tricks.

Doing tricks for men like Freddie Brooks was the lowest point of all from which to launch the day.

He went back through to the bedroom and began to dress.

Though he would never admit it, the way that Glenn looked was a major basis for the media interest in him. He was clean-cut, healthy and handsome, though he would never be so vain as to acknowledge it. The gay press loved his lean, athletic looks and were ever willing to publish his pictures.

At twenty-nine years of age, not far off thirty, he looked at least five years younger. He had the kind of juvenile, angular features that the papers were keen to label as pretty or boyish. Glenn did not feel young – in fact he felt every one of his years, though he was constantly mistaken for someone younger: early twenties. Practically a boy. He was not that tall either: at five foot eight his build was lean and proportionate. The short, close-crop cut of his light-brown hair did little to embellish his appearance with age.

His wide eyes were pure blue and it was only there, in the moody depths, that his maturity could be discerned.

He dressed for the interview in a casually cut, soft black suit and a baggy white shirt that he wore loosely opened. He didn't want to power-dress or appear too casual, but he had to give Brooks the message that he was no pushover. The thick sole and heels of the shoes he pulled on gave the illusion of extra height. The image was the best he could come up with in so short a time.

He browsed through his mail as he downed a quick cup of coffee. There was a letter from his agent outlining the publicity work he would be doing in London the next month. There were also a couple of fan letters. The remainder of the pile was just junk and bills. The former he deposited in the bin and the latter he left out on the table to be dealt with when he returned.

He was beginning to feel nervous.

Damn you, Freddie. I refuse to let you intimidate me this time. You sly bastard!

He called for a taxi and then hurried upstairs to clean his teeth and gargle with mouthwash.

His friends, and the few serious boyfriends that he had had over the years, were constantly berating him for his inability to drive. He spent an absolute fortune on taxi, train and bus fares and was consequently late for every appointment because of his reliance on them. But Glenn didn't want to drive. He had no interest in cars.

17

He hated them. He lacked any motivation to get behind the wheel of a vehicle and master it. He liked to sit back as a passenger and watch.

He checked his appearance one last time in the bathroom mirror. He didn't look too bad considering the excesses of the night before and his lack of sleep.

Was that a trace of fear lingering in his eyes?

No. Of course not. I'm not scared. Don't be stupid.

Do your worst, Freddie. See if I give a shit!

The horn of the taxi blared outside on the drive. Glenn quickly set the alarm and locked up the house. He got into the front of the car beside the driver and gave directions to his destination in Durham. He wasn't as good-looking as James from last night. This one was definitely not worth a shag.

Glenn yawned. Tiredness or nerves?

Pull yourself together.

As the car pulled out of the street he noticed a figure standing on the corner. He was a good-looking, beefy hunk, horny enough to turn most men's heads and gain gazes of approval. Glenn craned his neck to see him again. Was it the same man as last night? The one who had watched him from the shadows when he got home? He was standing with his back against the wall. He looked directly into the window of the car as it passed by him. He looked straight at Glenn.

He was gorgeous. Despite its short cut, his dark hair was unruly and tousled, as though he had just jumped out of bed. He had long, dark eyelashes and clear shiny eyes. His skin was lucid and coloured a gentle gold from the touch of the sun. There was a couples of days' worth of stubble on his strong chin.

There was definitely something familiar about this guy. Glenn was sure that he knew who he was. He turned in his seat to get a better look but the car rounded the corner and the man was lost from sight.

Curious, Glenn sat back in his seat. Who was he? A new resident on the estate? Someone he had seen around town, maybe, in Durham?

The roads were joyously quiet. In good traffic the ride from his house to the centre of Durham could be done in less than fifteen minutes. He looked down at his watch. Someone up above was smiling on him: he wasn't going to be late after all. He looked skywards and nodded gratefully.

When the driver dropped him off it was only a short walk across the bridge to the bistro where he had arranged to meet the reporter. The rendezvous was to be in a waterfront café that had the best view of the river and the town itself. Only a handful of tables were occupied; it was early and the lunchtime rush had yet to begin. The manager welcomed Glenn affectionately at the door. He was a regular customer and they knew each other well.

'Good morning, Glenn. Would you like a table?'

Glenn smiled. 'That's all right, Dave. I'm meeting someone. I can see that he's already here.'

Freddie Brooks did not look up when Glenn approached his table. His head was bowed in ignorance over his broad newspaper. Though Glenn would have liked to give him the benefit of the doubt and assume that the man had not realised he had arrived, he knew him well enough to be sure that Brooks was ignoring him deliberately.

'Hello, Freddie,' Glenn said, making a real effort to force some civility into his voice. 'I hope I'm not too late.'

The journalist looked up but he did not smile. 'I've been here a little while but it doesn't matter.' He waved at the chair opposite him. Glenn pulled it out and sat down. 'Forgive the informality of my dress: I usually make an effort, but I couldn't face that three-hour train journey in a three-piece suit.'

He was dressed in faded blue jeans and a jade-green shirt. It had occurred to Glenn the last time that they had met that Brooks would be so much more appealing if he ever bothered to smile. He was not unattractive. He had short auburn hair and flawlessly clear skin, yet his grey eyes were permanently cold and the corners of his mouth were down turned in an abiding sneer. His whole attitude was one of aloof detachment, but behind his cool façade his icy mind did not miss the slightest trick.

Dave came over to the table with the menu. 'Would you like to order any drinks? Coffee? Tea? Wine?'

Glenn would have killed for a glass of wine but he did not dare to order it. The last time that Brooks had interviewed him, he had

19

ordered a bottle of house white, to calm his nerves and loosen his tongue. His inhibitions were loosened too far and he ended up revealing things about himself that he would rather were kept secret. Freddie printed every intimate word, along with his personal analysis of Glenn as a sad alcoholic.

He wasn't going to make that mistake again.

'Just bring me a cappuccino, please, Dave.'

'I'll have another iced tea,' the reporter stated inertly. 'I'm surprised at you passing up on alcohol. Are you on the wagon right now?'

Glenn ignored the catty remark. He took off his jacket and hung it over the back of his chair. 'So how are you, Freddie?' His smile was fixed back in place. 'I haven't seen you for a while.'

'Fine. Can we get right on with this? I want to get back to London at a decent time this afternoon. If we hurry I can catch a train after lunch.'

'And bash your feature out on the way.'

'Exactly.'

At least they could get this over with quickly. 'Come on, then, you're the interviewer. What do you want to ask me?'

The little man took a small tape recorder and a narrow black notepad out of his black leather briefcase. He switched on the machine and consulted the prepared questions in his book.

'Let's get the plugs over and done with first,' Brooks said with a cold air of superiority. 'Tell me about your new book and when it's coming out.'

'Haven't you read it? I would have thought my publishers would have sent you a free copy.'

'They did but I haven't had time to read it. It's not really my cup of tea. Why don't you fill me in? Sell it to me.'

Great, thought Glenn: he's going to trash my book without even reading it. He took a deep breath. This was going to be just as hard as he had expected. 'It's called *Henry's Sorrow* and it's about a married man who's raped in his own home and has to watch as his wife is murdered in front of him. This happens in the opening chapter and the rest of the book deals with how he puts his life back together after such an atrocious experience.'

'Very sensationalist stuff. Some might say vulgar or tasteless.'

'I'm sure that some people will say that. I'm not interested in political correctness. I write about things that interest me.'

'Male rape and misogyny?'

'Yes,' Glenn said slowly, refusing to bite back, 'if they are handled sensitively. I'm interested in the human spirit and its ability to hold up and survive under the hardest conditions.'

'Rape and murder sells a lot of books.'

'If that's what people want to read about then that's what they'll buy.'

'You've sold a lot of books.'

'Yes, I have.' This was all a lot harder than Glenn had anticipated. He had not expected Brooks to go in so directly for the kill.

The reporter consulted his notebook. 'Before you wrote *Everyday Hurts*, which I think I'm right in saying was your first bestseller, which was then made into a glossy Hollywood film, and which then turned you into a *name* author, you wrote a couple of small-selling gay novels.'

'Yes, that's right. I did.' And I know exactly what's coming next, thought Glenn.

'Have you sold out your gay audience for the sake of mainstream success?'

Predictable as always. Come on, then, Glenn, stock replies for stock questions.

'No. I only remain true to myself and what I want to write. Besides, unless you have been reading a different book to the one I wrote, *Everyday Hurts* is very definitely a gay book. That is if you did read it.'

'But all of the homosexuality was toned down considerably in the film.'

'I had no input into that film. It was my book but not my movie. I'm a novelist, not a screenwriter or a director.'

Brooks paused for a moment to sip his icy tea and study the notes written in a minute hand before him. 'So,' he said after a careful silence, 'are you working on a new book now?'

Glenn relaxed back a little in his chair. It was a standard question, easy to deal with; he had a formulaic reply already prepared.

'Yes, I am. I haven't got very far, though. It's at an early stage, just research and planning at the minute. I have a few ideas to develop.'

'And can you let on what it's all about?'

Glenn hesitated before answering, wondering if it was wise to reveal too much. Brooks detected the pause and pressed him for an answer.

'It's actually a sequel. To *Everyday Hurts*.'

Brooks's eyes widened. 'Oh, how very lucrative. Guaranteed book sales, worldwide rights, Hollywood fighting over the screen rights. Very clever of you. It's quite a little gold mine.'

Glenn bit his tongue. 'I'm only telling a story. I'm not a businessman.'

'You're very defensive.'

Glenn forced a smile. 'You're very aggressive.'

'I am only saying that you appear to have deserted your gay readership in favour of bestselling success and that you no doubt have an eye on the sale of the film rights for all of your forthcoming books.'

It was hard for Glenn to keep the rising tone of anger out of his voice. 'I'm a gay man and I write for myself, so it's ridiculous for you to say that I don't write for a gay audience. Besides, you haven't done your research all that well. I published a volume of gay erotica last year, under a pen name, before I started work on my new book.'

Brooks was unfazed. 'Why a pen name? Why not Glenn Holden?'

'To dissociate the two genres. Most erotic authors write under a pen name.'

'It also avoids upsetting your straight readership, doesn't it?'

There was no point even arguing about any of this. Brooks was going to be proven right and have the final word whatever happened. A young waitress came over with their order. Glenn regarded the cappuccino with disdain. He wished now that he had opted for something stronger.

To think that he had passed up spending the night at Joe's for this. He could still have been there now, seeing in the day with great, satisfying sex. But no, he was here with this tight-arsed reporter.

'What does being a gay man mean to you?'

'I don't know, Freddie. I've never really thought about it. There really is no answer to a question like that as far as I'm concerned. I'm just a man.' The interview was way too aggressive but Glenn could think of no way to soothe the troubled waters between them. He wanted to relax but Brooks had him constantly on the defensive.

'Are you in a relationship right now?'

'No. I have a lot of good friends but there's no one special in my life right now.'

'Are you looking?'

'Not really.' Glenn paused for a minute. He wanted to think about some of his answers rather than just bark out one defensive reply after another. 'When I was younger, in my late teens and early twenties, I always had to have a boyfriend. I used to hate being on my own. I suppose that doesn't bother me so much any more. If I meet somebody, then great, but if I don't it won't be the end of the world.'

'Don't you worry about being old and all alone?'

'I think I have a few years left before I need to start worrying about that.'

A man came into the bistro and sat down a couple of tables back from Brooks. He was tall and well built, somewhere in his thirties. His eyes made contact with Glenn as he sat down and the two of them smiled at one another. Glenn felt a flush of blood to his face and a hardening in his pants. It was one of those casual opportunities that arose between strangers, a knowing look that overflowed with unspoken promises and carnal possibilities. If he hadn't been encumbered by Brooks Glenn would have exploited the situation to the full. He smiled once more before turning his eyes away from the stranger and focusing all of his attention back on to the interview.

Brooks was unrelenting.

'When did you first have sex?'

Shall I answer that or not?

'Sixteen.'

'Do you ever go cottaging?'

23

Glenn sighed. 'I thought this was a reputable magazine that you worked for, Freddie, not a trashy tabloid.'

'The question is relevant to my readers. Are you going to answer it?'

'No. I don't go cottaging.'

'Do you condemn the practice?'

'Of course I don't. It's a fact of life. It's just not something I enjoy. I think it's too clandestine, too secretive and hurried. I like time to enjoy sex properly, which means more than a quick wank or a blow job.'

Is that answer vulgar enough for you, you jumped up little twit?

The reporter regarded Glenn disdainfully over the edge of his nose. Glenn just wanted the ordeal to be over. He wanted a drink and he wanted to sit with the man two tables down, rather than the tight-arsed freak in front of him. He didn't want to reveal and reduce his personal life to this sordid level.

'I have heard a rather frequent rumour about you,' Brooks said coldly. 'It's something of a legend. I wonder if you would care to discuss it with me.'

'What's that, then?' asked Glenn carefully.

'That you were once so off your head on ecstasy that you sucked off four men in the toilets of a Newcastle nightclub in full view of the other punters.'

'*What!*'

'Is it true?'

'Who told you that?'

'It's common knowledge. But I heard it from someone who claims to have been there. An eyewitness. He said that you would have gone a lot further, too, but the bouncers threw you out.'

The man two tables down had obviously overheard the conversation. He stared down at the menu before him, red-faced and unable to look up.

Glenn was embarrassed. 'I . . . er, I.'

Brooks was gloating. 'So you don't deny it, then?'

'Yes, er, no. It . . . it wasn't how it sounds. You haven't got all of your facts right.'

'Not really intimate sex, is it? Or perhaps you were more interested in quantity rather than quality in those days.'

Glenn's embarrassment had turned to anger. 'Just be careful how you word that when you write it up, you talentless little hack. I'm neither confirming nor denying anything you say.'

Brooks switched off the tape recorder and placed it back in his case along with his notebook. 'I think we can finish it there. I've got enough material to work on and I don't want to miss my train.' He fished in his black leather wallet and pulled out a twenty-pound note. He dropped it casually on to the table. 'That should be enough to cover the bill. You can keep the change. You never know: there may even be enough left over for you to buy an E.'

He stalked triumphantly out of the bistro without saying goodbye.

Glenn was fuming. He pushed away the still full cappuccino and ordered a large vodka from the waitress. He had expected this to be bad, but it was far worse than he had ever anticipated. The interview had been nothing more than a formality for Brooks. He already knew precisely what he was going to cover in the article. It was more likely that the interview had already been written and would now only need a handful of slight adjustments and a couple of quotes thrown into it.

Bastard!

Glenn felt sick. He had been cheated, manipulated into looking sordid and cheap.

He glanced at the stranger two tables down.

He was no longer there. He had left without ordering. No doubt disgusted by what he had heard. Glenn could not blame him. The conversation had been tacky and degrading.

The vodka burned his throat as he knocked it back in one deep gulp. It set his stomach aflame and the warmth quickly rose up to his head. He sighed. At least it was over. Freddie Brooks was on his way back to London and Glenn would never consent to an interview with him again.

He looked at his watch.

The day was still young and he was determined that it would not be a complete waste. There was a lot more he wanted to fit in before it was over.

25

Three

Steam

The sauna had seen a steady influx of men, coming but not going, over the course of a long afternoon. By the time six o'clock came around and the hours of the working day were over, there was suddenly an even greater surge of paying customers, looking for a little out-of-hours stress reduction.

Glenn made his way down to the sauna at around six thirty, following a heavy ninety-minute session in the gym. His interview that morning with Freddie Brooks had left an uneasy ache in the pit of his stomach and an internal frenzy of aggression. He had to get the stress out of his system somehow. He had pounded the circuit of the gym, kicking, punching, thrashing and straining until the anger inside him eventually found a release. Afterwards, he was both exhilarated and drained.

Now, as he opened the double doors to the basement sauna and entered the humid maze of tiled rooms and billowing steam, his senses were immediately assailed by the no-holds-barred scent of masculine sex. The white walls and intimate inlays oozed with the aura of muscle, sweat and Eros.

Glenn was naked but for a narrow white towel wrapped around his tiny waist. His body was brimming with energy, the muscle glowing after being pushed to such physical extremes upstairs.

26

As he entered the sauna, immediately to the left was a row of marble-topped sinks and directly opposite that, on the other wall, a row of open shower cubicles. There were two men standing under the faucets, letting the water cascade over their hard bodies. A handful of other guys hung around on the low ceramic ledges next to the sinks, eyeing each other up appreciatively and making no attempt to conceal their half-stiff cocks. Every set of eyes instinctively looked up as Glenn entered, checking out his lean physique with undisguised approval. Glenn nodded to a couple of the men, returning their flirtatious glances.

He turned towards the showers. His body was hot and wet with sweat. He threw his towel down on to the floor and stepped beneath the cascading water, which was blessedly cool. Though not yet aroused, his own cock hung forward from his body, half hard with the excitement of anticipation. He ducked his head beneath the cool spray and allowed the refreshingly sharp needles to rain down on his tired body.

The boy in the shower to the left of him was putting on a shameless exhibition for the benefit of the guys on the ledge. He stood with his feet wide apart and spread his arse, pressing his fingers deep into the crack. He massaged soap deep into the crevice. Glenn glanced at the boy's cock. It was standing hard and straight against his stomach. The length of his shaft was entwined with thick, throbbing veins. He looked to be somewhere around nineteen or twenty. Glenn checked him out with approval and mild excitement, but he wasn't really interested. Not tonight anyway.

Feeling revived and suitably chilled, he turned off the water. He knew that the guys on the ledge were watching his arse with keen eyes as he bent over to retrieve his sodden towel. He didn't bother concealing himself as he walked slowly past them, his heavy cock swaying lazily from side to side, and entered the heart of the sauna. He could still feel their eyes on his arse as he was enveloped in a copious cloud of thick white steam. As he wandered deeper into the labyrinth, the bodies grew in number. So many men, of all ages, wandered past in the mist, showing off their semihard dicks and checking out one another. Glenn casually devoured each solid outline of flesh as it sauntered passed him. Several hands reached out of the fog and made a grab for his cock and his arse, but he shrugged them away and progressed further.

He found Dean and Gary in the Jacuzzi with a handful of other boys.

Gary saw him through the veil of steam first. 'Hi, Hon,' he called out, waving enthusiastically.

'Hey there.' Dean glanced back over his shoulder and smiled. 'How did it go this morning?'

'Please don't ask.'

A couple of men, sitting next to Dean, moved over, creating a space in the tub for Glenn. He dropped his towel and stepped down into the tumultuous water. He leaned back and sighed.

'Not good, huh?' asked Dean, wiping sweat out of his eyes.

'Oh, far worse than not good. Fucking diabolical.'

'So have you come here looking for some juicy cock to cheer you up?'

'It might take more than one to achieve the impossible.' Glenn laughed. 'No, tomorrow I have to go and pose for the pictures that will accompany the piece. I thought that, if I'm going to come across as a complete prick in the interview, I might as well look fabulous in the photos.'

'Good idea,' said Gary. 'No one will give a toss about the words if you give them a hard-on in the glossies.'

'I'm not so sure about that. The bastard's been digging for dirt. He even knew about what happened at the club that time.'

'What? Not that thing in the toilets?'

'Yep. He claimed it was common knowledge. *Everybody knows about it.*'

Dean and Gary burst into simultaneous fits of laughter.

'It's not funny,' Glenn sighed.

Of all the gay couples Glenn knew, Dean and Gary had that most rare thing: a lasting relationship. The two men had been together for the best part of ten years. They were two of the coolest people he had ever known. Dean was the younger of the two; in his early thirties, he had a raucous laugh and a wicked sense of humour. At five foot seven, he was short, stocky and muscular with big broad shoulders and a round, beefy arse. His chest was just a little bit hairy and his jet-black hair was cut into a neat crop. He had a pair of warm, rich, brown eyes.

Although he was only six years older, Gary was the 'daddy' of their relationship. He was longer and leaner with a broad, hairy chest and long muscular arms and legs. His hair was dark and short and the features of his face were more angular and serious than his lover's.

Underneath the water, the hand of the guy sitting to the left of Glenn had found its way to his thigh. He turned to check him out: he was in his twenties, good-looking and blond with clear, creamy skin. Even though he was a bit of a looker, Glenn wasn't interested; still he allowed the guy's hand to remain where it was. He would stop him when he went too far.

Dean was excited. He and Gary were throwing a party the following weekend. 'You haven't forgotten about it, have you?'

'Of course I haven't.'

'What are you wearing?'

Glenn shook his head. 'I have no idea. I haven't thought that far ahead.'

Dean tutted. 'You're as bad as Gary. He always leaves everything to the last minute.'

Glenn glanced sideways at the older man and smiled. 'I hope you've got *your* outfit sorted.'

Gary rolled his eyes. 'I'm gonna go for a little wander.'

'Cock hunting again,' Dean said with good humour. 'Don't go using all your energy. Save a little something for when we get home.'

Gary had a huge cock. He was proud of it and he liked to show it off. As he stood up, the water cascaded down his muscular body and streamed from the end of his monster dick like a raging torrent of piss. Every man in the Jacuzzi stared at the gargantuan shaft of semihard meat. The organ hung down long and low from the front of his pelvis. The shaft was a good ten inches in length and the enormous girth of it made him seem even bigger. Glenn had never seen another cock that was as thick as Gary's. It bore a striking resemblance to one of the impossibly huge dildos that were always used in Californian porn movies. There was no way that he could ever imagine a dick as big as that fitting inside his arse.

Gary climbed out of the pool and disappeared into the steam. The blond beside Glenn had obviously been affected by the size of Gary's dick and his hand slid further up Glenn's thigh. Glenn ignored him and turned to Dean.

'Doesn't it bother you?'

'What?

'There isn't a single man in this place that doesn't want to get his hands on your man's cock.'

Dean's hand slid into Glenn's groin beneath the water and located his now hard dick. 'Including you too, I see.' There was a wicked gleam in his eyes as he squeezed the shaft of Glenn's throbbing cock. 'It doesn't bother me. What kind of spiteful bastard would I be if I kept a monster like that all to myself?'

Glenn was right about one thing. The eyes of every man Gary encountered in the sauna were compulsively drawn towards his cock.

He cruised the hazy labyrinthine corridors like a shark stalking the ocean depths. Everywhere he turned there was somebody eyeing his erection with either awe or jealousy. There were guys here who would do anything to get a grip on what he had to offer. They flaunted themselves shamelessly, tempting him with their nudity and availability.

Gary was free to take his pick from the very best that was on offer, and he was going to spend some time looking around before he made his final choice.

He always got horny when he came to the sauna. The attention lavished on his cock made him hungry for sex. A quick fuck now would not satisfy the need, but it would buy him time. Emptying the heavy load of his balls into a hungry orifice would quell his passion for now. Tonight, when they got home, Dean would be treated to the full application of his hard desire. Gary would work his cock into Dean's well-practised arse and ride his body until Dean murmured into the pillow like a baby at the breast.

Right now he wanted to get off. As much as he liked Glenn, he was far too horny to sit in the tub swapping gossip and running over the party arrangements for the thousandth time. He was so ripe and ready to drop his load that his balls were hanging painfully in their sac.

Suddenly a boy caught his eye. He was young, no older than twenty, blond, with a lean, athletically toned body. He was lying face down on a sweaty white slab, exhibiting the perfect curves of his hard, round arse. He lifted his shoulders and propped himself up on his elbows. He appraised Gary with cool green eyes. He was trying to play it casual, acting as though he couldn't care less about the gargantuan piece of cock that was aiming straight at him. The upward tilt of his arse as he lay on the slab betrayed his cool. Gary knew exactly how badly he wanted it.

An older man, nearer thirty, appeared out of the wraithlike mist to stand at Gary's side. He was dark and lean with a solid, well-built chest. He slid his hand beneath Gary's cock and held the weight of him in his palm. He nodded towards the blond on the slab.

'He's gagging for it,' the man said in a lazy drawl. He squeezed Gary's cock, stroking it until it grew long and stiff, swelling to its fullest.

'He's gonna get it,' Gary said. '*Right after you.*'

He grabbed the thickset man by his hair and pushed him down to his knees. The man needed no further inducement to take Gary's hard cock in his hands. He stroked it gently, weighing up the magnitude of it, before his head moved closer. He opened his lips and took the fat head into his mouth. Gary looked down at his face as he tried to stretch his jaw wide. The man sucked his cock enthusiastically, sliding his moist tongue all over the swollen rod before trying to take the length of the shaft into his mouth.

He felt the man's hands on his balls, stretching his sac, kneading the heavy nuts in his palm. His fingers were travelling further back, delving into the crack of his arse.

'Don't even think about it,' Gary grunted. 'Nothing goes up my arse.'

The man did as he was told and Gary felt his fingers curl around the base of his shaft and gently jerk him back and forth. He dived down the shaft, swallowing as much of him as he could, and then easing back slowly to lick the pre-come that was oozing from his shaft at a mile a minute. His mouth was warm and smooth. Gary was ready to burst and he was going to let this stranger have it all. He grabbed a handful of hair and dragged the man's face back off his cock. Just as he was about to protest, Gary sprayed his load across the man's startled expression. Long, white ropes splattered into the man's hair, across his brow, down his cheek. He opened his mouth to catch the last residue of the orgasm as it spluttered from Gary's juddering cock.

With come dribbling slowly down both sides of his face, the man smiled. Gary spread his load across his face, rubbing it into his skin and hair with long, thick fingers. The man moaned appreciatively.

The young blond guy was now sitting on the edge of the slab, his legs hanging over the side. He had shot a load across his stomach and chest. He stared at Gary, with wide open eyes.

Gary smiled at him. 'Go find me a rubber, sunshine. I'm gonna fuck *you* now.'

Glenn and Dean had changed into white towelling robes and retired to the rest area outside. They sat opposite each other on scooped wicker chairs, drinking Diet Coke straight from the can. Glenn was now feeling less stressed. The heat of the baths had eased the ball of tension that Freddie Brooks had created in his stomach and purged the excesses of the previous night from his skin. Dean had spent the last fifteen minutes regaling him with details of the young lad he and Gary had picked up at the club the previous weekend. They had taken him home and ridden him until morning. Glenn was only half listening to the tale – he had heard it all before – different pick-up but the same story.

For a moment, back in the sauna, Glenn had briefly glimpsed a figure as it vanished down one of the corridors. His features had been obscured by steam, but he was convinced it was the same man. The one he had seen last night, outside the house, and then again this morning at the end of the street.

He told Dean, 'There was a guy back there in the steam room. I think he might be following me around. I'm sure I saw him outside my house last night and he was there again this morning.'

'What? A stalker?'

'I don't know. It does seem weird, though.'

Dean shrugged and took a slug of Coke. 'He's probably just moved in. Look on the bright side: fresh meat on the street. *And* he comes to the baths. Who could ask for anything more?'

'No,' said Glenn, 'I'm sure I recognise him from somewhere.'

'Ex-trade?'

'That's what I thought at first, but I usually have a better memory for faces than that. I'm sure I'd remember if I'd shagged him. I just can't put my finger on where I know his face from.'

'You know what the scene is like. Every face is a familiar one. What's wrong? Do you really think he's a stalker?'

Glenn laughed. 'No. It's just bugging me.'

'If he comes by again, point him out. I'll probably recognise his arse. Hey, I've probably *had* his arse.'

'I thought you were strictly passive.'

The familiar, cheeky grin that Glenn loved so much spread across Dean's face. 'So *he's* probably had *my* arse. It was merely a figure of speech.'

This time they both laughed and began to talk about the party that weekend once more.

The young blond sat on the edge of ceramic slab and ripped open the foil packet with his teeth. Gary's cock was standing erect, just inches in front of his face, so close that he could feel the warm heat of the young man's breath on his sensitive knob. He watched the guy as he took the rubber out of the packet and leaned forwards to stretch it over the wide head of Gary's cock and roll it down the broad shaft.

A dozen or so men had gathered round the slab to watch the big guy with the monster cock and the young blond with the hot arse. Those who had already seen the big fellow blown off a few minutes earlier knew that they were in for a treat.

Gary pushed the blond over on to his back. The young lad was wide-eyed and wondrous, his body a pliable tool for Gary to use in any way he wanted. He grabbed hold of the man's thighs and lifted his legs up to his chest, exposing his arse. His arsehole was several shades darker than the golden hue of his skin. The small ring was surrounded by a cluster of honey-coloured hair.

Gary spat on to his cock and smeared his heavy gob over the

rubber-coated organ. He knew that the boy was nervous – most men were when faced with the reality of cock so big. Gary didn't care: he knew from a lifetime of experience that the blond's fear would soon fade.

He pressed his cockhead against the waiting hole. The young man sucked in a lungful of air through clenched teeth. He slowly pushed his shaft inside. The other guy's arse was hot and very tight. Gary held his hips and gradually slid himself in further, listening as the blond sighed and gasped. He felt the muscles of the lad's arse stretch wide to accommodate him. Though he was already sweating heavily from the intense heat in the sauna, the temperature of both their bodies rose higher. Gary told the younger man how good his tight arse felt, as he worked himself in to the hilt. He throbbed hard within the delicate canal.

He gave the guy a few moments to get used to the presence of his dick inside his tight orifice and then he really began to let him have it. He held his hips tight and ground his cock back and forth, feeling the tight arse lips gripping from the root to the tip of his erection.

The men in the steam around them stroked their own cocks as they watched. One of the guys had already come and was letting someone eat the white cream that spilled from his organ. A couple of the other men had lain down, one on top of the other, and were studiously sucking each other's cock.

Gary teased the young man's arsehole to the max, alternating between short, sharp jabs and long heavy strokes. His balls smacked hard against the upturned buttocks with every internal thrust. The golden hairs of his crack gently grazed the root of Gary's dick. The lad panted and gasped beneath him, urging Gary to fuck him harder. Gary lifted the young man's hips higher and thrust his cock a little bit deeper, a little bit harder. The lad arched his back from the perspiring surface of the ceramic slab and surrendered to Gary's hands and cock.

Gary's thick, throbbing dick stroked the tenderest recesses of his arse and the young guy clenched his muscles, sucking the cock deeper into him. Gary thrust deep and the boy clutched him tighter. They were humping together. Gary grunted and thrust all the way, until his cock erupted and filled the rubber inside the blond's fine golden arse.

The lad grabbed his cock and jerked it off hard and fast. They both watched the come spill from his pink tip and rain down on either side of his flat belly. His copious load dribbled down over his stomach and on to the warm slab beneath him. His young body trembled, with Gary's big dick still buried deep inside his arse.

When Gary withdrew, his organ was still hard. There were any number of volunteers in the sauna willing to fulfil his remaining desire. He declined every offer. He was saving it now for Dean.

Glenn had closed his bedroom curtains against the dark night outside. His room was a sacred chamber, a place to relax and unwind. It was mellow in tone and warmed by the ambient glow of a dozen slowly smouldering candles. The soft voice and full-grown sound of Janet Jackson's 'Velvet Rope' oozed from the speakers of his stereo. It was late, but Glenn was not in the mood for sleep.

He was sprawled restlessly on his back on top of his king-sized bed, naked but for his black cotton shorts. He closed his eyes and lost himself for a blessed moment in the song of loneliness, while the chords of sexual frustration purred into his senses. He sighed and rolled over on to his side. He watched the slow flickering flame of one of the burning candles. The blistering flare character-ised his own sense of ennui.

He had intended to get to bed early and secure a decent night of sleep before he had to face the lens of the cameras in the morning. But sleep seemed intent on evading him. It had been a strange, unsatisfying day, a wasted day. He could not sleep when he was haunted by such an overwhelming sense of having achieved nothing.

He picked up the glass of Chardonnay from the side of the bed and drank slowly. He had opened the wine in the hope that it would relax him and ease his passage into unconsciousness. He was on his fourth glass and still no nearer to sleep.

On the bed beside him lay a worn, once white jockstrap. He had stolen it from Dean's bag while he was taking a shower after the sauna. Glenn brought the tired garment to his face and inhaled the deep, sweaty scent of his friend. The stimulant of the fragrance sent a thrill through his languorous body and his cock swelled inside his shorts. He pressed the jock tight against his nose and breathed deeply of its aroma.

Unlike his relationship with Joe, Glenn's friendship with Dean had never advanced to a sexual level, even though Glenn wanted to get Dean into bed more than any other man he knew. Unlike the crushes he often had on other men, the feelings he had for Dean had never faded, but had become stronger as the years passed and their friendship intensified. Glenn yearned to spend some time alone with Dean, to undress his body and explicitly explore every secret burrow and cleft of muscle.

He wanted to taste Dean's arsehole and suck his cock and savour the flavour of his skin. It was a special need and a secret that had lived within him for as long as he had been friends with Dean. Nobody knew how he felt – not Dean, not Gary, not Joe. Not anyone.

His passion for Dean was not an obsession. He didn't hold a grudge or harbour any malice towards Gary. It was just a nice thought, a fantasy that he kept alive in his mind, feeding it with used underwear. Dean never seemed to notice the loss.

Once Glenn had found a series of intimate photographs that Gary and Dean had taken of each other. He stole one in the hope that it would never be missed. It had been the source of an infinite number of orgasms since the day he took it.

He freed his cock from the restriction of his shorts, slid them down his thighs and kicked them off on to the floor. He was leaking a steady stream of pre-come on to his stomach. It matted the fine dusting of soft brown hair that trailed down from his navel into his groin. He smeared the juice across his belly and brought his fingertips to his lips. He licked each digit. He always tasted different from other guys.

He raised his legs and slipped on Dean's jockstrap. The well-worn garment fitted his waist and cock perfectly. He savoured the cut of the elastic straps into the flesh below his arse. He slid a couple of fingers into his cleft and ran them softly over the puckering of his rim.

He wondered idly if Gary had ever fucked Dean while he was

wearing this old jock. He spread his thighs as he envisioned the scene and pressed his fingers into himself, following the gentle incline of his passage towards his favourite spot. He located his secret place and stroked it smoothly.

He slipped his cock out of the side of the jockstrap. He was oozing pre-come heavily now. He caressed the sensitive head with his palm, smearing the clear juice over himself. His organ trembled in his hand. He opened his arse wide, sweeping his fingers over his prostate in delicate circles. He rocked his pelvis gently back and forth, an almost imperceptible motion.

He held his cock in a soft grip – there was no need to stroke it. He worked himself up to his orgasm slowly, building up the pressure inside. All the stimuli he needed were in his arse. When he came it was long and intense. His come vaulted from the tip of his dick in slow motion. He watched as it rose gently into the air before washing down over his stomach like warm summer rain. He released his breath in a gentle sigh.

He lay there for a while, not moving. His fingers remained inside himself and his come eventually lost its white hue and dribbled down the side of his stomach on to the bed. He closed his eyes, having finally rid himself of the tension of the day. His worries had been replaced by an easy picture of Dean in his mind. He lay still, not thinking, not functioning, just enjoying the perfect moment of rest.

Four

Pierced

The next morning, Glenn had another early start. Thankfully, he didn't have another hangover to contend with. When he had eventually managed to get off to sleep, his rest had been deep and beneficial. He woke up sometime around three when the outside security light came on. He got out of bed for a few minutes to look out of the window for evidence of any prowlers. There was nobody out there. The light had most likely been set off by one of the many neighbourhood cats.

He rose at six and spent an hour practising his yoga routine.

His expectations for the *GAYZ* photo shoot were entirely more positive than they had been for the interview the previous morning. The photographer was a man called Damien Marquez. Although Glenn had not met him before, he was most definitely aware of his impressive reputation and was a big fan of his work. Damien's pictures had graced the covers of glossy magazines all over the world. Stars like Kylie Minogue and Elizabeth Hurley had posed for his camera. Damien was famed for persuading his subjects to model for the most daring and controversial of shots. A collection of his work had been published in a coffee-table book the year before.

Glenn had been dubious at first when his agent informed him

that Damien was going to photograph him for the cover of the magazine. It had actually taken a while for the information to sink in. He didn't know what was more bizarre, the fact that he was going to be on the cover or that Marquez was taking the shots.

Damien had a studio in Newcastle, on Westgate Road, just up the street from the Tyne Theatre and Opera House. Glenn arrived by taxi at a little after eight that morning. Despite the photographer's fame and eccentric reputation, he wasn't feeling unduly nervous about the shoot. The ego of Damien Marquez could be nowhere near as exaggerated and spoiled as the reporter they had inflicted upon him the previous day.

He was dressed casually in a pair of cream, loose-fitting combat pants and a black French Connection T-shirt. His agent had notified him of the fact that there was no need to get dressed up beforehand. Damien was an artist and would have his own ideas about how he wanted his subject to look.

Glenn pressed the intercom box on the front door.

After a moment, the small eye-level speaker let out a static hiss and a male voice answered. 'Yes?' The man had to shout to make himself heard over the loud music blasting in the background.

'Hi. My name is Glenn Holden. I'm here for the *GAYZ* photo shoot.'

'Come on up,' the voice shouted. 'We're on the second floor. Damien's expecting you.'

An electronic buzz signalled that the door was open. There was no elevator so Glenn walked up the two flights of stairs to the studio. Up above someone was blasting out the Chemical Brothers. The music got louder the higher he climbed. The source of the noise was the studio on the second floor.

A young man dressed in jeans and a T-shirt was waiting on the landing. 'Hi,' he said, and Glenn recognised the voice that had greeted him over the intercom. 'I'm Jared. I'm Damien's assistant. Come on through. Damien's out on the balcony having a ciggie. He won't be long, unless you want to go out there and join him.'

'I'm trying to cut down.'

'Good for you. It's bloody frigid out there too. You won't catch me freezing my bollocks off for the sake of a quick puff.' The young man laughed as he looked Glenn quickly up and down, checking him out. 'Not *that* kind of puff, anyway.'

Jared was filled with the kind of energetic confidence that only those who are both very young and very pretty possess. Glenn noted that he was undeniably both of those things. He was tall, a little on the gangly side, Glenn thought, but athletic from head to toe. He didn't walk across the landing: he strutted. He was naturally blond, with a healthy, clear complexion. He had a broad infectious grin that lit up the whole of his face and radiated an incandescent light from the knowledgeable depths of his eyes. Glenn assumed that he couldn't have been much older than twenty.

The studio was an old warehouse that had been converted into four smaller units. Despite the open-plan construction, the rooms were surprisingly warm. The Chemical Brothers were pumping out of a very expensive sound system. Even with the volume turned up so high there was no distortion to the track. A huge white screen occupied the whole of one wall and stretched out across the floor. Three cameras were set up at different angles in front of it.

'Is that for me?' Glenn asked.

'Uh, huh.' Jared nodded. 'Damien thought he would shoot you against a plain white backdrop. I think he's planning to do something pretty simple with you. Is that OK?'

'Sure. You guys know a hell of a lot more about this than I do. I'll just do whatever I'm told.'

'You can trust Damien. He knows what it takes to get a great image. Did you see the shots he took of Sharon Stone for *Vanity*? You'll look fabulous whatever he does with you.'

A sudden icy draft blew through the studio and two men, both in their early thirties, stepped in off the balcony. They closed the door behind them.

Glenn knew without being told which one of them was Damien Marquez. He radiated a palpable aura of blatant sexuality. The sight of him gave Glenn such a rise that for a moment he thought that he might even be drooling.

Damien was a sex bomb on the verge of exploding.

He wasn't conventionally good-looking, but, whatever it is that makes a man irresistible, he had it in abundance. He was tall, well over six feet, and his rangy frame was fleshed out with long, beautifully toned muscle. His skin was dark and creamy, the rich colour of chocolate.

His clothes, what little he wore, skimmed his magnificent body. He was dressed in a pair of loose-fitting denims, cut off above the knee and hanging down low on his hips. His baggy white shirt was open, revealing the sculpted ridges of his stomach and the thick steel bar that pierced his navel. His arms, from his wrists to his shoulders, were covered in tattoos: black, tribal designs, more intricate than Glenn could fully appreciate with a casual eye. He had another visible tattoo, a Celtic cross, etched into the contours of his right calf.

His face was broad and angular, handsome and yet unnerving. There was a dangerous aspect to his appearance. Although he was smiling, Glenn had the impression that he would be very unpredictable. His smile could easily drop away, leaving only the mean, determined set of his broad mouth. His head was shaved down to an infinitesimal stubble. There was an uncertainty to his features, especially around his eyes, that could have been frightening. His eyes were dark, impenetrable pools that gave away nothing in their outlook. As well as the piercing in his navel, there was another impaled through his right eyebrow; the small steel ball bearings on either side of the bar protruded through the flesh above his eye.

The instant that he saw Damien, Glenn lost all sexual interest in Jared.

The young assistant introduced each of them. The other man with Damien was called Doug. He was good-looking and displayed a quiet manner. In other circumstances Glenn would have been attracted to him, but there was nothing about him that could compete with the dynamism of Marquez.

Glenn shook hands with both of them. Damien had a strong dry grip.

'I've been looking forward to meeting you,' Damien said. 'I'm a real fan of your books.'

'Thank you. I'm flattered.'

'No,' Damien said, '*I'm* flattered.'

Jared made coffee for everyone, while the other three sat down together on a huge leather suite in the corner.

'I just want to get a few ideas from you before we start,' Damien said, 'just to make sure that we're all on the right track here.' He was sprawled in an armchair directly across from Glenn. He sat with his long legs spread wide. Glenn's eyes were drawn to his crotch and the prominent swelling beneath his shorts. 'So, what do you want to achieve here today?'

As Jared joined them with a tray of drinks, Glenn explained how disastrous his interview had been. 'Brooks is going to crucify me in print. He wants to make out that I've compromised my sexuality and sold out for mainstream success.'

'He sounds like a fucking dickhead.'

'He is. And if I can I'd like to make him look like one, too. I'd like the photographs to contradict everything he says about me in the feature. I want something really provocative. Something in-your-face and proud.'

'Fucking classic.' Damien laughed. 'I love it. If you're prepared to go all the way with this we can come up with a cover that *everyone* is gonna be talking about!'

Glenn spent the next hour and a half with Doug, who turned out to be Damien's stylist. Between them, they came up with an image for the shoot. Damien had already decided that he was going to photograph him in stark black and white against a plain backdrop, so they needed to come up with a concept that would complement his vision and work within that frame.

Doug decided to keep it very simple. Rather than experimenting with hairstyles and make-up, he concluded that they would be better off accentuating Glenn's natural good looks.

'Would you be happy doing this with your shirt off?' Doug asked.

'What? Pose? With no shirt on?'

'Sure. You look like you've got a good body under that T-shirt. How about showing it off?'

'I'm not sure. I've never done anything like that before. I'd be embarrassed.'

'Rubbish. You'll look great. Take your shirt off and show me. Let's see what we have to work with.'

Glenn pulled the T-shirt over his head and draped it over the back of a chair. He looked at his reflection in the broad mirror. He had to admit it: he did look pretty good. The sessions in the gym and his early-morning yoga routines were paying off – although this wasn't quite what he'd had in mind when he had been working out for the picture shoot.

'I think you should do it,' Doug said. 'You've got a great chest and nice flat abs. You should show them off. Besides, you did say you wanted to assert your sexuality in these pictures and be provocative. If you put that body on the cover of *GAYZ*, I guarantee you sackloads of fan mail from guys all over the country. Not just that, your pictures will turn up all over the Internet. Everyone is gonna know who you are. Just think how many guys are gonna squirt over you.'

Glenn glanced towards Damien, who was setting up his equipment. The black man had stopped what he was doing and was regarding him with discernible appreciation. Glenn felt naked under his intense staring gaze. He felt a nervous apprehension deep in his stomach.

'You did say you were willing to go all the way,' said Damien, his black eyes unflinching in their assessment of his naked torso.

'OK,' said Glenn, 'I'll do it.'

Doug gave him a pair of baggy blue jeans that were two sizes too big for him, and a pair of snug white undershorts. He instructed Glenn to pull the shorts up high on his waist and let the jeans hang down low.

'It's kind of a slutty image,' he said, 'but the effect will be stunning.'

He moulded his hair with a combination of gel and soft wax, giving his short style a tousled, just-had-great-sex look.

Jared gave him a glass of champagne while he was changing into the clothes Doug had provided. 'It should relax you a little. Help you to loosen up before the camera.'

Glenn thanked him. 'It might take more than one glass.'

Posing half naked turned out to be easier than he expected. Damien talked to him throughout the shoot; his deep, mid-range baritone helped to ease him further. Very quickly he began to feel relaxed.

'I loved *Everyday Hurts*,' Damien said. 'That was a great book. OK, give me a full-on smile. Show a lot of teeth.'

Glenn was down on all fours, staring directly into the lens. He had worked up a sweat beneath the hot studio lights. He smiled, oblivious to the imagery he was creating. The camera clicked several times. The results were certainly stunning.

'Great,' said Damien. 'Put your finger in your mouth and suck it like it was a cock.'

Glenn did as he was instructed. He had stopped blushing at Damien's requests after the man had asked him to display the kind of ecstatic amazement he would have if he sat down on top of a fourteen-inch cock. He stuck the tip of his index finger in his mouth and sucked it lasciviously.

Damien clicked away, capturing the image for eternity.

'Most people tell me how much they like the film of *Everyday Hurts*,' Glenn said. 'They seem to forget it was a book first.'

Damien snapped off half a dozen shots.

'No way. The book is much better. Books nearly always are. I love that character in that story. Anthony Pierce. He really turned me on when I read it.'

'Anthony Pierce is the murderer.'

'He's still a sexy bastard.'

'No one has ever told me that before. I get a lot of mail about Matthew, the good guy. He's a very popular character. Especially with women and gay men.'

'I guess it's just me then,' Damien said. 'I prefer bad boys.'

Glenn licked his lips slowly. 'So do I.'

The temperature in the studio continued to rise. Damien took his shirt off and tossed it aside, carrying on working in just his shorts. Glenn stared at his bare torso, realising for the first time that as well as his navel Damien also had both of his nipples pierced. The small steel bars were speared horizontally through both of his tits; they flashed in the bright light of the studio. Visually the effect was stunning and incredibly erotic. Glenn had had only a minor interest in body jewellery: it did little to arouse him. But as he looked at Damien's swollen stubs he felt a hardness rising in his pants. His most basic instincts were excited. He fantasised about taking one of the nipples in his mouth and feeling the hardness of the steel against his teeth as he bit down.

His heart beat faster.

'Want to take this further?' Damien lowered the camera. His dark eyes looked directly into Glenn's, directly into his head where they could read every one of his illicit thoughts.

Glenn's mouth was dry. He swallowed, but could not speak.

'Take off your jeans,' Damien said.

'What?'

'Take your jeans off. If you really want to make this interesting.'

Glenn hesitated. He was hiding behind what little clothing he wore. The moment he dropped his jeans his arousal would manifest itself to the three other men in the room. He was sweating heavily. He looked into Damien's deep eyes, searching for reassurance, a sign that he was only joking.

'Do it,' the photographer said slowly.

Glenn inhaled and exhaled. Slowly in and out.

Avoiding eye contact with the three men, he unbuttoned the fly of his jeans. They slipped down over his thighs and he stepped out of them. Another deep breath. He straightened himself.

The prominence of his cock was displayed in a long bulge leaning to the left of his groin. The head had started to leak and left a large damp stain on the soft white cotton. Glenn felt his temperature soar even higher.

Jared stepped forward and offered him another glass of champagne. He drained the glass in one draught. Thankfully, it began to have an effect on him straightaway. He exhaled a deep sigh and loosened his shoulders.

'OK,' he said, 'I'm ready.'

He adopted his best professional attitude and continued to follow Damien's directions for the camera. It wasn't easy. His cock refused to soften and he knew exactly where the three pairs of eyes in front of him were looking. He couldn't deny the buzz he was getting from their attention either. He knew that his erection was only one of four in the room at that moment. When the pictures were published, his image would give men erections all over the world.

His confidence increased immeasurably. Damien didn't have to direct him any longer. He posed and pouted and groped his cock through his white cotton shorts like a seasoned professional. He gazed into the lens of the camera through half-lidded eyes. He had always had a fantasy about doing porn. This was the closest he was ever likely to get.

'Push your shorts down lower,' Damien said. 'Just enough to show some pubic hair.'

He tucked his thumbs into the thick elastic waist and slid them lower.

Click. Click. Click.

The camera captured every millimetre of flesh as it was exposed. A light cluster of brown hair curled over the top of the elastic. He pushed his shorts even lower until the thick root of his cock came into view.

'Take a picture of that,' he whispered.

Click.

After the shoot Glenn changed back into his own clothes. His hard cock was intent on staying that way.

Damien was sprawled back in his chair drinking champagne. Doug and Jared were working together in the far corner of the studio.

Glenn joined the photographer and refilled his own glass.

'How do you feel now?' Damien asked.

Glenn shrugged his shoulders. 'I don't know. Great, I suppose.' He laughed. 'I've never done anything like that before.'

'Don't worry about the photos. You'll get full approval of the final shots before I give them to the magazine.'

'Thanks. I'm not sure how I'll feel about those final few images in the cold light of day.'

Damien leaned forwards and smiled. Glenn got a sudden breath of his fresh, salty scent. 'Don't worry about it. You'll love them. I promise you that those pictures will make you an icon.'

He laughed. 'I'm not sure how I feel about that.'

Damien raised his glass. 'To Glenn Holden. Gay icon!'

They chinked glasses. Glenn blushed and averted his eyes.

He feasted his gaze on Damien's bare torso, once again drawn compulsively towards the steel bars that penetrated the dark-brown flesh of his nipples.

God. I really want to fuck this guy!

'How long have you had those? Your tattoos and piercings?'

Damien leaned back in his chair, stretching his spine. 'I've been getting tattoos since I was fifteen. They're by different artists, all over the world. It's a growing collection.' He laughed and then pointed to each piece of jewellery in turn. 'My bellybutton was the first piercing. Got that five years ago. Then my eyebrow. About two years ago. The nipples were the last. I had them done last year in San Francisco.'

He took each nipple between finger and thumb as he spoke, twisting the shiny bars.

'Doesn't that hurt?'

Damien shook his head. 'No. It doesn't hurt at all. It's nice.' He looked Glenn straight in the eye as he continued to play with himself. 'Feel for yourself.'

Glenn stood up, rising to the challenge. He approached Damien slowly. His heart was beating hard and fast. Damien leaned towards him, pressing his body close. So close that Glenn could feel his heat. He pressed his fingers cautiously against the swollen tits.

'Oh,' Damien sighed.

'Does it hurt?' Glenn's voice was little more than a whisper.

Damien grabbed his wrists, holding them in a vicelike grip, forcing him to apply more pressure to his chest. Glenn felt his hot, heavy breath on his face, its rhythm increasing. He gripped the bars between his fingers and twisted them slowly.

'Fucking hell,' Damien sighed. 'You have no idea how fucking great that feels.'

Glenn applied even more pressure, turning the bars further in his firm grip. 'Tell me.'

'Oh . . . It's as if my tits are wired up to every erogenous zone in my body. I can feel that right down in my balls. In my cock. My arsehole. Everywhere.' Tiny beads of sweat had started to form on Damien's brow. He sucked air deep into his chest and exhaled with a long sigh. He pressed his body into Glenn's hands. 'Right now, when you do that, my balls feel like they're gonna explode.'

Damien's strong arms wrapped around Glenn's body and pulled him tight against his chest. His huge hands grabbed his arse and kneaded the flesh between firm fingers. He kissed him. Glenn opened his mouth wide, allowing the kiss to go deeper. Damien's cock was pressing insistently against his stomach.

'I'm gonna fuck you,' Damien whispered against his lips, in the spaces between their kisses. 'Your arse won't know what's hit it when I shove my cock up there. I've got the rest of the day free and I'm gonna spend all of it inside you.'

Glenn was aroused to the point of combustion. The photographer's animal voice and lustful intentions struck the raw nerves of his sexuality. 'I'd love to spend the rest of the day with your cock inside me,' he breathed, grinding his body against Damien's huge, bulging dick. 'But there's something I want to do first.'

Damien gripped his arse so tight that his feet almost left the ground. 'What's that?'

Glenn kissed him with a fierce, barbaric intensity.

'I want to get my nipple pierced.'

'Are you sure you want to do this?'

'More than anything. If those little bars give you such a thrill, I can't wait to find out what they do for me.'

Glenn and Damien had been waiting for fifteen minutes. The artist, a man called Grant, was finishing off a tattoo in his studio. A couple of other men were waiting to go in, but Glenn was next in line. The walls of the waiting room were covered in art work. Apart from the catalogue of different designs available, the tattoo studio reminded Glenn of a dentist's reception room. The room was clean and brightly lit by overhead fluorescent tubes. It smelled strongly of disinfectant.

Damien had recommended the artist. 'He's clean and very professional. You won't have to worry about hygiene here.' He showed Glenn a tattoo at the base of his spine. It was another Celtic design, a black sun, about four inches wide. 'This is Grant's work. He did it for me a couple of years ago. He's one of the best I know.'

Despite his rigid determination, Glenn was nervous. He had never done anything as reckless as this before. He had never been a masochist – a little spanking was as far as his experimentation with pain had gone. This was mad. It was stupid. *It was gonna hurt like hell*. And yet the persistent throbbing of his cock reassured him that he was doing the right thing. When all the pain was over, the final pleasure would be worth it.

He could also look forward to the prospect of a whole afternoon with Damien and his big cock. When that big bastard shot up his arse he wouldn't even notice a little discomfort in his tit.

The door to the studio opened and a man in his early twenties came out into the waiting room. He was holding his shirt in his hand. He had a broad, gym-built chest.

'What have you had done?' Damien asked him.

The guy turned to display the swollen, newly etched work of an eagle in flight across his left shoulder. The wingspan of the tattoo was about nine inches in all. The newly coloured skin was raised and sore. It reminded Glenn of Braille: a blind man would be able to make out the design by following its swollen outline. Tiny beads of blood had begun to form on top of the freshly coloured skin.

'That's excellent,' Damien said. 'Nice job.'

Grant, a burly-looking man in his late thirties, followed the young man out of the studio. He was wearing rubber gloves and held a sterile dressing in his hands.

'All right,' he said to the man. 'You'll get your chance to show it off later.' He carefully applied the dressing over the tattoo. 'Keep that on until the bleeding stops.'

Glenn's stomach began to groan with a nervous mix of emotions, churning with fear and excitement.

Grant grinned at him, sensing his trepidation. 'OK, then,' he said in a softer voice than he had used on the other guy. 'It's your turn now. Follow me.'

Glenn stood up. Damien patted him on the back.

'There's still time to change your mind.'

'Not a chance. When I decide I want to do something, I do it. Even if it *is* stupid and irresponsible.'

'It's not irresponsible. Besides you can always take it out later if you hate it.'

'And go through all this pain for nothing,' Glenn said with nervous bravado. 'I don't think so. This thing is gonna stay in my tit for years.'

'Ha. Want me to come in with you?'

'No. Just be here for me when I come out. I might need your help to get me to the nearest pub.'

Glenn followed the tattooist through into his studio. Grant closed the door behind them.

The interior of the studio looked *exactly* like a dentist's surgery, right down to the blazing overhead lights, white-tiled walls and the huge contraption that passed for a chair in the centre of the room. The heavy scent of antiseptic and disinfectant was a strange comfort.

'Take a seat.'

Glenn regarded the chair with a blend of curiosity and mistrust. 'In that thing?'

'It's more comfortable than it looks.' Grant took off his rubber gloves and tossed them in the bin. 'So what's it to be? Left or right?'

'Right.'

'All right. I'll show you the choice of jewellery and then I need you to sign a consent form before I can perform the procedure.'

Glenn lay back in the rubber-coated chair. He raised his legs and tried to relax. He had never understood how some men got a real thrill out of sitting in a dentist's chair.

'Will this hurt a lot?'

Grant opened a cupboard and took out a tray of jewellery. 'I can't really answer that for you. It's different for everyone. It all depends on your threshold to pain. Some people scream the place down; others don't even flinch.'

He presented the selection of jewellery. Glenn couldn't begin to imagine what parts of the body some of the pieces were designed for. He pointed to a small steel bar with a ball bearing mounted on either side. 'That's the one I want.'

'OK. The bar that I use will be completely sterile so you don't have to worry about any contamination.' He handed him a consent form and biro. 'Have a read through this while I get everything ready for you. I need your name and address and a signature before I can carry out the piercing.'

Glenn's mouth was unnaturally dry. Despite his trepidation, his cock was still throbbing like mad. The next few minutes seemed to glide by in a dream. After consenting to the procedure, he took off his T-shirt and lay back in the chair. Grant pulled on another pair of gloves and cleaned Glenn's nipple and the surrounding skin with an antiseptic wipe. The nub of his tit was aroused and swollen. As Glenn looked down at himself, he could see his heart beating quickly in his chest. The tattooist then rubbed a thick white cream into the engorged appendage.

'This will numb you up a little. It'll help to dull the pain.' He smiled. 'Not that there'll be any pain. No one's ever passed out in my chair and I'm not about to let you be my first.'

He marked the entry and exit points on either side of the nipple with a narrow felt pen. Grant explained what he was doing at each step, reassuring him with his confidence. Glenn was concentrating on taking deep breaths, using the techniques of yoga to calm himself.

'This next step is the worst part,' Grant said, producing a narrow steel clamp. He gripped the nipple between thumb and forefinger and positioned the clamp above it. 'When I attach this it will cut off the blood supply to your nipple. That will numb you even further so, in theory at least, you won't feel very much when I pierce the flesh.'

He squeezed the hands of the clamp together fast and hard. Glenn let out a sharp hiss. The teeth of the clamp held his tit in a relentless grip. There was an intense, fiery edge to the pain.

'Breath through it,' Grant said. 'In another minute you won't feel it at all.' He left the clamp *in situ*, while he collected his sterile equipment together on a disposable tray. He removed his rubber gloves and replaced them with another pair from a sterile pack.

Glenn closed his eyes and concentrated on his breathing. The pain in his chest eventually began to lose its fierce edge and become a dull ache. The intensity of the experience was having a direct effect on his cock. He thought of Damien and all the restrained passion that he was going to release in bed with him that afternoon. He told himself it would not be long, but his cock was impatient. His underpants were already damp with the solution that seeped from its tip.

'You might want to close your eyes for the next part,' Grant said in a mellow tone.

'Is this it now?'

'Yes, another minute and it'll all be over.'

Deep breath. Slowly in and out.

Glenn closed his eyes. 'OK. Just get it over with.'

The sudden pressure against his clamped nipple was violent and intense. It felt as if someone had pressed a white-hot poker through his flesh.

'Aaah! Shit! *Fuck me!*'

'Nearly done,' said Grant softly. 'I've got the canular through your skin. That's it, the worst of it over. Just keep breathing. I'm inserting the bar now. Are you OK?'

'Only just,' Glenn hissed through gritted teeth. 'I must be insane.' His nipple was on fire. He couldn't feel Grant's fingers any more, just a flaming perception of white heat stabbing his chest.

Grant released the clamp. 'That's it,' he said. 'It's over. You can open your eyes now. You're not even bleeding.'

Glenn raised his eyelids slowly, fearful of the mutilation he was about to see. To his surprise the pain had receded quickly. There was nothing more than a dull, throbbing sensation in the affected area. Cautiously he looked down at himself.

His nipple was fiercely inflamed and swollen to nearly twice its normal size. The humble ball bearings protruded from either side of the tender tissue. His heart leaped at the sight.

'Shit!'

'Don't worry about the swelling: that'll go down in a few hours.'

Glenn's body was shaking with the huge surge of adrenalin that was pumping through his system.

'Wow,' he exclaimed, regarding the new addition with awe. It was breathtaking. 'I can't believe I've done it.'

'Are you all right? You don't regret it, do you?'

He laughed. 'No. No, I don't. Not at all. I just . . . can't believe it. It's fucking awesome.'

He stood up slowly and viewed himself in the full-length mirror. He suddenly saw his body in a whole new perspective. It was amazing how something so slight could alter his whole manner and appearance. In a bizarre way, it gave him a new self-awareness. He was unexpectedly in tune with all of his physical senses. His whole body was alert and active. And he was incredibly horny.

Grant covered the new piercing with a sterile dressing and

instructed him on how to take care of it. 'Keep it clean and don't fiddle with it, otherwise you'll infect it.' He gave him a leaflet on aftercare. 'Do exactly what this tells you and come back here if you have any problems.'

Damien stood up when Glenn walked back through into the waiting room.

'Well?'

Glenn grabbed him and kissed him hard on the lips.

'Come on, you bastard. Take me home and fuck me senseless.'

Five

Bound

Worked up into a frenzy, they could not keep their hands off each other. On the back seat of the taxi they kissed, groped and explored. The driver tried to ignore them as the heat of their passion intensified, but his eyes were drawn compulsively to the image in his rear-view mirror.

Glenn was out of his mind. Damien had freed him of all his inhibitions and the newly affixed piercing had awakened his senses. His entire body was an erogenous zone and it demanded sensual attention. He was teeming with sexual tension and desperate for a release.

Damien's hands were down the back of Glenn's combat pants, caressing his arse. He had already inserted a finger inside the tight opening. Glenn's rectum gripped his finger as if it was a cock. Damien pressed in deep, following the smooth curve of his inner walls. Glenn shuddered as he found the special place inside there.

'Oh God,' he sighed into Damien's open mouth. '*That* is like nothing else.'

'You're not kidding,' Damien said, stroking his prostate.

He fingered the swollen core. Glenn's cock was leaking like a garden hose as the black man manipulated his internal switches, controlling his pleasure.

'Just wait until I shove my cock in there, baby.' Damien forced his finger deeper. 'That really *is* like nothing else. Your tiny little hole won't know what's hit it. I'm gonna get you wet and loose and make you *beg* me to let you come. There's gonna be no bed for you either. I'm gonna have your arse in my Fuck Room.'

'What's your Fuck Room?' Glenn gasped.

'You'll see, baby. You'll see.'

Their kisses intensified. Glenn drew the other man deeper into him. He surrendered to the giant completely. He was willing to be his slave and serve him on the sole condition that he give him his cock in return. That hard piece of meat was all he asked for in exchange for total submission. His body was a compliant receptacle ready to receive anything and everything the photographer wanted to give him. He knew that he could take it and he was eager to prove it.

He slid his hands inside the fly of Damien's cut-offs, searching for the hard tool that was his sexual destiny. It was even bigger than he expected. When he curled his hand around the throbbing girth, his fingers did not meet. The strong pulse of the cock beat against his palm. He slid his loose grip up and down the shaft of flesh, feeling its size.

'It'll feel even bigger when it's inside you,' Damien whispered, sensing his trepidation.

Glenn didn't think that the shaft was as long as Gary's — that monster was still the biggest cock he had ever seen. Damien was maybe a couple of inches shorter, but he was easily just as thick. The proportion of length to girth actually made him seem thicker than Gary. Glenn rubbed his palm over the blunt head. It had slipped clean out of its protective skin in its eagerness to be free. The warm solution it secreted was thick and sticky. He rubbed the juice around the big crown.

Glenn loosened the buttons of Damien's jeans. 'I've *got* to see this thing,' he gasped.

He kept a tight grip on the swollen lance and extracted it slowly. It was an impressive sight, standing straight and ready. The skin of the shaft was like dark chocolate, while the fleshy head had the lighter shade of coffee. The thick rod and dark-brown balls gaped out of the open V of his fly. An impressive drool of pre-come soaked the bulky head and underside of the shaft; the veins were bulging all along the surface of his beautiful prick. It was breathtaking.

Damien pressed another finger into Glenn's arsehole.

'Think your little ring can manage a piece like that?'

'It has no choice,' Glenn said, staring wide-eyed at the heavy shank. 'One way or another, I'm having that thing inside me.' He held the cock in a tight grip and slid his hand up and down its length. Damien seemed to get bigger and thicker with every stroke.

Glenn didn't care that the driver was watching them in his mirror, or that whenever the car stopped for traffic any one of the other drivers could see what they were doing. He didn't give a damn about any of them. The only thing of importance was the giant cock in his hand and the secure knowledge that it would be inside him very soon.

The black man was near to a climax. Glenn's fingers were soaked with the juice that deluged from the bulging lips of his cock.

He raised his free hand to his freshly pierced nipple, fingering it gently. The pain heightened his senses and increased his arousal. Damien finger-fucked him with straight, rigid fingers. He yielded completely to his manipulations, relaxing his sphincter and allowing the man deeper into his body. He rocked his hips gently on Damien's fist. If this was just a prelude to the passion they would share, then he had found his utopia.

Glenn worked Damien's cock, bringing him closer to the brink with each stroke, stretching him, teasing him, increasing the pressure. The man's breath deepened and his scrotum contracted around the base of his cock, hugging his balls in a taut grip. At the final moment Damien became completely still. His brilliant white come oozed up his cock and spilled out over Glenn's fingers, dribbling down the back of his hand to his wrist. The cock kept pumping and his come continued to flow until, at last, Damien exhaled slowly and the moment was over. Spent, he closed his eyes, breathing in and out through his mouth, relaxing back into the seat.

Glenn released his tight hold. The sperm was thick and strong-smelling. He lifted his hand to his mouth and tasted the juice that dribbled down the back. Its taste was as intense as its odour. He devoured all traces, greedily working his tongue between his fingers until his skin was clean. He bent over into Damien's groin and worked his tongue all the way over his still hard shaft, darting into the tiny pisshole and eating up every last vestige of cock cream.

And then they kissed again. Exchanging the taste of come between their wet, open mouths. Glenn sat back further on to Damien's hand, feeling his fingers probe deeper.

'You'd better pull your pants up,' Damien said. 'We're nearly there.'

Just like his studio, Damien's apartment had been converted out of an old warehouse. The entire four-storey block of textile buildings had been bought up and adapted in the early nineties, around the same time as the profitable quayside development project further along the river.

Damien's residence took up the whole of the third floor. It was obvious to Glenn as soon as he stepped out of the elevator and into the lobby that the decor of the apartment was as eclectic and unusual as the man who owned it. As the doors of the lift opened he was confronted with a huge black-and-white photograph of a pair of male buttocks. The picture took up almost the whole of one wall, from floor to ceiling, behind its glass frame. Two hands rested on the taut buttocks and spread them wide open. The eye of the camera captured every intimate feature of the crevice, revealing in vivid clarity each wrinkle and line of the puckered hole and the tell tale stubble of dark hair that had been so carefully shaved. There were no secrets or subtleties left to the physical image: it was all there to be seen, blown up in crystal-clear sharpness.

Glenn couldn't help staring at the photograph and being drawn into its frank sexuality. The exposed area of flesh was like a visual magnet, drawing the viewer into its dark depths. There was no mystery to the exterior of the image, but the potential of that arsehole and the erotic power of the photograph was tremendous.

Damien wrapped his arms around Glenn from behind and nuzzled the back of his neck. 'Do you like it?'

'Wow!' he exclaimed. 'It's amazing. Did you take it?'

'No. A very good friend of mine took that shot. The model's a familiar one, though.'

Glenn leaned back into Damien's embrace, pressing his hips into his groin, grinding his arse against the hard bulge. 'Is it you?'

'Yes. It was few years ago, though.'

'Beautiful,' Glenn said.

Damien guided him into the apartment. 'It won't be long until you see it in the flesh.'

There was no real theme to the decor. The apartment with filled with pictures and artefacts that Damien had collected as his work took him all over the world: a photograph from India, a rug from Turkey, a coffee table from Brazil, art from Chicago. There was a handful of pictures of Damien posing with celebrities.

'I'll give you a tour afterwards,' he said. 'First I want to tour your arse. What kind of music do you like?'

'Pretty much anything.'

'What kind of music do you like to *fuck* to?'

'Dance I suppose. Something hard with a strong beat.'

Damien smiled. 'You'll get something hard all right.'

He selected a CD. It was a white-label compilation. 'A friend mixed this for me. He's based in London but he DJs all over the world. He sends me CDs every now and again. I think you'll like it.'

The first track began to blast. Glenn had no idea what it was, but he liked the powerful beat. It set the mood for the kind of sex he desired. His mind was working along a single track, and sex was the only consideration. What Damien was promising was more than just simple sex, more than a blow job and a fuck. He was promising a journey, a trip to a place where body and mind were united in ecstasy.

'So. Where is this Fuck Room?'

'You'll see,' Damien said. 'Take off your clothes first.'

Glenn lifted his T-shirt over his head and threw it aside.

'You've got a great body.' Damien's eyes were inspecting him carefully. 'I'm gonna enjoy it.'

The implication of his words caused Glenn's heart to beat faster. It was a long time since he had experienced this kind of sexual chemistry with another man.

He carefully removed the dressing from his new piercing, the sight of his swollen nipple deepening his state of arousal. He couldn't wait for the injured flesh to heal, so that he could touch it and twist it and explore the possibilities of pleasure it would offer.

He continued to undress, taking off his boots and pants. Once again he stood in front of the photographer in nothing but his damp white shorts. Damien told him to turn around.

'Slide your shorts down slowly over your arse. I've been waiting all day to see this and I want to enjoy it.'

Glenn did as the big man instructed. He hooked his thumbs beneath the thick elastic waistband and slowly pushed his shorts down. The warm cotton slipped over the creamy curve of his buttocks as he proudly exposed himself. He eased the shorts down around his ankles and stepped out of them, kicking them aside. He waited breathlessly for Damien to respond.

'Bend over slowly. I want to see all the way into your crack.'

Glenn bent his knees and leaned over. He could feel the heat of Damien's eyes on his buttocks, photographing him in his head, admiring his arse while it was still a virgin to his cock. He reached behind and took hold of his buttocks in either hand. He spread himself wide. There was something so profound about an exposed arsehole. Showing the most secret region of the body to another being was almost as intimate as fucking itself. As he displayed his moist, golden-haired hole Glenn had nothing left of his sexual self to conceal.

Damien could now see everything that there was to see. And he understood it.

'Get down on your hands and knees,' he said.

Glenn bent down and assumed the position on the floor. He waited there, prone and exposed. Cool air caressed his funky arsehole. Damien slipped away into another room and returned a few moments later. Glenn felt a pressure against the soft flesh of his arsehole and then something short and blunt slid up inside him. Damien wedged the object into his rectum like a cork.

'What's that?' Glenn gasped.

Damien slapped his buttocks, the force of his palm stinging Glenn's flesh.

'It's a special little toy,' Damien said, 'to get you loose and ready for me.'

Glenn clenched his arsehole softly, getting a feel of the intrusive object. Whatever it was, it was short, maybe about five inches in length, and thick, especially around the base.

It was a butt plug. He had once dated a man who was really into them but he had never really bothered much himself.

Damien twisted the base of the toy and suddenly it began to vibrate inside him.

'*Oh my God!*'

The thick plug trembled inside his sensitive anal cavity, putting pressure on his prostate. The pleasure caused by such exquisite stimulation radiated outwards, from the core of his arse throughout his entire body. He gripped his buttocks tight. The taut nucleus of pleasure was concentrated down in his bowel and pulsated through to his balls. His nuts shivered in their sac, vibrating to the steady pulse inside him.

It was too intense. He closed his eyes and breathed deeply, willing himself not to come. He was on the very brink of an orgasm and it took every ounce of will to prevent himself spilling over the edge.

Damien smacked his buttocks again. The sudden pain brought him back to his senses.

'Don't you dare blow your load all over my floor. You don't come until I tell you.'

'OK,' Glenn gasped.

Damien pressed hard at the base of the toy, forcing it deeper inside. Glenn's thighs were trembling under the burden of such unwavering sensuality. He concentrated on the music to take his mind off the orgasm he wanted to unleash. The unknown track that had opened the compilation had moved into the Brothers in Rhythm mix of Kylie's 'Too Far'. Glenn acknowledged the relevance of the darkly poetic track on the moment in hand.

Damien told him to stand up. It wasn't easy. He tightened his sphincter around the bottom of the anal plug. He was frightened that if he dropped it Damien might take it away from him. Slowly, carefully, he uncurled his spine and rose to his knees. The vibrations intensified as he straightened himself up and his buttocks tightened further. He reached behind and held the rubber plug in place as he rose to his feet. The effort of pure will it took to delay his orgasm was tremendous. His balls were ready to release their flood at any moment. He remembered the disciplined techniques in yoga and put them into practice, clearing his mind and concentrating on his breath.

Damien's hands slid round Glenn's body, caressing his arse, his hips, his stomach. He moved down lower, towards his cock. He drew his fingers lazily along the shaft, tracing the seam. Still Glenn managed to hold off his release.

Damien seemed pleased. He held up a pair of black latex shorts. 'I want you to put these on,' he said.

Glenn took the pants from him. They were backless.

Damien smiled, nodding his head slightly. 'They'll keep your cock nice and secure. Prevent you getting any ideas about wanking yourself off. But they'll still give me clear access to that nice butt of yours.'

Glenn raised one leg and stepped carefully into the latex piece. He felt the plug slip from his rectum as his sphincter loosened. He reached behind and grabbed the vibrating rubber core before it came free and pushed it all the way back inside him. He stepped his other foot into the legs of the shorts and pulled them up over his thighs. They were very tight-fitting and it was a struggle to draw them up over his hips. There was a zip fastening at the side, which he undid to enable him to pull the shorts into place. He zipped them back up. It was like wearing a rubber jockstrap. His cock was squeezed tight within the restrictive pouch but his arse was free and exposed.

Damien caressed the restrained bulge of his dick. 'I'm impressed,' he said. 'They really suit you.' He moved towards a closed door against the far wall and indicated for Glenn to follow him.

Walking with the rubber plug vibrating against his prostate wasn't easy. He had to grip his buttocks tight and take small steps. He was afraid both of coming inside the tight shorts and of dropping the toy out of his arse. A yard seemed like a mile.

Damien had opened the door and disappeared inside. Glenn kept breathing deeply and taking slow, controlled steps. His face was flushed with the exertion; beads of perspiration broke across his brow and rolled down his cheeks.

At last he reached the open doorway. Damien was waiting just inside.

'Welcome to my Fuck Room,' he said with a smile.

The walls of the room were dark blue, and the lighting was low. There were no windows. Spread out across the shelves was a great array of sex toys: dildos, Thai beads, suction cups, bottles of cream and lube. There were vibrators in every size and colour imaginable, from slim six-inch fingers to huge, thirty-inch, double-ended dildos. On a steel rail in the corner hung a complete wardrobe of rubber and leather wear: harnesses, pouches, masks, jocks, boots, gags, whips. Against the far wall was a huge widescreen television set and video. In front of the TV was a long, leather-topped bench.

Damien beckoned him towards the bench. He approached with slow, careful steps. Damien patted the black leather surface.

'On your stomach,' he ordered.

Glenn had to hold the butt plug in place with his hand as he lifted one leg and straddled the bench. He leaned forwards, pressing his bare stomach and chest against the cold surface. He winced at the sudden pain as his nipple pressed against the leather covering. He repositioned himself to take the weight off the affected area. His arms and legs hung down on either side of the bench.

Damien caressed the line of his spine, drawing his fingers through the sheen of sweat.

'This kind of game is all new to you, isn't it?' Glenn nodded. 'You'll get used to it.'

Damien restrained his hands beneath the bench, fastening his wrists together with a pair of thick leather cuffs. He drew the buckle tight, locking Glenn's arms into position. He did the same with his legs, binding them at the ankles with a pair of heavy cuffs. He was secure.

Damien switched on the television and inserted a tape into the video.

'Here's something to get you in the mood, baby. I'll be back in a few minutes.' He gave Glenn's buttocks a slap as he walked by. 'Don't even think about getting yourself off on that bench while I'm gone. I don't want you to spill a drop of your precious load until I've truly worked your arse into a frenzy.'

He was gone, leaving Glenn bound and alone with the images on the television screen. It didn't take him long to realise that the porno tape Damien had left him with was a home-made one. The volume was muted but he recognised the location on screen: the Fuck Room.

He lifted his head and craned his neck to see the large set clearly. Damien was on screen with two other men. The camera obviously was hand-held so there had to be at least one other person in the room with them. Damien was wearing a black leather hood that completely covered his head but for two narrow eye slits. There was no mistaking that body, though, and its canvas of tattoos.

The two men were in their twenties and similar in build and looks. They were both lean, blond and tanned – and completely naked. They had a sun-kissed, Californian-porno-hunk look. They were both crouched on the bench on all fours, backsides thrust in the air. Damien was riding one of the blonds while he stuck an enormous dildo up the arse of the man nearest to the camera. He was giving it to them both with equal force.

The camera moved in closer, ignoring the boy with the dildo to concentrate on the other two men. The image swam out of focus as the camera zoomed in for a close-up of the penetration. The picture sharpened again and Glenn was looking directly at the thick shaft of Damien's cock as it slid in and out of the blond's arse. His golden buttocks quivered with every thrust of Damien's hard hips. Damien slapped the man's arse again and again as he fucked him, and the sun-tanned flesh began to redden. The black man was banging the man's hole with a ruthless determination.

The view was moving again as the camera operator came round in front of them to capture the look on the blond's face as he took such a brutal pounding. His face was red and wet, his blond hair plastered across his sweaty brow. His eyes were shut tight and he was breathing heavily through gritted teeth. The blond was beautiful with the fine, chiselled features of an angel. He had a clear, golden complexion, and pale, natural lashes and eyebrows. His teeth were white and even.

The boy opened his eyes. The ecstasy he was experiencing could be seen clearly in their pale-blue mirrors. He smiled at the camera, both exhausted and satisfied. Damien grabbed a fistful of hair and yanked his head backwards. The guy grimaced as he fucked him harder.

'Enjoying the movie?' Damien was back in the room.

Glenn twisted his head to look at him. He was wearing a harness of leather. The straps came over his broad shoulders, round his waist and up between his legs to fasten in front of his navel. His hard cock was strung up in a metal ring and jutting straight forward. The rod of meat was enraged and bulging.

'Who are these guys?' Glenn asked, surprised at the weakness of his voice.

Damien stood over him. 'Matthew and Derrick, a couple of friends of mine from America. They came to stay with me for a few weeks earlier this year. Matthew is the one I'm fucking right there. I'd love to introduce you but they've gone home. Maybe next time.'

Damien took hold of the butt plug and turned it slowly round 360 degrees inside his arse. A long sigh escaped from somewhere deep inside Glenn's chest.

'Maybe I'll let you keep this little toy,' Damien said. 'You seem to like it so much.'

Glenn groaned in despair when he realised that Damien was taking the vibrating plug out of him. He felt the strain as the thick base popped out of his tight ring and then the rest of its length slid out of him effortlessly, leaving a vacant space inside. He pressed his face into the deep leather, which smelled strongly of sweat and masculine sex, and waited for what was going to happen next. Damien was busy behind him. He twisted his neck but couldn't see what the black man was holding.

Damien chuckled and stepped nearer. 'Think you can cope with this?'

The dildo was over ten inches long and moulded to look like the real thing in every way, from the foreskin over its bulbous head to the bulging veins along its flesh-coloured shaft. There was even a huge rubber ball sac at its base. Damien teased him with the toy, rubbing it down his face, across his lips. Glenn flicked his tongue into the realistic piss slit. It was crafted out of malleable rubber, the long shaft yielding like real flesh against his skin.

Damien tore open the foil wrapper of a condom and stretched the sheath over the body of the fake cock. He squeezed a glob of K-Y on to the head and spread it all over its length.

'You'll need a lot of lube to get this baby inside you,' he said.

Glenn squirmed. His arse was loose and open. The removal of the plug had left a hunger inside and he was ready to take anything. He wanted the dildo inside him and anything else that Damien wanted to put in there.

Damien smeared some more lube into his arsehole and shoved it up inside him, getting his passage sticky and loose.

'Are you ready for this?'

'Oh yeah.'

The blunt rubber head pressed against his sphincter. Despite its relaxed condition, the tight ring offered some resistance to the huge foreign body. Damien thrust forwards. Glenn's arsehole surrendered and the long piece of latex slid all the way into his rectum. Glenn gasped as it shifted his insides. He strained at the cuffs binding his limbs, grinding his pelvis into the bench beneath him. Damien inserted the false cock all the way in until the rubbery scrotum pressed against his underside. He left it deep inside, allowing Glenn's body to get a feel for it, while he kneaded the hard flesh of his buttocks. His arse was full to bursting.

Glenn glanced at the TV screen as Damien started to slide the dildo back and forth. His arse opened and closed around its immense girth. Damien timed his strokes to the hard beat of the music.

On the home-made video Damien had swapped blonds. It was now the turn of Derrick to get his arse pounded for the benefit of the camera. He was lying on his back. Matthew held his legs up in the air while Damien let rip into his body. The guy was taking a hard drumming, but the expression on his face revealed that he was loving every second of it.

Damien started to slow down with the dildo. He slipped it back and forth slowly, sliding slickly up to the root and then languidly out again. It grazed Glenn's prostate with a divine lassitude. He pushed his hips up from the bench, trying to gobble it back up with his arse as it was lazily withdrawn.

Damien retracted the dildo one last time and took it all the way out.

Glenn cried in dismay.

'Don't worry, baby,' Damien said softly. 'Here comes the best part.'

He reached under the bench and released the straps around his ankles. He straddled the bench behind Glenn and eased up his hips until he was standing. With his hands still bound on the floor, Glenn was bent over almost double.

Damien already wore a condom. He positioned himself behind Glenn's raised buttocks. He pressed his cock to the open hole and slid his hips forwards. With one stroke he entered him to the hilt.

Glenn sighed. This was the real thing. No dildo could ever replicate the throbbing heat of a real cock. Damien held his hips in an iron grip and started to thrust back and forth. He bore the weight and tightened his arse, giving himself over to the other man. They were both sweating heavily. Damien rode him hard, his hips slapping noisily against his wet buttocks.

Glenn reached an even higher level of ecstasy. He thrust his arse back harder, trying to swallow the cock with his anus. He kept pushing back, matching his lover stroke for stroke. They reached a frantic pace.

'Do you wanna come now?' Damien said breathlessly.

'Uh huh,' he grunted.

Damien unzipped the fastening of his pants. He pressed his hand inside between leather and flesh and squeezed Glenn's soaking cock. He pumped the rigid organ quickly. After so much pleasure, Glenn couldn't hold off any longer. He screamed out loud, almost passing out with the intense flood of relief. He spurted wildly, filling his pants and Damien's fist with his hot come.

Damien grasped his arse in his come-filled hands. His cock thickened inside him and suddenly the black man was releasing his own load. Glenn could feel each pulse of his cock as it erupted its white lava inside him.

Glenn's knees weakened and finally gave way. They both collapsed into a sweaty, heaving heap.

The only light in the room came from the television screen where Damien had just shot a load over the faces of the two blonds. The CD player had finished its cycle and the apartment was quiet.

They lay together on the floor, nestled in each other's arms, their nakedness covered by a blanket. Damien lit a cigarette, the ashtray resting on his stomach. He exhaled a lazy cloud of smoke and passed the cigarette to Glenn.

He inhaled, relishing the potency of the smoke in his lungs. 'I was trying to quit,' he drawled, flicking the ash from the tip.

'Try another day.'

'It looks like I'll have to.' He stretched slowly, savouring the looseness of his body. There was a delicious vigour and strength to his physique that stemmed directly from the core of his freshly fucked arsehole. He tightened his sphincter, welcoming the wetness there.

'Are you writing another book?' Damien asked.

'I've started to make notes. It's nothing more than an outline at the minute. I'm too busy promoting the new book to write full time right now.' He rested his hand on Damien's cock, which was finally soft. He cupped the cock and balls in one hand and massaged them in his palm.

'Mmm.' Damien drew on the cigarette. 'So what's it about?'

'Which one?'

'The new one. The outline.'

'You shouldn't ask me that. Don't you know writers think it's bad luck to discuss their work before they've written it?'

'Why?'

'It can jinx the project.'

'Bollocks. You can at least tell me a little bit of what it's about. After all, we're friends now, aren't we?'

Glenn squeezed the big man's balls. 'I suppose we are friends now. Luckily for both of us, I don't have a problem with fucking my friends.'

Damien leaned over and kissed him on the lips. 'Very lucky.'

'I've been toying with the idea of writing a sequel to *Everyday Hurts*. I've been working on a few ideas but I haven't made up my mind if I want to do it yet.'

'You should.' Damien was enthusiastic. 'I'd love to know what happens to those characters next. I hope you plan to bring back Anthony.'

'I'd be using nearly all of the characters from the first book. But I'm still not sure if I want to do a follow-up.'

Damien stroked the curve of his spine. 'I would do it if I was

67

you. Those film people will only come up with a sequel themselves if you don't do it. It might as well come from the original creator.'

'That's what I've been thinking myself. Those men are a part of me. I don't want to turn them over to someone else. I already did that with the script of the first book.'

'You've definitely got the right idea,' Damien said, kissing him again.

Glenn glanced at his watch. 'I should really be making a move. It's nearly seven o'clock.'

Damien hugged him close. 'Don't you want to stay with me?'

'I'm tempted. But I don't think my arse could take another session like this afternoon's so soon. I'd love to see you again, though.'

Damien squeezed his buttocks. 'I'll hold you to that.' They kissed. 'How's your nipple feeling?'

'It's a bit sore but I'll survive.'

'No regrets?'

Glenn stroked Damien's thick, flaccid cock. 'No way. I don't believe in them.'

Six

Reflections

On the way home Glenn stopped at the local supermarket. It was nearly eight o'clock and the assistants were getting ready for the store to close. The cashiers were already shutting down their checkouts. He hurried round the aisles with a trolley. He hated grocery shopping and wanted to get it over with as quickly as possible. Sex with Damien had given him a ravenous appetite and he knew that the refrigerator at home was empty, apart from two bottles of Chardonnay, a litre of gin and a couple of milkshakes.

He grabbed one of the last remaining loaves from the bakery and sped round to the deli counter for some cooked meat and pâté. He grabbed a few other essentials: bacon, eggs, fresh fruit and vegetables. On his way to the checkouts he stopped in the drinks aisle and dumped two bottles of champagne into his trolley, a bottle of blue-label vodka, a bottle of rum and a two-litre bottle of cola.

One of the grocery assistants approached him as he was leaving. Lee was a nice kid in his mid twenties. Glenn had gone out with him for a few weeks about three years ago. Lee was a voracious predator in bed, never satisfied with what he received. Even Glenn, who had a highly active sex drive of his own, found it hard living up to his demands.

Lee also wanted to be a writer but he couldn't seem to get a break and had to support himself by working at the supermarket. Glenn had read some of his work and it was pretty good. Lee had written a horror novel that was very impressive but he couldn't find a publisher to take it. His raw, remorseless style of writing was suited to the horror genre. His book was stark and terrifying in its portrayal of violence and fear. Glenn had even shown it to his own publisher, but they had surprised him with their lack of interest.

'Hi, Glenn. How are you?' Lee always looked uncomfortable in the regulation store uniform.

'I'm fine. How are you doing? Did you try that list of agents I gave you?'

'Yeah. Still waiting to hear back. The same old news.'

As a teenager Lee had been thin and awkward. It was amazing the transformation a few years had brought to his features. He had filled out across his shoulders and his face seemed to suit its new-found maturity. Although their relationship had ended years before, they still peppered their friendship with the occasional bout of passionate sex. Lee had a serious boyfriend now, but his hunger for sex meant that they weren't above an infrequent threesome.

Glenn considered asking Lee what time he finished work. It had been quite a while since the last time they had fucked. But then he remembered his tired arsehole. His mind was still enthusiastic but his body needed time to recuperate. Lee was an aggressive little top and Glenn just wasn't up to the job. He would have to wait for another night.

'Are you going to Gary's party on Saturday?' Glenn asked.

Lee nodded. 'Yes. I'll see you there?'

'Yes. Bye for now, then.'

It was dark when he arrived home. He switched off the alarm and carried his groceries straight through into the kitchen. He put the bottle of vodka in the freezer and stuffed everything else into the fridge. He couldn't wait for anything to cook so he made himself a sandwich with the meat he had bought and poured himself a glass of wine. He never seemed to cook when he was on his own. It would have been nice to have some company tonight.

Glenn ate his sandwich and carried his glass of wine upstairs. He ran the bath and, while he was waiting for it to fill, he went through into his study and switched on the PC. He signed on to

AOL and downloaded his email. He scanned quickly through the list of senders. Boring. There was nothing there that couldn't wait. He turned off the computer.

Grant had told him to avoid using any kind of oils or creams in his bathwater to avoid infecting his nipple. When the tub was full, he poured in three large capfuls of antiseptic and stirred it round. He stripped off in the bedroom and stuffed his clothes into the washing basket. He gazed at his full-length reflection in the mirror, turning left and right to admire himself.

Although it was still very painful and swollen, the piercing really had given him a new perception of the way that he looked. He held himself differently, his shoulders well back, chest forward. He wasn't a vain man but he had to admit that it did look very sexy. He couldn't believe that he had never thought about piercing before. At least he had it now and it would always be there as a constant reminder of Damien − a souvenir of the long, strenuous afternoon they spent together.

Though there was little chance that he would *ever* forget his time with Damien.

It would be days before his arsehole returned to normal.

Glenn put his glass on the side of the bath and eased himself down into the steaming hot water. The muscles of his legs and back and buttocks were all aching from being restrained in one position for so long. Even his cock was sore after the unexpected intensity of his orgasm. He sipped his wine and allowed the hot currents to soothe his tired body. He spread his legs and let the water caress his abused hole.

He was careful not to douse his nipple under the water for too long. Grant had warned him to keep it clean but not to soak it. He would purge it with pure water after his bath.

He shut his eyes and tried to think of other things.

The idea of a sequel to *Everyday Hurts* had been bugging him for a while. After the success of the first novel and the subsequent movie adaptation he had been feeling the pressure to write another book. As well as requests from his publisher and the film studio he received letters every week from fans of the book who wanted to read more about their favourite characters.

After a couple of moderate successes with his first two novels,

Glenn had been completely unprepared for the explosive impact *Everyday Hurts* made. The book was a psychological thriller. A cat-and-mouse story involving a lawyer and a brilliant killer. Even though Anthony Pierce is guilty of stabbing his girlfriend to death in a cold-blooded attack, his young lawyer Matthew Reed turns up evidence that could get Pierce acquitted. Matthew is convinced that Pierce is guilty even though he has no motive for the murder and has to battle with his own conscience when it comes to suppressing evidence or not. Pierce, realising that Matthew is sexually attracted to him, manipulates the lawyer into successfully defending him. At the end of the book when Pierce walks free, both Matthew and the reader know that he is guilty of the crime and capable of killing again.

By the time the film adaptation of *Everyday Hurts* went into production the novel had already gone ballistic and was a number-one bestseller on both sides of the Atlantic.

As far as Glenn was concerned, when he finished the book, that was it. Anthony Pierce walked out of court a free man and Matthew had to live with the knowledge of what he had done. It was the end of the book and the end of the story. He went on to write other things.

But the pressure to write a sequel was persistent. His agent had warned him a few weeks ago that the film company were considering putting a follow-up into production even without Glenn's input. If he wanted to hold on to the story and the development of his characters he had to act now.

Despite his reluctance, he started to form a few ideas, making notes, jotting down potential storylines. He rejected a lot of his own suggestions until he came up with a strand that had a grain of potential to it. He would pick up where the first book left off, with Pierce's release. Then Pierce would begin to stalk his lawyer, manipulating him through fear and sex and then eventually murdering him in the course of the story. Killing off the novel's most popular character would be a controversial move but it was the only satisfactory storyline that he was interested in developing.

He tried not to worry about it. It would be months yet before the idea advanced beyond the stage of some hastily scribbled notes and a vague outline. His time over the next few weeks was not his own. He had to make the most of his last few days of freedom before the publicity machine for his new novel went into overdrive.

He finished the wine and put the glass down on the floor.

Once he had fulfilled his commitments to the present book he had intended to take a holiday and have a few months off before starting work on anything else. Now it didn't look like he was going to get the chance. If he started work on the new novel, it would be at least eighteen months of hard graft before he had time to sit back and relax.

He had been looking forward to a break from serious writing. Throughout his career he had experimented with erotica – writing stories for magazines, mainly in America, under the pen name Kyle Hanson. For a while now he had been toying with the idea of editing the Kyle Hanson stories down into one volume. He had unofficially pencilled it in as his next project in the break between novels. That idea would have to be put on hold now.

He lay in the bath until the water started to lose its temperature and then climbed out. He towel-dried his aching limbs slowly. He wrapped the towel around his waist and filled the sink with clean water. Carefully he cleaned his nipple with cotton balls. The piercing was extremely tender and he didn't want to put too much pressure on it. Grant had recommended that he use an antiseptic spray on it for the first couple of weeks. He would have to go out to the chemist in the morning and buy a can.

He went down to the kitchen to refill his glass and then returned to the bedroom to finish drying. He wasn't fond of pyjamas, so rather than put on another set of clothes at that time of night he stepped into a pair of fresh white boxer shorts and threw himself down on top of the bed.

Before he had decided what to do next, the telephone rang. He rolled across the bed and picked it up. It was Dean. Glenn suddenly became attentive at the sound of his voice.

'Hi. How did it go today?' Dean sounded happy and in the mood to talk.

'It was great. More than great, actually.'

Dean was on to the cryptic tone of his voice immediately. 'You shagged the photographer, didn't you?'

'No, I didn't. Well, not exactly. He shagged me.'

'Ha. I can't *believe* you. You act like butter wouldn't melt in your mouth and then you go round dropping your pants for famous photographers. Anyway, I always had you down for a top. Come on, then. What happened? Tell me all about it. God knows, I tell you enough about my sex life. What's he like? I don't think I've ever seen a proper photograph of him.'

Glenn described Damien's looks. 'It's quite difficult to put into words, because to look at him you couldn't really say that he was handsome. He's just got *something* very special.'

'Like what? Is he hung?'

'He's hung. Massive in fact.'

'I like big guys. It gives Gary something to be jealous about. A bit of healthy competition does him good. So when can I meet him?'

Glenn laughed. 'I don't know if you can. I'll have to ask him for you.'

'When are you seeing him again?'

'Sometime over the next week. I'm not really sure. I'm going back to see the pictures when he develops them.'

'I bet. Are you going to assume the position again?'

'I might. I haven't ruled it out. It all depends how well I recover from this afternoon's adventure.'

'Glenn, you really shock me. I honestly thought you were the dominant type.'

Glenn sipped his wine. Talking about Damien had given him another hard-on. He ran his hand over the bulge. 'What makes you think that?'

'I don't know. I just assumed you were.'

'I'm easy, mate. I can go either way. It just depends on my mood. I'd give your butt a good seeing-to if I got the chance.' He spoke light-heartedly. Dean failed to realise the deeper consequences of what Glenn had just said.

Dean chuckled down the phone. 'You wouldn't know what to do with my butt. It would eat you up alive.'

Glenn decided to change the subject before he revealed too much. 'I've got something else that will come as a surprise.'

'Nothing you can say can shock me now.'

'Do you want to bet on that?'

'I'm not a betting man, but I'll make good on all my innuendo if you can top what you've just told me.'

'I had my nipple pierced this afternoon.' There was a stunned silence on the end of the phone. 'Dean. Are you still there?'

'You're winding me up.'

'No, I'm not. I've got a nice little bar sticking through my tit right now.'

'Ha ha. You really have lost your mind. That Damien must be a hell of a shag if he has this effect on you. It sounds to me like he's fucked your brains out.'

The two men continued chatting for the next half an hour, mostly about sex.

'When we got home from the sauna last night,' Dean said, 'Gary was like an animal. He always gets horny when he comes back from the baths, but he hasn't been like this in ages. He grabbed me as soon as we came in the door and ripped my pants off. He gave me a right banging over the back of the sofa. My arsehole's been slack all day.'

'What brought that about?'

'Apparently, he got into quite a scene in the steam rooms while we were still in the tub. He fucked some guy right there on one of the slabs. He got such a kick out of it he came straight home and treated me to the same thing. What can I say? I'm lucky to have such a caring boyfriend. Isn't it about time you found yourself a boyfriend? It can't be much fun rattling round that big house on your own every night.'

'I've had boyfriends.'

'Yeah, but none that ever last. Wouldn't you like someone to come home who'll take you over the sofa every night?'

'I couldn't cope with that every night,' Glenn said bravely. Dean had struck a sensitive nerve.

'You know what I mean. There's more to life than just cock. What about Damien? Is that going to go anywhere?'

'Dean, I only met him for the first time this morning.'

'And you've already got horizontal and intimate with him. There must be *something* there between you.'

Glenn sighed. 'Maybe there is. We'll see in time. I'm not going to rush it.' His glass was empty again. 'I'm gonna go now. I'm pretty tired.'

'Hey. What about your stalker? Have you seen any more of the mysterious stranger?'

'Oh. I'd forgotten all about him. No. Not seen him around today. That's another man I must have scared away.'

'Yeah, well I don't doubt that. Listen, go to bed and get a good night's sleep. I'll see you at the weekend. Bye, darlin'.'

'Bye.' He listened to the hollowness on the line as Dean hung up before slowly putting down the receiver.

'Oh shit,' he said aloud.

He wondered if Dean had any idea at all about the way he felt for him. If he did, he certainly didn't give anything away. Glenn knew how much Dean loved Gary. There was no way he would ever get a look-in there. It didn't stop him wanting, though.

He reached down for the envelope that he kept hidden under the bed and extracted the photograph. It was a ten-by-eight enlargement. It must have been taken about five years ago. Dean had a neat little beard that he had long since shaved. He was kneeling on the floor and leaning forwards with his elbows resting across the bed. He was looking back over his shoulder, gazing into the camera with his liquid-brown eyes – eyes that were full of love for the man behind the lens. Gary must have taken the shot not long after they came back from holiday because Dean had a rich, golden-brown tan that was pronounced even further across his broad, sunburned shoulders. His chunky buttocks were creamy white, revealing the line of his shorts. The crack of his arse was open just wide enough to see the trace of brown hair within. The photo wasn't sufficiently sharp to see his precious brown ring.

Glenn had every detail of the photo committed to memory. He had caressed that arse a million times in his fantasies, stroked it, kissed it, ridden it, loved it. He worshipped the body in the photograph. He would give up everything for just one night alone with that body. It was the only wish that he wanted to become reality.

He put the picture back in the envelope and returned it to its hiding place under the bed.

It was getting late. Almost midnight. His schedule for the next day was clear. He was actually free right up to the middle of the following week, when he had to do an interview for a local radio station.

He had told Dean that he wanted to go to sleep, but that had been a lie. He knew that it would be a while yet before sleep was ready to take him. His body was tired but his mind, as usual, was active. It was always the same at night.

He went back down to the kitchen to refill his glass. Taking the bottle with him, he went up to his study and took out his notebooks for *Everyday Hurts*. Every one of his novels began this way, with book after book of notes and ideas. He worked out the story and plot in the finest detail on paper before committing a single sentence to the word processor. He kept all of his notes, even after he had finished the final draft of the book.

With the prospect of a sequel on the horizon he wanted to reacquaint himself with his lead characters. He sank back into his armchair with the reading light behind him and started to work through the old books.

The hour got later and the level of the wine in the bottle decreased.

At 2.15 he was jolted out of his reflections by a sudden noise. He put down the book and listened, certain that the sound had come from downstairs.

Silence.

He waited.

Listening.

Nothing.

He looked at the clock again. His mind was tired and starting to play tricks on him. He stood up slowly and stretched, deciding to finally call it a day. He left the notebooks out on top of his desk and turned off the light.

This time the sound was unmistakable. It came from below. Something had been knocked over.

Glenn froze; his blood turned to ice.

Someone was in the house.

He didn't move or make a sound. He just waited.

Nothing.

Carefully he turned on the light again. He needed a weapon. He looked around the study. *Shit*. There was nothing of any use. He reached for the telephone.

Then stopped. Listening.

There was nothing to hear. What if he had just imagined it? The police wouldn't treat him too kindly. It was late and he had been drinking. They weren't going to be very sympathetic if they came out and found nothing.

He picked up the empty wine bottle by the neck. Wielding it before him like a club, he stepped lightly towards the study door. He turned the handle slowly and drew the door towards him.

He had left the landing lights on and those down in the kitchen; other than that, the house was in darkness. He leaned over the top of the banister rail and looked down on to the floor below. The living-room door was open but he could see nothing of the blackness beyond. Light poured out of the kitchen doorway. There was still nothing to hear.

I must have imagined it, he convinced himself. It's late. The mind plays funny tricks at this time of night.

He descended the stairs slowly, still gripping the neck of the empty bottle tight. He stopped halfway down to listen. Nothing. He continued. At the bottom he waited, glancing uneasily between the brightly lit kitchen and the pitch-black living room. His heart was thumping like a hammer, the blood thundering through his head.

He chose the kitchen first. Stepping round the doorway in a wide arch. It was empty. He crossed to the door and tried the handle. Locked. He gave a sigh of relief.

He must have imagined it all. Maybe the noise had been outside – a cat or something – and his fatigued brain thought it came from in the house.

He was breathing more easily now.

Still, better check out the front of the house, just in case.

He walked back through into the hall with increasing confidence. He stepped into the living room and turned on the light.

The man was standing over by the window.

Glenn almost jumped out of his skin.

He recognised him immediately: the man who had been following him around.

So Dean had been right after all. He was a stalker. He was dressed in dark-blue jeans and a black jacket.

Glenn raised the bottle threateningly towards him. His hand was shaking with the sudden surge of adrenalin. Images raced through his mind of other celebrities who had fallen victim to stalkers. The potential of this situation was terrifying.

'What the fuck are you doing here?' Despite his terror, he was thankful for the anger that manifested itself in his voice.

The man raised his hands, showing that they were empty. 'Take it easy. I'm not going to hurt you.'

'You won't get the chance, you bastard.'

'Look, you don't understand. This isn't what it seems.'

'Like fuck it isn't. You've been following me around for days. You break into my house. And you say it's not what it fucking seems.'

'Please,' the man pleaded, 'I need your help.'

'You'll get all the help you need from the police,' Glenn said, edging nearer to the phone. 'I don't want to hear it. This is my house. How dare you break in? What's wrong with people like you? You're sick.'

'No,' the man shouted, 'don't phone the police.'

Glenn ignored him and picked up the handset.

The man suddenly lunged across the room towards him. Glenn hurled the empty bottle at his attacker. It missed the main target of his body and just glanced off his shoulder, shattering on the floor. The man grabbed for him, but was hindered by the coffee table. Glenn ducked out of his grip. He dropped the phone and ran for the door.

'Wait, please,' the man shouted.

Glenn was in the hall. Where could he go? The front and back doors were locked and there was no time to open them.

His attacker was right behind him. He leaped for the stairs, narrowly missing the man's outstretched hand. He stumbled but did not fall, taking the stairs two at a time. Terror and adrenalin were giving an unnatural velocity to his limbs.

The man was halfway up the stairs behind him.

Glenn burst through the bedroom door, slamming it shut in the face of his pursuer. He lunged for the telephone beside the bed.

Before he could dial a single digit the man grabbed him from behind, tearing the phone from his grasp. They both lost their balance and fell across the bed.

The man wrapped his arms around him. Glenn fought back, smashing a hard fist into his face. He rolled out from under his attacker to the edge of the bed. He jumped up and lunged for the door. The man caught him by his underpants. The cotton tore as he dragged him back towards him. Glenn lost his balance and fell, sprawling to the floor bare-arsed, his pants tangled around his knees.

The man was on top of him like a tiger, pinning his arms and legs to the floor. Glenn tried to struggle but it was useless. His attacker outweighed him and he couldn't move.

'Calm down!' the man shouted, pressing all of his weight on top of Glenn's naked body. 'I didn't come here to hurt you. I came looking for help.'

'By breaking into my house in the middle of the night.'

'I had to get near you. It was the only way.'

Glenn stared up into the man's hazel eyes. It was strange but he didn't look like a psychopath. There was also an unexpected softness to the features of his face. But Glenn could feel the strength of the man's body as it pinned him down hard. There was no use fighting back from this position.

'Will you at least listen to me?'

'I don't have much choice,' Glenn said, 'do I? You've got me trapped.'

'I'll let you go in a minute. I just need to know that I can trust you not to phone the police if I let you go.'

'I'm listening.'

'Do you know who I am?'

Glenn looked up at his face. 'No. There's something ... Something about you that I recognise. But no, I don't know who you are. I just know that you've been following me.'

'You should recognise me.'

'I don't.'

'My name is Matthew. Matthew Reed.'

What was going on with this guy?

'Matthew Reed is a character in one of my books.'

The man nodded. 'I know. You created me.'

Glenn couldn't stop himself from laughing. 'You really are a nutcase.'

'Come on. Look at me. Can't you see it? I'm the exact image that you had in your head when you wrote that book. You can't deny it!'

Glenn couldn't really argue with that. Now that the man had pointed it out, he realised he was right. 'That character was good-looking, well built, dark. A lot of men fit that description.'

'I can tell you things about myself that you never put in your book.'

Glenn was uneasy. 'Like what?'

'My middle name is Iain. Spelled with two Is. I fell in love when I was fifteen with a man called Paul. He broke my heart after three months, but gave me the confidence to accept my sexuality. I'm submissive in bed. A bottom.'

Glenn was dumb struck. 'How do you know all this? Have you been reading through my notebooks? Have you been in the house before?'

'I've already told you how I know. I *am* Matthew.' He relaxed his grip on Glenn's wrists. 'I was circumcised when I was nineteen. I don't think you ever included *that* in your notes, but it's part of my character.'

Glenn was beginning to doubt his own sanity. The man was accurate in every detail. And he did look *exactly* like he had intended that character to look. When the man let go of him and rolled over on to his side, Glenn didn't try to get away. He leaned over and looked behind his ear.

There it was. The birthmark he had given Matthew Reed.

Glenn was struggling to comprehend any of this.

'What else do you know?' he said quietly.

'I know that in your next book you plan to kill me. That is why I'm here. To beg you not to do it.'

Seven

Matthew

The ice cubes cracked and splintered as Glenn poured vodka over the top of them. He half filled two tumblers with the spirit and then topped up the rest of the glasses with tonic. He took a long draught from his own drink before carrying both glasses though to the living room.

The man who claimed to be Matthew Reed had cleaned up the broken glass and was sitting on the edge of the sofa. Glenn gave him the drink and he smiled nervously.

'Thanks,' the man said.

They were both tense. Glenn sat down in the armchair and nursed the tumbler on his lap. He had pulled on a pair of old jeans and a white vest. He was struggling to come to terms with what was happening. Common sense was telling him that he should throw the man out into the street and call the police. He was obviously touched and Glenn could only make it worse by humouring him. He needed psychiatric help, not someone to pander to his fantasies.

But something was niggling at his conscience. There was no way the man could know the specific details of the Matthew Reed character that he did. Even if he had been reading through his notes on the character, this guy knew intimate aspects that Glenn had not even committed to paper. It just wasn't conceivable that he could know these things.

His appearance was even more unsettling. The reason Glenn had thought he recognised him when he first saw him on the street was because he did. The man looked *exactly* like Matthew Reed: his size, his hair, every feature of his face. A fraud could have based his appearance on physical details from the book, like the neat cut of his hair, the black band tattooed round his right biceps. But there were other details that could not be faked: the firm set of his fleshy lips, the deep moodiness of his dark-brown eyes, the birthmark. These were the mysteries that Glenn's intelligent mind could not rationalise.

He sipped his drink.

'Look,' he said, '*Matthew*. If you want me to believe any of this you're going to have to convince me. I can't just accept the fact that a fictitious character could come to life and then break into my house. Matthew Reed is not a real person.'

'I was real to you when you created me. When you wrote that book you didn't just create a character. You created a whole new world. A universe that is just as real within its own dimensions as your own is to you. That world was real to you when you invented it and it's real to millions of people who have read that book. And it's real to all of us living within it.'

Glenn shook his head. 'Fiction is fiction. That world and those people only ever existed in my mind.'

The man stood up and put his hand on Glenn's shoulder. 'You can feel that, can't you? *I'm* real, aren't I? I'm not in your mind now.'

'That doesn't make you who you say you are.'

The man sighed. Glenn could see the pain clearly in his soft brown eyes. 'How do I convince you?' He sat back down for a moment, quietly thinking. Suddenly he looked up smiling, as an idea formed. 'OK,' he said, putting down his drink on the coffee table.

He stood up and slowly peeled back his T-shirt, revealing the hard ridges of his stomach. He pulled it off over his head and threw it down on the floor. He presented himself to Glenn, all taut muscle and hard tits.

'Look at me,' he said. 'I'm what you made me. This is the body you gave me.'

He was right. His body was an exact manifestation of Glenn's desire. Everything he wanted in a man was accumulated in one perfect physical package. His pecs were like two huge plates of hard flesh. His tiny brown nipples were swollen and surrounded by a cluster of soft brown hair. His stomach was a terrain of clearly defined ridges covered with a light dusting of hair that descended below the waist of his jeans. His arms were huge, filled with thick muscle from shoulder to wrist.

'Be honest,' the man said: 'isn't this the body you created for me?'

Glenn stared at his torso with wide eyes. He swallowed, his mouth dry. 'Yes,' he said. 'That's exactly how I pictured you.' He drained his glass dry. 'I need another drink.'

The man followed him through into the kitchen without bothering to put back on his T-shirt. He leaned against the bench, his arms folded across his broad chest.

Glenn took the bottle from the freezer and refilled his glass, mixing an even stronger drink this time.

'So do you believe me now?'

Glenn stared at the perfect male specimen standing in his kitchen. 'I don't know if I believe what you're saying, as much as I doubt my own sanity.'

'I don't know what else I can do to prove it. I thought just the sight of me would be enough to convince you. After everything else I've told you, I thought that would be enough.'

'It's not an easy story to swallow.'

The man stepped towards him. Two huge hands fixed on his shoulders. They stood face to face. The man was an inch or two shorter than Glenn but he looked directly into his eyes. The look on his handsome face was completely earnest.

'I *need* you to help me.'

Glenn was trembling. He was scared. Not physically afraid of the stranger in his house, but scared of the place in his own head that was starting to believe this fantastic fable.

Suddenly they were even nearer as Glenn allowed the man to draw him into his arms. The man's lips came closer. They touched;

their mouths joined in an open union. Glenn could feel the strength and energy of the man affecting him. When the warm kiss ended Glenn was shaking.

He *knew* from that kiss this was true.

The stranger was Matthew Reed.

Glenn's eyes were wet. A single tear rolled down his face like rain on a sheet of glass. Matthew wiped it dry with gentle fingers.

'Why are you crying?' he asked softly, his warm breath caressing Glenn's damp cheek.

Despite his confusion and astonishment, Glenn smiled. He leaned into Matthew's broad chest and allowed himself to be held. They stayed like that for a while, neither of them speaking. Glenn rested his head against Matthew's shoulder, feeling the heat of his skin against his face. He could perceive the strong, peaceful beat of his heart against his own chest.

They drew apart slowly. Glenn gazed into Matthew's face with astonishment. The other man smiled with kind eyes, his broad lips bracketed with soft dimples. Glenn ran his fingers along his face, tracing the clean line of his jaw. His stubble rasped beneath his fingertips.

'You're so beautiful,' he whispered.

'I'm how you made me.' Matthew kissed the tips of his fingers as they explored his lips.

'I can see that.'

They went back through into the living room. Glenn sat cross-legged on the sofa. He was exhausted but his mind would not stop racing, trying in vain to make sense of the night's events.

'All right,' said Glenn, 'against all better judgement, and at great risk to my sanity, I believe what you're saying. Why is this happening now?'

'Because, when you started work on the sequel to my story, everything in my world changed. Before that everyone had their own will and their own life within the context of that world. When you finished the first story you left us to make our own lives. The future was our own.'

'So what's different now?'

'None of us are in control of it any more. You govern our will and our lives again.'

'Because I drew up a story outline for your characters?'

'Yes. Although you haven't started to write the book, just by outlining the events of the story, things have already started to change for us. If you go ahead with the novel, it will all change for ever. Do you understand that?'

'Kind of,' Glenn said. 'I understand what you're saying. I don't understand how it can be happening or why you could be here in the flesh right now.'

'I'm here because I have to be. Anthony wants to kill me and you're the only one who can stop him.'

Glenn shook his head. 'I can't grasp this.'

Matthew took hold of his hand. 'Just promise me you won't write that book. You're the only one who can possibly save me. You loved me when you wrote that first book. How can you let me die now?'

Glenn closed his eyes. 'It's late. I'm going to go to bed. If I wake up tomorrow and you're still here, if it doesn't turn out that I've just dreamed this whole episode, *then* I'll help you.'

Matthew squeezed his hand tight. 'If you were dreaming you wouldn't be able to feel me. But thank you, anyway.'

Glenn uncurled his legs from under him and rose to his feet.

'Can I sleep on your couch?' asked Matthew. 'I don't have anywhere to go in this world. I've been roughing it since I got here.'

Glenn laughed. 'Bloody hell. I think I've got a more surreal imagination than I ever gave myself credit for.' He held out his hand and helped Matthew to his feet. 'You can come to bed with me. That way I'll know as soon as I wake up tomorrow whether or not I'm completely mad.'

Matthew struggled to push his tight jeans down over his bulging thigh muscles. Underneath he was wearing a pair of pale-blue shorts. He folded up his jeans and placed them over the back of a chair. His entire body rippled with muscle as he moved. His thighs were smooth but his calves were covered in the same dusting of light-brown hair as his chest and stomach.

'Wow,' Glenn exclaimed, 'you really have got a magnificent body.'

Matthew smiled and flexed his muscles, posing for him like a bodybuilder. 'I've got you to thank for that.'

Glenn was underneath the duvet in his boxer shorts. Matthew lifted up the covers and climbed in with him. He shuffled across the bed and enfolded Glenn in his big arms. Glenn felt strangely secure and comfortable in his protective embrace.

'Do you want to fuck me before you go to sleep?' Matthew asked, kissing Glenn's cheek and slowly working his way around his mouth.

'*What?*'

'I know you used to fantasise about me all the time.'

'How do you know that?'

'I probably know you better than you know me. I'm really horny. Feel.' He guided Glenn's hand down to the hard protuberance in his shorts. 'See.'

'Matthew, I'm really tired. You've given me an awful lot to think about tonight.'

'I said you could fuck me. You know how much I like it.'

Glenn protested feebly.

Matthew sounded hurt. 'Don't you like me any more? I used to be one of your favourites. I always thought you wanted to fuck me. You spent so much time giving me a great body and a perfect arse.'

'I'd love to fuck you. But I'm exhausted.'

'Will you do it tomorrow?'

'If you're still here.'

Matthew held him tighter. 'I'll still be here.'

Eight

Morning Glory

Glenn woke up slowly, gradually freeing his mind from the dark embrace of sleep and a fog of confused dreams. Matthew was lying against his back, a protective arm wrapped around his shoulder, cuddled in a spoon position.

So the handsome stranger was still here.

It hadn't been a dream. Meaning one of only two things: a fictional character had walked out of the pages of a novel, crossing the boundaries of reality and imagination, in search of his creator; or Glenn Holden had finally lost his mind. Well *that* prospect had been on the cards for a while.

Glenn stretched slowly, feeling the hard body of the other man pressing against the curve of his spine. Matthew's hard cock was resting in the cleft of his buttocks with only their shorts to prevent it slipping inside him.

The light in the bedroom was gloomy, the grey shafts of morning light failing to penetrate the heavy curtains. Glenn could hear the steady rattle of rain against the window. He turned over on to his back slowly, glancing over Matthew's shoulder at the bedside clock. It was half past eleven.

Matthew stirred, murmuring something in his sleep.

Glenn turned to look at the face on the pillow beside him. His sleeping partner looked so peaceful and innocent. He studied the features that he had moulded in his mind years earlier. Matthew's soft brow was clear and untroubled. His dark hair was damp and unruly through sleep, its untidiness increasing his naïve attraction.

The personification of Matthew Reed was a revelation, a manifestation of pure desire. When Glenn created him he had drawn on his fantasy of the perfect man. Now the perfect man was right here in bed beside him.

Glenn leaned nearer and placed a soft kiss on his stubbled cheek. The smooth brown eyes fluttered open, moist and dark with sleep.

'Sorry, I didn't mean to wake you.'

Matthew's broad lips widened and curled into a clear, infectious smile revealing his strong, even teeth and bracketing his mouth with two very sexy dimples. He wrapped his arms around Glenn and lifted him on to his chest, their stomachs and hard cocks pressed together. 'You can wake me up like that whenever you want.'

Excited by the strength of his body and the strong salty scent of him, Glenn started kissing him, fervently, with passion. He squashed the tender nub of his nipple against the mountainous peaks of Matthew's chest. His cock seemed to be leaking a gallon of pre-come into his shorts. He pressed his hips down on to the body beneath him, grinding, savouring the friction of their two hard shafts.

'Are you gonna fuck me now?' Matthew asked breathlessly.

Glenn thrust down even harder, crushing his cock hard against the other man's throbbing dick. 'How long have I got you?'

'As long as you want me.'

'Then there's no hurry,' Glenn said. He was unquestionably looking forward to fucking the perfect example of manhood beneath him and being ridden like an animal in turn, but right now he had an even greater desire than fucking. He wanted to taste his man right from the source.

He flung back the bedclothes. The covers slipped from their bodies and slid into a heap on the floor. Glenn slithered down Matthew's magnificent torso, descending towards his groin. The front of his shorts was dark and damp. Matthew lifted his hips from the bed and Glenn slipped his pants down. He gasped at the sight that he uncovered. Matthew's cock jutted up, nude and erect, reasonably long and impressively thick. It was perfectly in proportion to his stocky build.

Glenn wrapped his hand around the impressive tool, stroking it with a slow fist.

'Is it as nice as you imagined it?' Matthew asked.

Glenn squeezed the shaft, milking a big drop of pre-come from the tiny slit.

'This', he said, 'is better than I ever imagined.'

He leaned forwards and kissed the fleshy knob at the end, sliding the tip of his tongue into the mouth of the pisshole. He worked his tongue over the organ, tracing the seam along the underside, licking him from his balls to his tip. The cock throbbed at the wet caress of his tongue. He lingered over the sensitive head, giving him quick little licks to the swollen tip. Matthew's pre-come was dense and phenomenally sticky. It oozed rapidly on to Glenn's tongue, kindling his hunger.

He closed his mouth over the head, sealing his lips. He opened wide and followed the graceful curve of the head, over the crest and down along the shaft. Matthew's thighs jerked involuntarily. Glenn drew back along the shaft, keeping a tight seal on his lips and closing his mouth around the head. He took another taste of the sticky juice that wept from the pisshole.

Matthew's hand was on the back of his head, fingers curled in his hair, urging him to take his cock deeper. Glenn descended slowly, guided by his lover's hands until he felt the wet heat of his cock against his tonsils. He took a deep, rattling breath, sucking air past the obstruction in his throat.

He drew back, his soft lips sucking Matthew's cock up and down, slowly to the root, slowly to the crown. He gripped the organ tightly at the base as he worked it with his lips. He licked a finger on his free hand and pressed it into the cleft of Matthew's buttocks. Finding the hole, he entered it. He pressed inwards, against the resistance of the muscle, sliding into the hot, wet slippery passage.

Matthew tightened the grip on his head, gagging Glenn with his meat as it poured past his lips and down his throat. The thick cock speared his gullet. Glenn's face was pressed into the tidy bush of pubic hair; he inhaled the salty, sweaty essence.

Glenn glanced up into his lover's eyes. Matthew's broad handsome face was turning red. Glenn tightened the seal of his mouth, nearly making him come, getting him ready to shoot.

Matthew grunted as Glenn delivered a powerful jab to his prostate. He was flooding Glenn's throat with pre-come in the build-up to his orgasm. He was nearly there. Glenn worked his arsehole and his cock in unison. Paroxysms of pleasure racked Matthew's body as he took the brunt of Glenn's attention from in front and behind.

Matthew was breathing fast and furiously. Glenn knew that he had him. He was surrendering to the start of a shattering, rapturous orgasm. His grip tightened; his cock grew stiffer; his arsehole locked rigidly around Glenn's finger. He cried out as he started to ejaculate. Glenn sucked greedily as Matthew flooded his mouth in long, spurting bursts. The taste was what he had been waiting for.

With one hand buried deep in Matthew's arse and lips locked fast around his squirting manhood, Glenn released his own cock from his shorts. He wanked himself with a rapid hand. A few hard, fast strokes was all that it took. He sprayed his white hot load against Matthew's tense thighs.

Trembling in the dying seconds of ejaculation, he fell forwards across Matthew's hairy stomach. Matthew's heart hammered hard against his face.

They lay together in a hot, sweaty heap until their breathing decreased to a normal rate. Glenn lifted his head slowly. Matthew was smiling down at him. Glenn crawled over his body until they were face to face. The essence of Matthew's come was still strong in his mouth. They kissed, sharing the flavour.

Glenn rolled over on to his side. He fondled Matthew's softening cock and low hanging ball sac, smearing his own semen into the loose skin. He licked his fingers clean – his own flavour was less savoury than his lover's.

'What do I have to do now?' Glenn asked.

'I thought we were gonna screw around all day.'

Glenn squeezed Matthew's nipple, causing him to let out a

playful squeal. 'You know what I mean. What do I do with my book?'

'I'm not sure. I don't have all the answers myself. If you just stop working on it, that might be enough.'

'But you said that things had already started to change in your world.'

'They have. But if you don't set it out in print then our destiny will still be our own. We can determine what happens to ourselves.'

'Won't you still be in danger? If Anthony Pierce already has the idea to kill you, what's to stop him going through with it?'

'Nothing. But I'll be in a position to protect myself. My death won't be such a sure thing.'

Glenn cuddled up even closer to Matthew. 'This is the most bizarre conversation I've ever had. If I put this plot in a book, no one would believe it.'

Matthew laughed. 'Think how complicated that would be for your characters. Having to inhabit a reality within a reality.'

Glenn stretched and sat up slowly. 'I don't even want to think about *that*. I'm going to make some breakfast. Do you want some?'

'Yeah. I'm going to need to keep my strength up. After all that you've done for me I'm going to show you a *lot* of appreciation.'

Glenn walked through into the *en-suite* bathroom and took a slow, satisfying piss. He pulled on a towelling robe and returned to the bedroom. Matthew was sitting naked on the edge of the bed.

'Have you got anything I could wear?' He spread his arms to display himself in all his nude glory. 'Or do you want me to wander around like this?'

Glenn opened the wardrobe and tossed him a navy-blue robe. 'There you go. If you wander around naked the whole time, you'll rob me of the pleasure of undressing you.' He leaned over Matthew and kissed his smooth brow.

'Thanks. All I have to wear are the clothes I arrived in.'

'I might have a few things that would fit you, but I think we're probably different sizes. If you want to hang around for a few days I can always take you shopping.'

'Do you want me around for a few days?'

'If that's OK with you.'

Matthew enfolded him in a warm hug and kissed him. 'I'll stay with you as long as you want me.'

They went down to the kitchen together. Glenn poured them both a glass of orange juice and Matthew sat at the table watching him while he prepared their breakfast. He turned on the grill and opened a pack of bacon.

'What will you do if you don't write the sequel to my story.'

Glenn laid the slices of bacon out on the grill tray. 'I'm not really sure. To be honest I didn't really want to write a follow-up. I was doing it under pressure. Now I'm free to write the kind of story *I* want to write.'

Half an hour later, Glenn served up a full breakfast of bacon, scrambled eggs, tomatoes, mushrooms, toast and fried bread. They were both ravenous and wolfed down their food with two pots of tea. Conversation between the two of them was surprisingly easy. Although they had met for the first time only the night before, they both knew each other so well.

Glenn realised that this was what companionship was. To have someone there with you in the morning. Someone to talk to who'd listen and understand. It had never been like this for him with any other man, even the ones that he had some kind of lasting relationship with. It had never been this easy. The nearest he had ever come to this kind of companionship was when he was with Joe. But that was just friendship: once the sex was over there was no lingering intimacy between them. They just went back to being friends, joking and fooling around.

He wondered if this was what it was like for Dean and Gary. Was this the kind of love and understanding that had kept them together for so long? He had often envied what they had, never really knowing what it was. Maybe he was about to find out.

Matthew played with his foot beneath the table, looking directly into his eyes when he spoke, and smiling. The reality of having this perfect man around for the next few days was like a sublime dream. There was so much that Glenn wanted to share with him. He would show him what life in the real world was like: real people, real places, real fucking.

When they had finished breakfast Matthew went upstairs to the bathroom and Glenn loaded the used plates and cutlery into the dishwasher. He could hear Matthew in the shower as he tidied up the kitchen. After a few minutes he followed him upstairs.

The robe that Glenn had given him was draped across the bed. The door to the *en-suite* bathroom was open. A thin wraith of steam billowed out of the shower and through the open doorway. Glenn could just about make out the bulky form of the other man through the steamed-up pane of the shower door.

He slipped off his robe and dropped it on the floor. With the water turned up so high Matthew was unaware of his presence in the room. He crept closer to the door. Matthew gave a startled little jump as he slid the shower door open. He smiled.

Glenn had surprised him right in the middle of washing his genitals. Soapy water coursed over the length of his heavy cock and balls and dripped like semen from the bulky head.

'Mind if I join you?'

'I'd mind more if you didn't.'

Glenn stepped into the stall and drew the door shut behind him. They embraced beneath the hot jets of water, kissing. Glenn slid his hands all over Matthew's expansive back, caressing and exploring the cuts of muscle, descending the curve of his spine down to his beefy buttocks. He lowered his head to his mountainous pecs. Matthew's nipples stood out hard from his wet hairy chest. Glenn closed his mouth over the left bud and bit down. The big man moaned. Glenn raised his head to his mouth again, continuing the long, eager kiss.

'You're fucking gorgeous,' Glenn whispered.

'So are you.'

Matthew squeezed a handful of shower gel into the palm of his hand and slavered it over Glenn's semistiff cock. He slipped back the foreskin and worked the soap all over the crown. The friction of his palm was like warm, wet velvet. The cock began to lengthen and swell. In seconds it was fully erect. He drew the foreskin smoothly back into position. Matthew shuffled round so that Glenn was directly under the shower head. He stroked and caressed his cock until all of the soap had been rinsed away.

Glenn leaned back against the tiled wall and spread his legs. Matthew moved down his body slowly, hot water cascading over them both. He kissed Glenn's neck and chest, circling round his pierced nipple, but careful not to hurt him. He moved his face down his stomach, lingering for a moment, working his tongue into the pit of his navel before descending further. Glenn watched his head travel lower. His scalp shone through his fine, wet hair. At last he reached his throbbing cock, and took it straight into his mouth. He slid his face all the way down the shaft until he had the whole of Glenn's cock wedged in his throat.

He worked his jaw back and forth, exploring the fleshy organ with his tongue, swirling round the head. He darted beneath the foreskin. Glenn shuddered at the abrasion of his tongue on the sensitive glans. The tip flicked over his pisshole. He moved up and down the throbbing length, hot and heavy and thick.

Matthew drew back for air. 'I want this in my arse,' he gasped.

They moved out of the shower and on to the bathroom floor. Their wet bodies slipped over one another as they rolled back and forth, kissing and humping each other's thighs.

Matthew lay down on his back and hitched his knees up to his chest, proudly displaying his noble arsehole. Glenn gasped at its beauty. His ring was an oasis between the pale hemispheres of his arse. The tight ring was the milky colour of coffee, surrounded by a light forest of dark-brown hair. Glenn lowered his face to it, inhaling the clean soapy scent. The arsehole twitched as his breath whispered softly across it.

Glenn drew his tongue slowly through the forest of curls, skirting all the way around the main attraction. Matthew sighed, hooking his arms around his knees, he hitched his arse higher, offering him more.

Glenn could see the shell-pink hue of the inner walls. He worked his tongue in decreasing circles, coming nearer and nearer to his prize. He spread his hands across Matthew's cheeks and buried his face in the crevice between. He lapped at the magnificent hole like a thirsty dog, tasting its manly flavour. The orifice quivered on the tip of his tongue. He pressed into the ring of muscle, which opened to take him.

'Oh yes,' Matthew gasped. 'Fuck me with your tongue.'

He thrust into the hole, bearing deep into the inner passage. Matthew twisted beneath him, lifting his hips up on to his face, impaling his arse on his rigid tongue. Glenn burrowed deep into the musky hole.

Matthew rolled out from beneath him and turned over on to his hands and knees. He thrust his arse back towards Glenn. 'Don't just eat my arse,' he said breathlessly. 'Fuck it!'

Glenn quickly reached up and grabbed a tube of lubricant and a condom from the bathroom cabinet. He squeezed a huge blob of lube into his hand and worked it over his fingers. Matthew crouched over in hungry anticipation. Glenn slicked up his fingers with the lubricant and then smeared it all over Matthew's butt, he slid a finger in and out of the hole, pushing through the tight opening. He slid another finger into him and then another, stretching and widening the ring with a circular wrist action.

Glenn withdrew and opened the condom wrapper, straining the rubber sheath down over his cock. He covered himself in lubricant and straddled Matthew's arse. He pressed his cock down into the cleft and found the opening. Matthew's arsehole gripped his cock as he passed through the sphincter and into his rectum. He slid all the way into him until the sac of his balls pressed against his buttocks.

Matthew looked back at him over his shoulder, his brown eyes shining and hungry.

Neither of them moved, getting used to the tight sensation of their union.

Matthew's arse was so tight. It held him in a perfect grip, tighter than any other hole he cared to remember. Glenn drew in a deep breath of air. He was liable to come quickly inside such a pert arse and he wanted to pace himself. He slid his hands over the splayed buttocks, caressing the hard flesh. He looked at his cock: barely a centimetre of its shaft could be seen, surrounded by the wide lips of Matthew's arsehole.

Matthew lifted his arse higher, pressing his hips back against Glenn's pelvis.

'Come on,' he said. 'Fuck me with that thing.'

Keeping a tight hold on Matthew's hips, Glenn withdrew, slowly, carefully, savouring the friction, until only the bulbous tip of his cock remained inside. He slid back in just as slowly, repeating the motion back and forth. They both sighed and gasped as the arse lips slid along his dick. Matthew rested his head on the floor and relaxed into the gentle pace, quelling his impatience. The head of Glenn's cock grazed his prostate with each slow propulsion.

The moist heat of the bathroom started to rise. Glenn began to build up speed, increasing the rhythm of his hips. The four walls of the room echoed with the steady slap of skin on skin and the deep-chested grunts of the two men. The hot grip of Matthew's hole tightened on his cock, holding him all the way from root to tip. Glenn took a tighter hold of his beefy arse, ramming his cock home a little deeper, a little rougher. Matthew thrust back against him on every stroke.

Their passion increased, banging each other hard. Glenn's view of his cock slipping between chunky cheeks of muscle was obscured by the sweat that poured down his brow and into his eyes. Matthew's prone body glowed red with exertion and glistened with the raw sweat of sex. Glenn gave his wet arse a slap and he swore his appreciation.

'Slap,' he demanded.

Glenn smacked him again, and again. His creamy arse flushed beneath his palm. Matthew's fingers started to manipulate his own cock, jerking himself to the rhythm of their sex.

'Slap,' he cried. 'Slap. *Slap*.'

He ground his arse furiously against Glenn's cock and hand, demanding more of him and more. The cracks echoed throughout the room. They both voiced their pleasure loudly.

'Oh shit,' Glenn cried, 'I can't keep it up. I'm gonna come.'

Matthew tightened his arsehole, fisted his cock. His knees started to buckle as the pleasure finally became too much for him. He screamed and arched his back as his come flew all over the floor. The tightening of his arse tipped the balance of control for Glenn. His cries rose in intensity as he joined Matthew in orgasm. He rammed his cock home one final time and started to ejaculate in long waves, filling the condom with his seed. His knees trembled as he emptied his balls into Matthew's raw arse.

They both heaved and sweated and gasped, regaining their composure in the aftermath of such strenuous sex. Glenn withdrew his softening cock slowly, holding on tight to the base of the come-heavy condom. He was about to tie it off when Matthew stopped him.

'I want to taste you,' he said.

He took the rubber out of Glenn's hands and held it up above his face. Tilting his head back, he emptied the contents into his open mouth. The off-white juice dribbled down into his waiting gullet in a long, lazy trail. Matthew squeezed out the body of the condom until he was certain he had emptied it of every drop. He swallowed and licked his lips.

'Delicious,' he said.

They helped each other to stand and crawled back beneath the covers of the bed. Matthew took a packet of cigarettes out of the pocket of his jeans and lit up. He smoked it slowly.

'I forgot about that,' Glenn said as he curled up against Matthew's chest, hugging him like a big, human bear.

'What?'

'That you were a smoker.'

Matthew exhaled a lazy cloud. 'You don't mind, do you? I'll put it out if you do.'

'No, it's all right.' Glenn took the cigarette from his fingers and inhaled on it himself. 'I've been trying to cut down lately, but when I wrote *Everyday Hurts* I was a forty-a-day man. Therefore, so were nearly all of my characters.'

'So why have you cut down?'

'I have enough vices to begin with and thought I'd cut down on smoking 'cause it's the one I'd miss the least. I enjoy my other vices too much to give them up.'

'So which is your favourite?'

Glenn nuzzled his face against Matthew's mountainous chest and chewed on a fleshy nipple. 'Oh, that's easy.'

'So what is it?'

He slid his hand down over Matthew's hairy stomach and into his crotch.

'Cock!' he said.

Nine

Killing Time

The living-room blinds were closed against the bright, intrusive light of the midday sun.

The closing credits of *Everyday Hurts* rolled slowly over an otherwise black screen to the accompaniment of the film's haunting and melancholic score.

They were lying on the sofa, naked. Matthew sat between Glenn's open thighs, leaning back against his stomach. Neither of them spoke until the last frame of the film had rolled and the credits faded to black. Matthew leaned over and grabbed his cigarettes from the coffee table. He balanced the ashtray on his bare thighs and lit up. He sucked slowly and exhaled a dense wreath of smoke through his nostrils. He passed the cigarette back over his shoulder to Glenn.

Glenn retrieved the remote control from the floor and switched off the DVD. He silenced the television and then softly stroked the broad line of Matthew's neck.

'Are you OK?'

Matthew took the cigarette back from him and puffed thoughtfully. 'Yes. I guess so.'

'Maybe this wasn't such a good idea.'

'No, it's all right. I wanted to see it. It's just strange to see something that is supposed to be your life playing on TV.' He rested his head back against Glenn's chest, solicitously avoiding his tender piercing. 'That actor looks nothing like me. He acts nothing like me. None of the cast of this film are right. Not even the fella playing Anthony. He might be dangerous, but one thing I will say about Anthony Pierce is that he's a sexy bastard. This guy in the film just doesn't have it.'

Glenn kissed the top of his head. 'I've never considered it to be a particularly well-cast film. Relocating the story to America doesn't work, either.'

'No, it doesn't. Still, I'm glad I've seen it. It's interesting.'

'I've always felt rather distant from it. It's somebody else's work rather than my own. It did make me a lot of money, though. I should be grateful for that.' He ran a hand over Matthew's chest, cupping a hard breast.

'Who do you prefer?' Matthew asked casually.

'What?'

'The movie Matthew or me?'

Glenn pinched his nipples causing him to yelp with delight.

'You're my perfect creation,' he said. 'Don't forget it.'

There was one day left until the party. Saturday was the big day.

Everything that could be arranged in advance had been. Dean had confirmed the food order with the caterers. The gardener had come round on Thursday afternoon and had worked until ten at night making sure that the lawn and the flower beds were perfect. Mrs Jackson and Mrs Benchley were in the middle of a cleaning blitz right now, ensuring that every room in the house would be spotless. Gary was taking care of the music himself. Everything was arranged and running to plan.

But Dean had a panic on his hands.

When he woke up that morning, he decided that the clothes he had chosen to wear – black leather trousers and a tight white vest – were no good. They made him look too 'cloney' and seemed to add ten years to his appearance. He had to find something else. Quick.

He left the two cleaners with instructions on what to do and drove off to Newcastle in search of some new clothes. As he journeyed up the motorway towards the city he considered giving Glenn a call to meet him there and help him decide on what to buy. He was just about to dial the pre-programmed number on his phone when he changed his mind. He wanted to surprise his guests with what he was wearing. That meant that no one, not even his best friend Glenn, could see it beforehand.

After three hours of wandering the city, from shop to shop, trying on different combinations, he finally made up his mind. He settled on a pair of flat-fronted, charcoal-grey trousers that were tight across his thighs and arse and flared slightly below the knee. To go with the pants, he chose a sheer, silver grey, sleeveless T-shirt that moulded itself to every bulging muscle on his chest and stomach, and a pair of square-toed, shiny black boots.

At last, happy with his purchases, he decided that he needed a drink to relax.

It was half past two.

Although Newcastle's gay scene was more than adequate at night, during the day homosexual options were more limited. Unlike Manchester, it just didn't have the volume of gay-friendly establishments to offer anything in the way of variety.

It came down to a choice of three: the Venue, the Roxy or the Barking Dog. He opted for the Venue.

Dean carried his shopping bags back to the car and stuck another hour's worth of money into the parking meter before walking up towards the pub.

The Venue was a small basement bar adjoining the Mineshaft nightclub. Dean walked down the steel steps and through the heavy double doors. Loud dance music was playing as he entered. It was early on a Friday afternoon and already an impressive crowd had started to gather. There were no windows and the dark bar was atmospherically lit. It always reminded Dean of a dungeon. Like all gay bars, the place stank of stale cigarette smoke.

He walked slowly towards the bar, taking his time to catch a good look at all the faces gathered there. He gained several approving smiles and glances as he surveyed the room. He was wearing a pair of washed-out jeans and a white Armani T-shirt that was a size too small for him. The tight cotton was stretched impressively across his taut chest, barely concealing the body that was trying to burst out of it.

He checked out the kid behind the bar as he ordered a bottle of beer. Not bad. Tall and slim with peroxide-blond hair. His name tag called him Spike. He considered buying Spike a drink but was put off by the young guy's effeminate voice and mannerisms. Not really his type. Dean liked his men a little rougher. Brawny.

He took his beer and stood at the island in the centre of the bar.

A handful of other men were gathered there, all turning to give him a cursory once-over. Dean smiled and put down his bottle. He hadn't come here with the intention of cruising: he just wanted a drink to relax him after the time he had spent in the shops. But now that he was in an exclusively gay environment, surrounded by other predatory men, he instinctively started to weigh up his options.

Two men playing pool in the corner had potential: they were both tall and well built, exactly how he liked his trade, but they were both a bit scruffy and neither man was particularly handsome. Another guy was throwing money into the slot machine. Again, he had the right build and proportions but the slot machine was a turn-off. Dean had never understood the obsession a lot of men and women seemed to have for such a trashy form of gambling. If they ever won any money, they only threw it straight back in the slot.

His keen eyes resumed their search. There were a couple of young men in the corner, but they had eyes only for each other. Cute. A man over by the smoke machine. No. Too skinny. There was a man sitting against the back wall with a couple of girls. Maybe; maybe not. He could take or leave him depending on what else he found.

Although he loved sex and he enjoyed a lot of variety, Dean liked to maintain his standards. Unlike some of his friends, or even Gary for that matter, he couldn't just fuck about with anyone for the sake of it. Why should he? He had a gorgeous man at home, so there was no way he was going to scrape the bottom of the barrel elsewhere.

If he didn't find anyone up to scratch then he would do without. It was simple.

Then he saw him.

He was standing over by the bar, next to the telephone. Dean mustn't have noticed him on the way in. He was well over six feet tall and built like a tank. He had a short thatch of tousled blond hair and bright eyes that were regarding Dean with common interest.

Bingo, he thought. You're all mine, baby!

Glenn and Matthew sat out on the patio drinking beer and enjoying the pleasurable heat of the afternoon sun. Matthew had squeezed into a pair of Glenn's shorts. They didn't really fit his broad figure. Geri Halliwell was on the portable CD player. They wanted to get a breath of fresh air and some sun on their skin, having spent the early part of the day indoors.

After rising late and watching the DVD of *Everyday Hurts* they had gone back to bed and Glenn had ridden Matthew's arse for the best part of an hour. Afterwards they had dozed for a while in each other's arms.

Glenn relaxed in his chair, his eyes resting behind his sunglasses. He was a contented man. 'Do you want to come to a party with me tomorrow night?'

'Where?' Matthew asked slugging on his beer.

'Some friends of mine are having a get-together at their house. Dean and Gary. They're a couple of really nice guys.'

'Won't they mind me coming? They don't know me.'

Glenn laughed. 'Of course not. They'll both probably try to shag you, but they won't mind.'

'What will I wear? I can hardly go in these tiny shorts of yours.'

'We can go shopping in the morning to get you something if you like. Don't worry about it, though. You look gorgeous just as you are.'

'OK.'

Matthew stood up and stretched out on the lawn. Glenn watched as he performed fifty slow press-ups. The taut muscles in his shoulders and back stretched and rippled as he raised and lowered his own weight, his breathing deepening with the effort. When he was finished he rolled on to his back and spread himself out in the warm rays of the sun, one arm flung out at his side, the other draped across his eyes, shielding them from the sun. His chest expanded with his deep inhalations.

'What else do you do to keep in shape?'

'I run,' he said, 'and work out with weights.'

Glenn stood up and lay down beside him on the grass.

'I was thinking,' he said. 'How about going out tonight? I could book a table for two somewhere. We could maybe go clubbing afterwards. What do you think?'

'It sounds nice.'

'Great. It'll make a change to get out of the house. We can't stay home and fuck every night.'

'Why not? It beats all the other entertainment I can think of.'

Glenn smiled. 'Because, unlike you, I have some limitations. If we keep going at this rate you're gonna wear me out.'

Matthew rolled over and grabbed the front of his shorts.

'Maybe. But there's no better way to go.'

For the next ten minutes they eyed one another across the moody bar, waiting to see who would give in and make the first move.

Dean was confident that he would not have to wait long. He sipped his beer and sized up the other man, biding his time. He stood with the confident stance of a mature man. It was hard to be sure in the shady light, but Dean put his age at somewhere between thirty-five and forty. He was certainly no older than that.

He stood with one arm resting against the counter, his long legs splayed. His faded jeans glided up the sinewy contours of his legs to a sizeable protuberance in the groin. He was wearing a black, slim-fitting shirt, the cut of which revealed a hard body underneath. His arms were long and sinewy like his legs. Dean liked a man who took care of his body. This one had a brawny, lean look about him, as though his muscle was developed by rowing and diving rather than religiously cultivated in a gym. The top few buttons of the shirt were undone, gaping open to reveal a nice tawny-blond chest. His rugged forearms were covered in the same spread of dark blond hair. Dean imagined how those dark blond curls would form a divine nest around the root of his cock and balls and nestle warmly in the cleft of his arse.

His cool blue eyes made contact with Dean's dark pools and

held it. Dean's heart jumped. Without the exchange of a single word, the chemistry between them was immediate – a natural, animal instinct. It was a base power that could not be forced or faked.

Dean sipped his beer.

His large nipples were projecting through his shirt like missiles, preset on their target – a clear invitation to the stranger.

He smiled.

The man pushed himself back from the bar and stood up straight. Invitation accepted. His long legs covered the distance between them in two lengthy strides. He moved up close to Dean and set his bottle down on the beer-stained surface of the island. Dean caught a faint fragrance of Obsession.

'Hi,' the man said, his voice was deep with a regional accent; not too heavy.

'Hi.'

'Are you alone?'

'Yes. Are you?'

'Yes. Can I buy you a drink?'

'That's nice of you, but no, thanks. I was planning to leave soon.'

The man ran a long finger along Dean's forearm, tracing the line of thick muscle to the elbow. 'Are you going somewhere else?'

Dean leaned his lower body closer, their groins almost touching. 'Maybe,' he said, raising the beer bottle slowly to his lips. 'It depends.'

'On what?'

He brushed his inner thigh against the man's leg. 'On whether or not you come with me and what else you suggest.'

The man's fingers travelled over Dean's broad biceps and down his chest where he drew a gentle circle around his left nipple. 'I'd suggest anything at all with you.' His broad lips broke into a smile that was cut on either side by two very sexy dimples. 'My name is Carter.'

Dean leaned even closer. 'I'm very pleased to meet you, Carter. I'm Dean.'

'So do you want to get out of here? We could go somewhere more private.'

'Mine or yours? Which is closest?'

'I live right here in town. My boyfriend is at home right now. He's sleeping. He was at work all last night.'

'Do you want to wake him up?'

Carter cracked his sexy smile again. 'Do *you* want to wake him up?'

'Would he like it if I did that?'

'I can't see him having any major objections.'

They finished their beers. 'What's your boyfriend like?'

Carter's eyes beamed when he spoke. 'He's called John. He's thirty-six and he's a big guy like me. I think you'll like him. I definitely know *he'll* like *you*.'

'So what does he do to be working night shifts?'

'He's a police inspector.'

Dean set down his empty bottle. 'I like the sound of him already.'

They walked out on to the street and climbed into Dean's car. His stomach was churning with anticipation and excitement. They leaned across the seats and kissed, open-mouthed and passionate. They sighed and groaned, both breathing heavily. Dean ventured a hand down to the bulge in the front of Carter's pants. He was pleased with what he found. It was going to be a worthwhile afternoon. Carter's police inspector boyfriend was just a bonus.

Carter gave directions. It was a relatively short journey. They had an apartment down on the quayside, overlooking the river. Dean knew the area well.

'How will John react to this?' Dean asked.

Carter's broad lips broke into a sexy smile. 'I have no idea. There's only one way to find out.'

'Do you guys have regular threesomes?'

'Not regular, but sometimes. John is usually in on the choice of men though. I haven't ever given him a surprise like this before.'

'What if he doesn't like the surprise?'

Carter ran a firm hand over Dean's stomach and chest, squeezing a swollen nipple. 'Don't worry. He'll like you all right. I know him well enough.'

Dean locked up the car and they went into the apartment block, taking the lift up to the fourth floor. Carter inserted his key into the lock and turned it slowly. He quietly opened the door and they slipped inside. The apartment was immaculate – stylishly decorated and spotlessly clean. It pleased him to see that these guys didn't like a mess. Dean hated untidy trade. Fucking in a pigsty was a big turn-off.

The living room was bright and airy with a large window that looked out directly across the River Tyne.

The two of them were upon each other in seconds, their mouths locked in a passionate kiss, their hands all over each other's body. Dean embraced Carter's broad back, feeling the trim muscle of his shoulders, descending down the long curve of his spine to the hard mounds of his arse. They stripped, tossing their clothes on to the floor. Dean flung open Carter's shirt and tore it off him. He rived open the front of his trousers. His hand went straight inside and found what he was searching for. He withdrew Carter's cock and dropped straight down to his knees in front of it.

It was a beautiful piece of meat: long, lean and golden-skinned. Dean peeled back the foreskin and took the pink swollen head straight into his mouth. He swirled his tongue around the ridge and licked the juice out of the little slit.

He rose to his feet again and they stripped each other bare. Carter's body was magnificent; he looked even better out of his clothes than he did in them. He was graceful and lean, with sinewy, athletic muscle. He was covered in a fine pelt of dark-blond hair that was spread evenly across his stomach and down his legs, growing thicker across his broad chest and around the root of his tasty cock.

'So where's your boyfriend?' Dean whispered quietly.

Carter pointed towards the closed bedroom door and held a finger to his lips. 'Ssshh!' he said. He took Dean's hand and guided him silently to the door. He listened for a moment. 'I think he's still asleep. I can't hear anything.'

Dean felt a thrill right down his back and all along the nerves of his cock as Carter carefully turned the handle and pushed the door inwards. The curtains were closed but, in the shadowy light of the bedroom, Dean could just about make out a broad figure huddled beneath the covers on the bed.

Carter drew Dean towards the bed. All that he could discern of the body beneath the duvet was the top of his bleached-blond head. The peroxide-coloured hair was unnaturally white against the dark pillow. Carter sat down on the edge of the bed.

'John.' He said softly.

The body beneath the covers did not stir.

'John,' he gently drew back the duvet.

Dean felt another surge of excitement. John was just as gorgeous as Carter. Like his lover he was big and muscular. Even in sleep, Dean could see the strong set of his face and the mean determination to his features. This was a driven man, a man who went for it in a big way. He was going to be an incredible fuck. He stirred as Carter touched his shoulder, gently shaking him awake. He murmured something unintelligible.

Carter beckoned Dean closer.

Dean looked down on the slumbering face. He had a wide mouth, with thin, almost cruel-looking lips. The intelligent lines of his brow furrowed as he struggled to wake up. His blond hair was damp and unruly through sleep. Dean leaned over and placed a kiss on his handsome brow, tasting the essence of sweat on his skin.

John's eyes shot open. A look of alarm and confusion flickered across his face as he stared up into the eyes of a stranger.

'Who are you?' he gasped, not yet fully awake.

'Sshh,' said Carter, soothing his lover. 'It's all right. Don't be scared. I've brought a friend to see you.'

'Who is he?'

Carter drew back the bedclothes from John's naked body. 'It's someone very nice. You'll like him.'

Dean's eyes were drawn straight down to John's cock. He was not disappointed. It was lying hard against his stomach, the big head resting in the cleft of his navel. It was a lot thicker than either Carter's or his own. It had the dimensions of a beer can.

Dean and Carter climbed on to the bed together and lay down on either side of John. Three mouths opened and joined in one kiss, their tongues, probing, searching, getting a feel for one another. John slid an arm around the two other men and pulled them both hard against his body.

Dean explored John with his hands. His chest was broad and smooth; he had hard little nipples; the left tit was pierced. Dean fingered the steel bar, thinking for a moment of Glenn. His hands descended over the hard ridges of his belly until he found his cock. He took it in his hand and squeezed the fat shaft. It reassured him that his fingers could not close around its girth. Dean liked his men to be big. Carter's hand closed over his own and they jerked the thick shaft together. John moaned softly into their mouths.

John put his hand on both of their shoulders and shoved them down his body. The two of them shuffled down until their faces were level with his cock. They held him in a firm grip and licked his pink head like a lollipop, working him from either side. Dean licked him from root to tip, pausing for a moment over the head to kiss Carter full on the lips before returning his attention to the other man's cock. Dean and Carter worked John's dick in perfect unison, slavering up and down the hefty tool.

Carter closed his mouth over the fat tip and started to swallow the shaft. Dean shuffled down lower, shoving his face between the big man's legs. John's underside was completely smooth. Dean wondered if he shaved his arse and balls himself or did his lover help him with the razor? His big bountiful balls rolled within a thick, chewy sac. Dean nibbled on the succulent flesh. He opened his mouth and sucked one of his big nuts into his mouth, feeling the weight of it on his tongue. He spat it out slowly and sucked in the other testicle, unable to fit both of them inside him at the same time.

He dipped his head lower, following the seam of flesh below John's balls. He flicked his tongue along his smooth underside. John spread his thighs wide, allowing Dean's mouth into the crack of his arse. The cleft was warm and damp, with the funky smell of sleep. Dean inhaled the manly essence as he followed the seam all the way up to John's tight hole. The orifice was smooth and finely drawn. Dean ran his tongue around its musky perimeter. He heard John groan.

Dean loved to eat out other men's arses. It was a pity that Gary never let him anywhere near his precious hole. Such a waste.

John grabbed hold of Dean's hips and lifted him up to straddle his chest. Dean marvelled at his strength. While Dean worked his tongue around John's hole, John lifted his own arse to his face. He gasped as the man's big, wet tongue lapped at his arsehole.

Carter had released John's cock from his lips and was joining his lover in his appreciation for Dean's arse. They both kissed and stroked his butt. Dean gasped as he felt a thick tongue enter his hole. He buried his face into John's arse with equal passion. John's tongue fucked him like a miniature cock. Dean gave up on what he was doing to John's butt and just surrendered to the hands and mouths of the two lovers.

John lifted him up again and rolled out from beneath him. He threw him face down on to the bed. Strong hands drew him back on to his hands and knees and he felt a thick finger skirt over his arse lips and wriggle its way into the muscular hole.

'He's a tight little fucker,' John said. 'We'll have to get him loosened up.'

He spat on to his hand and shoved another finger into Dean's arse, prizing the tight walls of man flesh apart. He pushed deeper and deeper, fucking him with his fingers.

Carter opened a drawer on the bedside cabinet and took out a stash of condoms and lubricant. He stroked the back of Dean's head while his lover buried his hand up his arse. 'I'll fuck you first,' he said. 'I'll loosen you up for John's big cock.'

Dean didn't say anything. He knew that he was more than capable of taking the monster between John's legs and more. He wanted both Carter and John to pound his arse. It made no difference to him in which order they performed.

Carter rolled on a rubber and smeared himself in lubricant. He handed the tube to John, who removed his fingers from Dean's rectum, covered them in lube and then reinserted them, shoving the lubricant deep inside him. Dean worked his arsehole, bearing down, squeezing and relaxing it around John's fingers, getting himself good and sticky.

John pulled out again and climbed around the bed. He sat down in front of Dean, legs open, cock ready. Dean took the hint, opening his mouth and champing down on his thick tool and baldy nut sac. As he sucked on each testicle in turn he felt the pressure of Carter's cock against his arsehole. Dean and Carter pushed against the resistance at the same time and suddenly he was in. Sliding in all the way to the hilt. He grabbed hold of Dean's hips and started a hard, rhythmic fuck. Dean spat out John's balls and grabbed a deep breath. There was no build-up or time to relax his hole around Carter's cock. Carter was horny and giving it to him hard.

Dean steadied himself against John's chunky thighs before bowing his head into his groin again. John held his cock at the root and teased him with it, keeping it just out of reach of his open mouth. He smacked it against each of his hollow cheeks.

'Please,' Dean begged. '*I want it!*'

John put a heavy hand on the back of Dean's head and shoved his cock into his mouth. He stuffed Dean's head down, wedging his cock into his throat. Dean was impaled on the two men, stuffed full from either side. He fought the urge to gag and sucked in air past the obstruction in his throat. He massaged John's heavy scrotum and sucked his cock.

Carter was pounding his arse hard and fast, working both of them up into a profound sweat. He withdrew his cock all the way out until his swollen head popped free from Dean's hole and then lunged back in up to the hilt. His hips slapped against Dean's buttocks with each thrust.

John held Dean's head down on his cock and encouraged his lover. 'Fuck him hard,' he said. 'Something tells me he can take it and he likes it.'

Dean did like it. It was an effort to keep up with the demands of the two men but he committed himself to them entirely, pushing his body further.

John loosened the grip on his head. He reached into the drawer and grabbed a rubber for himself. Dean relaxed his aching jaw while John stretched the condom over his thick girth. He squeezed some lubricant from the tube and coated himself with it.

Carter pulled his cock out of Dean's arse. He smacked his buttocks, pushing him forwards. Dean didn't have to be told what to do. He placed his knees either side of John's waist and straddled the monster cock. He backed his hips up slowly, feeling the wide blunt head against his hole.

John took a small bottle of poppers from the cabinet. He took off the lid and held the open bottle to Dean's nose. He inhaled the amyl nitrate through each nostril in turn. The rush to his head was instant and his body relaxed further. With proficient skill he eased his arsehole and pressed himself down on to John's cock. The narrow opening widened over the bulbous head. There was a split second of pain, and then it was in. He slid gracefully down the shaft until he felt the smooth caress of John's scrotum against his buttocks. He breathed heavily.

John tensed inside him, filling him further. Dean rolled his eyes to the ceiling. He arched his back, steadying himself against John's knees. He started to lift up and down. He felt every centimetre of John's dick as it slipped past the lips of his arse. He continued to rise until he felt the wide head and then lowered himself back down.

'That's *so* fucking nice,' John drawled. He inhaled from the little bottle.

Dean started to increase momentum, sliding up and down the shaft. He was breathing quickly with the effort. His eyes were stinging with sweat. He flung himself forwards, falling across John's chest, searching for a kiss. John's mouth was open for him with an intensity that matched the depth of his cock in Dean's arse. Their bodies heaved and contorted, grinding against each other.

When John wrapped his arms tight around his back and held his body in a firm grip, Dean knew what was coming next. He anticipated the pressure of Carter's cock against his already full arsehole an instant before the reality. Dean was suddenly both frightened and excited. The head of Carter's cock was persistent, forcing its way in through the obstruction. Dean's arsehole stretched wider. John offered him the bottle of poppers and he filled his lungs gratefully.

At first, as Carter's cock entered his rectum alongside John's monster dick, the pain was excruciating. Dean cried through clenched teeth. As Carter wedged his cock in deeper and the amyl nitrate started to take effect, the pain decreased and was replaced by pleasure – double pleasure. The two men rocked their cocks inside him, slowly increasing the in and out movement. Dean ground his body against them and bit into the hard muscle of John's shoulder. He clenched his arsehole, working both of their dicks.

Double penetration. Couldn't be beaten.

Their pleasure had reached such a peak of intensity that no one could sustain it for long. Carter and John came together. Their cocks lengthened and swelled inside Dean's bowel and suddenly they were both there, gushing hot milk inside him.

Their orgasms were a catalyst for Dean. His stomach muscles clenched violently and he started to shoot big, gobby wads across John's belly. His body trembled with the release of tension. He screamed something incomprehensible before collapsing into a puddle of his own come.

Carter and John withdrew their cocks slowly. Dean was exhausted. The three men lay down on the bed and waited for their breathing to return to normal. Dean felt a huge empty space inside his arse.

'You're amazing,' Carter said. 'Most guys have trouble with John's cock. No one has ever been able to take us both.'

Dean smiled. 'It's a first for me too.'

'You're gonna be sore in the morning,' John said.

'I'm sore now.'

All three of them laughed. Dean slowly sat up and glanced at the clock. It was after six. 'I should get going. My boyfriend will be home soon.'

He climbed off the bed. He found his clothes strewn across the living-room floor. He began to pick them up and put them on. Carter and John pulled on towelling robes and followed him through.

Carter perched on the arm of the sofa. 'How do you feel about meeting up again sometime? Maybe with your boyfriend?'

Dean pulled on his jeans. 'That would be great. I'm sure Gary would love you guys.' He fished his wallet out of his pocket and handed them a card. 'My number's on there. Call any time.'

Dean finished dressing and kissed the two men goodbye at the door. He stopped just as he was about to leave.

'How do the two of you fancy coming to a party tomorrow night?' he asked.

Ten

Night Life

Glenn and Matthew decided to cancel their plans to go out for dinner.

Matthew borrowed some clothes from Glenn's wardrobe; a pair of navy blue combat pants and a short-sleeved white shirt. The pants were on the small side and he was almost bursting out of the shirt seams. The buttons were taut across his hard stomach and he couldn't even fasten them across his chest. With the white cotton stretched impossibly tight across his massive pecs, the look was stunning. The pants were just as tight, concealing very little of his bulging crotch and chunky buttocks.

He turned from side to side in front of the full-length mirror, sizing up his appearance. After trying on several different pairs of trousers and shirts these were the best fit he could find.

Glenn lay on top of the bed, admiring Matthew's impressive profile.

'You should stick with that,' Glenn said. 'You looking fucking hot.'

Matthew brushed a hand across his prominent chest. 'I'm not sure about this. It's a bit tight. A bit obvious.'

'It's fine,' Glenn said. 'I mean it, it looks great on you.'

'Yeah, I suppose it'll be OK for a nightclub, but do you really think I could get away with looking like this in a restaurant?'

'Mmm. You have a good point. I know I wouldn't be interested in eating *food* with you looking like that.'

'I'm being serious.'

Glenn smiled. 'So am I. All right, then, we can eat something here before going out if you don't feel comfortable. Tomorrow we'll go shopping and get some new clothes.'

Glenn cooked them up a light dinner, stir-frying an assortment of vegetables he had left over in the fridge. It was basic food but they washed it down with a delicious bottle of South Australian Chardonnay before getting ready to go out.

Damien Marquez had called earlier that afternoon. He was very excited with the way the photo shoot had turned out.

'You won't believe it when you see these shots,' he enthused. 'They're incredible. *You* are incredible. Man, I knew they were gonna be good but I didn't expect them to be this fucking good. Can you drop by sometime tomorrow and approve the contact sheets? I can't wait to see your face when you get a look at these babies.'

'Sorry, Damien, I'm gonna be busy all day tomorrow. I've, er . . . got a friend staying with me for the weekend and we're going to a party tomorrow night.'

'How long is your friend gonna be around?'

Good question, Glenn thought. 'I'm not sure. A few more days at least.'

'Well drop by the studio on Monday and I'll have the contacts ready for your approval. Bring your friend with you,' he said, his voice dropping an octave. The implication of his invitation was clear.

'OK. I might do that. See you on Monday, then.'

Damien and Matthew. Mmmm. Nice thought.

Matthew was still feeling self-conscious in the tight clothes. Glenn decided to ease his discomfort by wearing something equally revealing and tight himself.

'I bought this last summer,' he said, pulling the tiny garment out of his wardrobe. 'But I haven't had the nerve to wear it before now.'

There was very little to the sheer black top. It was made of a fine mesh with short sleeves. The cut of the garment was narrow. When Glenn pulled it over his head and down his torso, the slim-fitting outfit concealed nothing. It skimmed the contours of his chest and stomach, barely reaching the level of his waist. His skin shone straight through; his navel and nipples could clearly be seen. Every ridge and cut of muscle was on show. The shiny new nipple stud glinted through the narrow mesh.

When he pulled on a pair of old blue jeans that hugged the curve of his buttocks, and a pair of shiny black boots, the final effect was stunning. He could hardly believe that the jaw-dropping reflection in the full-length mirror was his own.

Their taxi arrived and took them to Newcastle, arriving at the first bar at just after nine. The Roxy was an old-fashioned kind of gay bar. The clientele were generally older than those found in the other bars on the scene, especially in Celestial, a trendy young bar straight upstairs from the Roxy.

Glenn had a soft spot for the old pub. It was the first bar he had ever gone into when he'd first come out on the Newcastle scene. It wasn't as fashionable as the other bars around and it was desperately in need of a refit, but he always liked to call in, just for one drink at the start of the night.

The sight of Glenn and Matthew walking through the front door, dressed as they were, was enough to turn every male head in the place. They were both greeted with smiles and leering glances as they made their way through the eager crowd to the bar. The place was packed. Glenn ordered a couple of beers and they found a spot to stand in the corner by the cigarette machine.

Matthew turned slowly, having a good look around at the place. They were easily the youngest in there, by about ten years, and the bar stank of stale smoke. No one, apart from a handful of guys at the front, was paying very much attention to an ageing drag queen who stood up on a podium, badly mouthing the words to 'Take That Look Off Your Face'.

A tall man in his early fifties groped the prominent stub of Matthew's right nipple as he walked past. He winked and headed off towards the toilets.

'So,' said Glenn, shouting above the music. 'What do you think?'

Matthew looked bemused. 'Are they all like this?'

Glenn laughed. 'Unfortunately not. This place is unique. I thought I'd chuck you straight in at the deep end.'

'You're all heart.'

Glenn slid his arm around Matthew's waist and kissed him on the lips. 'I just want to show you a good time. We're starting right at the bottom. The only way is up from here, so just think what a great night we're going to have.'

Rather than going upstairs to Celestial next, Glenn decided to take Matthew a hundred yards down the road to Babycakes. Babycakes was a disco bar on the corner of town, right next to the Redhuegh bridge. As they walked through the front doors he could sense straight away that Matthew was infinitely more impressed with Babycakes' bright lights and modern music than he had been in the previous pub.

It was even busier in here than the Roxy and they had to force their way through to the bar. They were eventually served by a cute-looking teen called Phil. As Glenn paid for their drinks the DJ announced that the stripper would be on stage in ten minutes.

'What kind of stripper?' Matthew asked.

Glenn gave him his drink and took his free hand. 'Come on. There's only one way to find out.' He shoved his way through the tightly packed bodies until he found them a good spot at the front of the stage to view the action.

The bar was buzzing and there was a nice Friday night atmosphere going. The packed crowd was in a jovial mood, anticipating the arrival of the stripper with good humour. The DJ played his last track, a reworking of 'Use It Up and Wear It Out', and then cut the music.

The introduction of Nico was received with a roar of enthusiasm. He made his entrance into the spotlight wearing green and white army combats to the accompaniment of a heavy house beat. The army issues covered his flesh from the neck all the way down to his stout black boots. He wore a cap on his head and his face was concealed behind a pair of dark shades.

All Glenn could make out was that he was dark-skinned with a strong, square-set jaw. Matthew cheered as Nico launched into his routine.

The hat was the first thing to go, flung aside to reveal a sexy black crew cut. Nico moved fluidly across the stage, dancing to a standard well above that of the usual male stripper. When he performed a neat high kick, his foot shot well above the height of his head. He shed his camouflage jacket to reveal a magnificent torso. He had the kind of body that took hours of hard work each week to cultivate and maintain. His skin was smooth and hairless and glistening with baby oil.

He kicked out his leg and slid down into a perfectly executed set of splits before leaping back to his feet and ripping off his pants. A tiny black thong concealed the treasure of his groin.

Glenn was usually unmoved by strippers. Their manufactured brand of sexuality failed to excite, so it caught him completely by surprise to realise the growth he was cultivating in the front of his underpants. He was amazed and aroused at Nico's agility and obvious athleticism.

The stripper's body was totally smooth. From his neck down to his feet, he had taken great care to shave away every trace of body hair. His sleek, oily thighs rippled as he danced across the stage. He pulled out a bottle of baby oil and leaped down from the stage into the audience. He began a quick circuit of the bar, stopping various customers and persuading them to rub the oil into his hairless arse and solid limbs.

Glenn leaned against Matthew, feeling sensuous and very horny. 'He's great, isn't he?'

Matthew rested a hand in the curl of Glenn's back. 'I prefer you,' he said.

They were both startled when Nico suddenly appeared in front of them, his perfect body glistening with sweat and oil. He paused for a moment, looking them both over. He made an unexpected grab for Glenn. Pulling him closer, he suddenly ducked down and fastened his mouth over his clearly visible nipple. He nipped the hard bud. Glenn arched his back and gasped, his flesh yielding beneath Nico's sharp teeth. His insides jumped − a little stab of something beginning in his chest and travelling down to his stomach.

Just as suddenly the stripper released him and bounded back on to the stage. Glenn stood breathless in his wake, both nipples hardening through the transparency of his top.

Matthew hugged him from behind, nuzzling the back of his neck and pressing his bulging groin into the tight cleft of his buttocks. 'Did you enjoy that?' he whispered with a kiss.

'Yeah. I think I did.'

Nico was ready to get completely naked for his appreciative audience. He turned his back on the crowd and bent over, sliding the thong down over his hips. As he slid the garment lower and peeled the narrow strip of material out of the crack of his arse, Glenn caught a brief glimpse of his hole. The vision was over in a second, but a second was all that it took to ingrain the picture on his mind — its size, its shape, its honey-brown colouring. It was a beautiful sight.

Nico tossed the black thong aside and pirouetted round to introduce the audience of Babycakes to his manhood. A tumultuous cheer greeted the display of his cock. Just as Glenn had expected, the stripper's pelvis was devoid of pubic hair; his cock and balls were completely smooth, too. Nico boasted a good seven inches of semihard meat. He had tied his cock off at the root with a leather strap to prevent himself from reaching a state of undiminished arousal.

He strutted across the stage, grinding his hips and slapping his cock against his belly for the benefit of the elated mob. Glenn and Matthew, along with the rest of the spectators, pressed closer to the stage, desperate for a closer look.

The climax of Nico's performance was a magnificent act of exhibitionism. He stood at the edge of the stage and thrust his arse towards the mob. Now Glenn could see his hole in all its juicy splendour, the smooth puckered muscle and slightly pouting lips. As Nico pressed his hips further back Glenn could just about make out, at the centre of the honey jewel, just beyond the rim, the slightest glimmer of pink inner flesh.

'Wow,' he gasped. 'He's gorgeous.'

What Nico did next caused his eyes to widen further and his jaw to drop in disbelief. The stripper pushed his cock down between his legs, showing it off along with his fruity arsehole. Then he pressed it further back, bending the semihard shaft around towards his hole. A hush fell across the pub as the head of his cock inched nearer and nearer to his hole. No one could quite believe that it was possible – there was no way he could follow all the way through.

The half-hard head brushed against the opening. Nico teased his arse, rubbing the tip of his oily cock against his hole. Then he pressed back all the way. The head of his cock was swallowed up by the open mouth of his arse. After a second of silent disbelief the crowd erupted, yelling, screeching and screaming their approval.

'*I don't believe it*,' Matthew gasped in awe.

Both Glenn and Matthew burst out laughing and raised their hands above their heads to applaud and cheer the performer.

Nico pushed as much of his cock as possible into his arse, about two inches, and held it there. He rotated his hips slowly from left to right, giving everyone a clear view of the awesome spectacle.

After a couple of minutes of nonstop applause, he withdrew his cock, took a bow and left the stage. He returned a moment later, a towel wrapped around his narrow waist to take his final bow. Glenn had seen nothing like it; it was the wildest applause he had ever witnessed for this kind of act. The entire bar was cheering and clapping. Matthew whistled, while Glenn's hands ached from clapping so enthusiastically.

Nico gave a final wave and then vanished behind the curtain.

'Wow,' said Matthew. 'I think I should practise that trick.'

'I think it takes a special knack,' Glenn said. '*Jesus!*'

'You could always write it into my character profile for me, then I'll be able to do it – no problem.'

'Wouldn't that be cheating?'

'Cheating's allowed as long as it's in a good cause.' Matthew pouted.

Glenn squeezed his butt. 'Wouldn't it be more fun to practise?'

'Hmm. You do have a point there.'

With the strip show finished, the crowd in Babycakes began to thin out. It was almost eleven o'clock, the disbanded patrons were either rushing off to catch last orders in Celestial or heading up to one of the nightclubs in the hope of avoiding the queues that always built up after eleven. Glenn and Matthew made their way to the Mineshaft.

The Mineshaft was a dark club – black floors, black walls, black ceilings. Very black. As soon as you went down the steps and into the foyer you were greeted with the scent of damp, dry ice and amyl. And your feet always stuck to the ancient carpet. The only other club Glenn knew that compared to it was the Cockring in Amsterdam.

Friday night in the Mineshaft was HI-NRG and disco. Glenn and Matthew entered to the sound of Déjà Vu's 'To Deserve You'. Although the club was only halfway full when they arrived, within fifteen minutes the place was packed.

Glenn bought a round of beers at the bar and a fresh bottle of poppers, which he stuffed in his jeans pocket. With their drinks in hand, he took Matthew for a tour of the club. Although only on one floor, as opposed to the various levels of the Cockring, the Mineshaft was a big club. The large dance floor was right in the middle, forming the crux of the venue. There was standing room at either side of the dance floor and then two bars at opposite ends of the floor. To the right of the floor was access through to the Venue bar, which formed part of the complex, and to the right was the entrance to the back bar with pool tables and slot machines.

Glenn and Matthew both drew lascivious looks and stares and countless admiring glances as they slowly made their way through the club. The dance floor was now packed with boys and girls dancing with euphoria to Tina Cousins's 'Pray'. Most of the men on stage had taken off their shirts and ground their bare torsos to the trance beats.

A big man dressed all in black tapped Glenn on the shoulder as he took Matthew through into the back bar.

'Hello, stranger.'

Glenn turned. 'David. Hi.' He embraced the darkly dressed man.

David Redfern was an old flame. Glenn had had a thing with him several years ago. It didn't really get past the sex-and-infatuation stage and they managed to remain friends afterwards.

'I haven't seen you in here for a while,' David said, looking Glenn up and down, checking out his body. Although the relationship had long since perished, their common interest in sex hadn't. He turned his gaze to Matthew, viewing him with increasing interest.

'I don't come to Newcastle much these days. I felt like a change tonight and I wanted to show Matthew round.' He introduced Matthew to his ex-lover. They shook hands.

'I like this,' David said, brushing a finger over Glenn's pierced nipple.

'Careful,' he said. 'It hasn't healed yet.'

'I didn't know you were into all that. You surprise me.'

Glenn shrugged. 'My tastes have changed.'

'So I see.' David glanced at Matthew again, his dark eyes meticulously taking in every detail of his compact figure. 'I don't suppose you fancy meeting up later. The three of us could get together when the club closes. It could be fun.'

It was a tempting offer for each of them. David was tall and handsome with a dominant demeanour. He was well over six feet and built like a brick shithouse. He was a straightforward man who liked a good, straightforward fuck. He didn't waste time with foreplay and sex toys. David liked to get right down to the business: ram it in and start banging.

It was an interesting scenario. The thought of a threesome with Matthew and David intrigued him; Glenn would be the versatile party between an exemplary top and a model bottom. The sexual possibilities of such a divine union sent a sudden thrill right down to his groin.

He sensed that Matthew shared his excitement.

They needed time to talk.

'We're gonna go and dance for a while. If you're still around later, we can have a drink and see what happens.'

'I'll hold you to that.'

David squeezed both of their arses as Glenn slipped his arm around Matthew's waist and led him away. They made their way back through to the main floor of the club.

'Who was he?' Matthew asked, when they were out of David's earshot.

'He's an old flame of mine. We had an affair a few years ago. It didn't last very long. He's a bit of a heartbreaker.'

'Why? Were you in love with him?'

'No, not really. I was infatuated with him for a while. But I think that had more to do with his big fat dick than romance.'

'Is he good?'

'Yeah,' Glenn replied without hesitation. 'His style is pretty basic. He just sticks it in and lets you have it. But yeah, for a nice rough, satisfying fuck, he is good. I think you'd like him.'

'Do you want to go with him tonight? After the club?'

'Do you?'

Matthew paused for a moment, considering. 'Yeah. I like big guys like that.'

They had reached the edge of the dance floor.

'Let's see what happens. It's still early. There's no point limiting our options just yet!'

They pushed through the crowd and jumped up on to the packed stage, throwing themselves into the music. They both inhaled from the bottle of poppers and went crazy to Utopia's 'Feel the Need In Me'. Blood pounded through Glenn's head. He gyrated to the hedonistic rhythm. They couldn't talk above the music.

They began to heat up, their lust bringing them closer together. The music filled their bodies, their gyrating hips not missing a beat. Each one of them made the other the focus of his dance. The world was closing in around them, condensing into a tiny square yard on the dance floor.

Glenn moved his hands around Matthew's waist, resting his palms on his arse, feeling the taut muscle of his butt beneath the tight fabric of his combats. He felt the strain at his groin as the heat of the dance floor and the disco rhythms began to affect him on a deeper level. He brushed his throbbing crotch against the bulge in the front of Matthew's combats. The whole atmosphere of the club infused itself into his cock like a potent drug. He was horny as hell.

The music passed into another track but his mind had ceased making any distinction.

He saw David Redfern at the edge of the dance floor, watching them. Glenn pressed nearer to Matthew, putting on a show. Their bodies swayed, rubbing together with increased fever. He moved closer. Matthew's mouth was open, his lips parted, ready. They kissed and their tongues found each other.

Matthew's hands were down in Glenn's groin. He burst through his fly and slid his hand in between tight denim and hot flesh.

Glenn sighed as strong fingers curled around the shaft of his cock. His ground his hips against Matthew's hand, working his cock into his fist. His jeans were damp with sweat and pre-come. His hands were on Matthew's arse, pulling their bodies tight together, as though they were meant to be one.

Glenn glanced over Matthew's shoulder, towards David, challenging him through a sea of sweaty faces and limbs. David was watching them with obvious intent. It was evident in his dark eyes how badly he wanted them. He nodded towards the far corner, to the dark passage that led to the toilets.

Glenn smiled. He kissed Matthew and whispered in his ear, 'Let's go. David can't wait any longer.'

Matthew glanced back over his shoulder towards the edge of the floor. He saw David, waiting for them. He smiled.

They climbed down off the stage and slipped through the throng of sweaty bodies. David slid a strong arm around each of their shoulders, kissing them both in turn: Glenn first and then Matthew – full open-mouthed kisses.

'Into a cubicle,' he said, '*now*. I'm gonna have the two of you.'

The toilets were busy and they had no time for discretion. David marched Glenn and Matthew past the crowd of men gathered around the urinals and shoved them into the first empty cubicle. The stall was tiny. Glenn was pushed over the toilet bowl, when David followed them in and slammed the door behind him.

David unzipped his pants, releasing his fat cock. 'All right,' he said. 'Matthew, you're first.' He ripped open the wrapper of a condom and unrolled the rubber on to his thick shaft.

Glenn slid down on to the toilet seat. Matthew was standing in front of him. Glenn reached up and unfastened his belt and trousers. He pulled his pants down, struggling to tear the ill-fitting trouser legs down over Matthew's solid thighs. Eventually he managed to get them down around his calves. Matthew leaned forwards, resting his hands on Glenn's shoulders and spreading his feet as much as his pants would allow. He bent his knees and steadied himself.

David opened a sachet of lubricant. He squeezed half the contents over his cock and stuffed the remainder into Matthew's arsehole.

Matthew gripped Glenn's shoulders tight and readied himself. 'OK,' he gasped. 'Give it to me.'

Glenn watched the expression on his face. The sudden tension as the fat head of David's cock forced its way past the resistance of his arse. He grimaced for a second and then relaxed as the big shaft slid comfortably into place. Glenn knew from experience that David didn't offer his sex partners any time to catch their breath, no fleeting moments that gave their arseholes time to adjust to the massive intrusion. He started to pound Matthew's arse, picking up a hard and forceful rhythm.

Matthew dug his fingers into the muscle of Glenn's shoulder. His breath hissed through his gritted teeth. He bore the brunt of David's cock with greedy desire. His own cock slapped back and forth against his stomach as he tried to stand his ground.

No man could stand up to such a ferocious pounding for very long. He screamed and his cock suddenly shot out a direct load that hit Glenn straight in the face. He continued to squirt, firing blast after blast of cock cream on Glenn's brow and into his hair. Glenn opened his mouth and caught a couple of long streams. He savoured the taste on his tongue before swallowing.

David pulled quickly out of Matthew's arse.

'Time to change over,' he said. He ripped off the condom and started to unroll a fresh one.

Glenn stood up and changed places with Matthew, shoving his jeans down around his ankles and positioning his arse for David's cock. When David rammed the corpulent piece of meat into him he was suddenly flooded with memories of their time together – all the great, hard and fast sex they had shared.

He loved the bare feel of David's flat pelvis slapping against his buttocks and how it was a struggle to remain standing with every forward thrust. David held him in his huge hands and increased the pace, hammering in short sharp stabs. He roared in Glenn's ear as he reached his climax and Glenn felt the swelling in his hole as the condom filled up with spunk.

His own orgasm needed no provocation. His cock leaped and started to spit all over the floor. Matthew moved forwards with an open mouth to catch the brilliant white spillage as it dribbled from his dick. As the orgasm finally died, he took Glenn's cock in his mouth and licked away the last sticky residue.

David withdrew from him and they pulled up their pants and left the toilets.

David bought a round of drinks and all three men shared a cigarette in the Venue bar. From there Glenn and Matthew lost track of him. They returned to the dance floor and continued dancing until well after two o'clock. By then they were both tired. Rather than hanging round and hunting for another fuck, they headed off home, to enjoy the gentle pleasure of each other's body before drifting off into an exhausted sleep.

Eleven

Surprise

Glenn couldn't face the Saturday afternoon crowds in New-castle so he took Matthew into Durham to buy some new clothes. They had stayed in bed until late that morning following their night at the Mineshaft. They arrived in Durham around one o'clock.

'Why don't we go and get something to eat first?' Glenn said. 'There's no point trying to buy clothes on an empty stomach. What are you in the mood for?'

Matthew shrugged. 'I'm not really that hungry. Just something light will do.' He was dressed in his own clothes: the jeans, T-shirt and dark jacket that he had arrived in.

Glenn took him to a busy wine bar down the road from the bus station. It was one of a large chain of such bars, but he preferred the bright, airy premises to some of the poky bistros on the other, more trendy, side of town.

They ordered their food and drinks at the bar and sat at a table in the window, overlooking the busy street outside. Matthew took off his jacket and hung it over the back of his chair. He offered Glenn a cigarette.

'No, thanks. I've had a few lapses lately but I'd like to stick to my resolution.'

'Do you mind if I do?'

'Go ahead. I can hardly refuse you a cigarette when I'm the one who made you a smoker in the first place.'

Matthew lit up. He smiled, exhaling a long breath of smoke. 'That's true.'

A good-looking waiter arrived with the wine Glenn had ordered and two glasses.

'Cheers,' Glenn said.

'Cheers.'

They chinked glasses.

'Tell me about that fella last night,' Matthew said. 'David.'

Glenn sipped the cold, crisp wine. It was delicious. 'Why? Did you like him?'

'I don't know. I didn't have a chance to get to know him.' Matthew puffed on his cigarette. 'He seemed like a nice bloke, though, and he was a good shag.'

'Yeah.' Glenn grinned. 'He is a good shag. He always was. I'm glad to see that he hasn't changed in that respect. For a good, hard, horny fuck he still can't be beaten. What do you want to know about him?'

'I don't know really. Just a bit of background. I like to know something about the men I have sex with. I'm not too keen on anonymous lovers.'

'I'm afraid to say that there's not that much to know about David. What you see is pretty much what you get. He's a nice guy and he's a good fuck but that's about all there really is to him. I don't want to be rude or patronising about him, but he's not the brightest man I've ever known.'

'What happened between you?'

'Not much, beside a hell of a lot of fucking. When I first met him I couldn't get enough of that big fat thing between his legs. I wanted it all the time and the good thing was that he was always able to deliver. When the novelty of the sex wore off, though, we didn't have a lot to talk about.'

Matthew looked at Glenn with laughing eyes. 'It would be a long time before the novelty wore off a cock like that.'

'You'd be surprised. You can't shag for ever.'

'You said he was a heartbreaker. You must have felt something for him, then.'

Glenn fingered the base of his wineglass, twisting it slowly round. 'I thought I did at first. I think it's quite easy to think you're in love with such strong masculine men. But it wasn't really love. I was very fond of him. He's a nice guy and I did like him a lot. But it would be wrong to say that I was ever in love with him. I was just infatuated with his body.'

'Have you ever been in love?'

'Oh, come on.' Glenn laughed.

'I'm interested,' Matthew said. 'You know everything about my past – I'd just like to know a little bit about yours.'

Glenn spread his hands. 'I've thought I was in love hundreds of times and I never have been. Once I got over the novelty of sex there was rarely much else left to those relationships. I love my friends more – at least I have something more than just shagging with them.'

'What about when you were young? Didn't you ever have a great first love?'

'Come on, you don't want to know this crap.'

'Honestly I do. I'm interested in you.'

Glenn sighed and shook his head. He took a deep breath and tried to compose himself. He leaned forwards and lowered his voice to speak. 'The first man I fell in love with was called Mark. I didn't have sex with him or anything. He lived at the end of our street. He was married. I was thirteen and I thought he was the most gorgeous man I had ever seen. For three years I had a huge crush on him. I used to watch him all the time. I would follow him when he took his dog for a walk. I used to lie in bed and fantasise about him every night. They weren't sex fantasies – I didn't really think about sex then. I used to dream about holding his hand and kissing him – romantic stuff like that.'

'So what happened?'

'Nothing happened. I grew up and got over it.' He sipped his wine. 'I had my first proper boyfriend when I was sixteen. He was called Paul and he was twenty. I really thought he was the one for me; I don't know why now, though. He was a little squirt.'

Matthew was laughing. 'Has anyone ever told you that you have a very jaded attitude towards relationships?'

'I don't. I just don't know why I was so hung up on him. He wasn't my kind of man at all. When I look back on it now the only reason I think I chose him was because he was so small and unintimidating. It was my first time, after all.'

'So how was your first time?'

'To give poor Paul his due it was actually OK. Pretty nice. I was terrified of the whole cock-up-the-arse thing. But he took his time and was really gentle with me. It didn't hurt a bit.'

'So what became of him?'

Glenn smiled. It was a long time since he had deliberated over any of this. 'The bastard dumped me. He got back together with his old boyfriend and that was the end of me. It took me about two days to get over my broken heart. Within a week I had a new man. And that is pretty much the story of my life. One sex-driven relationship after another.'

'So there has been no great love of your life?'

Glenn paused. The answer of course was yes. But he replied, 'No.'

Dean was sprawled out on the living-room carpet listening to a tape of Barbra Streisand in concert. He had a pile of video tapes on the floor in front of him that he was sorting into two separate stacks: one stack was the good stuff, the other was crap. Gary was sitting on the sofa, loading compact discs into the ten-disc cartridge of their stereo system.

Although Gary had been moaning about it for weeks, Dean's early organisation and arrangements for the party had paid off. Everything was now in order and they had both been able to enjoy a relatively stress-free day.

'What about this one?' Dean picked up a tape and shoved it into the video. 'It's been that long since we've watched some of this stuff I can't even remember which one is which.'

The television screen flashed with static for a moment and then the hazy image of two bearded men having sex filled the screen. One of the men lay on a towel by the side of a Californian swimming pool, his legs slung over the shoulders of the other, bigger, man, while he got his arse pounded.

'Oh no,' Dean said, 'we can't use this, it's ancient.'

Gary chuckled astutely. 'What is it?'

He pressed stop and ejected the cassette. '*Mr Manrammer*,' he said, reading the name on the spine.

They both laughed.

'I'm not even sure where this one's come from. I don't remember buying it.'

'Haven't we got anything better than that?'

Dean tossed the tape on to his crap pile. 'I've come up with a few good ones but it isn't easy. We haven't bought any new porn for ages. I'm gonna order some new tapes off the Internet.'

'It's a bit late for tonight, though, isn't it?'

'Yeah, but no wonder we haven't been watching much lately if this is the cream of our collection.'

His intention was to have the television on all through the party playing back-to-back porn for anyone who was interested in watching it.

'So what are we gonna do?'

Dean indicated to the other stack of tapes – the good pile. 'Well, I thought we could have a theme. I've found five Kristen Bjorn videos and three Matt Bradshaws.'

'So what's the theme?'

'If I can find any more of either kind, we'll make it a Kristen Bjorn or a Matt Bradshaw night.' He stood up and picked up the phone. 'I'll call Glenn, see if he has any.'

He dialled Glenn's mobile number.

'Hi, babe, it's me. Where are you? Oh, right. Listen I just wanted to ask you a favour. Have you got any Kristen Bjorn videos? Of course I mean porn. Uh huh. All right. What about Matt Bradshaw? OK. Will you bring them with you tonight? Great. What? Oh, our porno collection is tragic. Thanks, Glenn. You're a star. See you later. Bye.'

He hung up.

'Well?'

'Kristen Bjorn it is. He's got *Carnival in Rio*, *Hungry for Men* and *Hot Times in Little Havana*. That should be enough to keep us going.'

Gary had finished loading the cartridge. 'How many people have you invited?'

'I'm not sure. Maybe about forty.'

'Do I know all these people?'

'Of course you do. There's Glenn for a start. Though apparently he's bringing a date with him. Joe, Lee and Eric, Patrick, Thomas and Liam, Adam, Paul and Kevin, Christopher and Edward, Mark.' He continued to reel off names. 'There will be a handful of guys you don't know, but that makes it more fun, doesn't it? Besides, I've got a surprise for you.'

Gary pulled Dean down on to the sofa with him. 'Oh, yeah. What kind of surprise?'

Dean snuggled into his bare arms. 'Don't worry, it's a nice one. I've invited a couple of guys I met yesterday.'

'Where?'

'When I went shopping. I knew you'd like them so I couldn't see the harm in asking.'

'What? You had trade yesterday? In Newcastle?'

'Uh huh.'

'Why didn't you tell me?'

'I'm telling you now, aren't I?'

'What are they like?'

Dean kissed Gary's bare chest. 'Just great. I don't want to spoil it for you but they're both fucking gorgeous. They're called Carter and John. John's a policeman.'

'Hang on a minute. Are you sure that's a good idea? Inviting a copper to one of our parties? What if he busts us for possession?'

'He won't. He had dope of his own at home. Just relax. Besides, if you don't get along there'll be plenty of other men there for you. You can take your pick of the best.'

Gary held Dean close, his hands resting in the curl of his spine. 'It looks like you've thought of everything.'

'Of course. I'm the perfect host.'

Gary leaned his mouth down close to Dean's. 'I love you, hon.'

'I love you too.'

Their lips met and they both pressed deeply into the kiss.

★

'So what kind of clothes do you want?'

Matthew looked around. 'I need something dressy that I can wear tonight, but I also need some more casual stuff to wear from day to day.'

The clothes shop was on Elvet Bridge. One of several designer retailers in that area of the city. The ground floor was ladies' wear and the men's attire was upstairs. A couple of very good-looking boys, decked out from head to toe in designer gear, were standing in attendance by the counter.

'Just let us know if you need any assistance.' The darker of the two men beamed.

Glenn smiled and told him that they just wanted to look around. He hated it when sales assistants stood over him, putting on pressure to buy.

'All right. Let's look at the casual stuff first. What do you like?'

Matthew shrugged. 'Just the usual. Jeans, shirts, T-shirts. And underwear. I'm desperate for some new underwear.'

'I don't know.' Glenn grinned. 'I think I prefer you without them.'

'But think of all the fun you'll have taking them off me,' Matthew said with a wink.

He selected two pairs of jeans, five white cotton T-shirts and five pairs of Calvin Klein underpants. He left them with the two boys at the counter while he set about the more difficult task of finding something for the party.

Glenn watched Matthew searching through the hangers. He stopped occasionally to examine some garment in more detail before replacing it, seemingly unsatisfied. Glenn browsed through the shelves looking for something he could wear himself.

He found a pair of trousers. They were black and loose-fitting with a drawstring cord at the waist. He quite liked them so he flung them over his arm. He would try them on. He found a plain black top made from cotton lycra. It was sleeveless and slim-fitting. He decided to try that on too.

'Well?' he said to Matthew. 'Have you found anything?'

'Maybe. What do you think of these?' He held up a pair of trousers and a shirt. The trousers were black with a pleat front; the shirt was plain white with a round collar and cutaway sleeves. 'I quite like these too,' he said, holding up a pair of black patent-leather shoes. They were square-toed with laces.

'They're nice,' said Glenn. 'Are you gonna try them on?'

Matthew nodded. 'Yeah, I think I will.'

The darker of the two assistants conducted them through to the changing rooms. He looked both men up and down with apparent interest. The name on his badge said Robert.

There were six small, adjacent stalls, curtained off for privacy. Glenn and Matthew carried their costumes into two cubicles right next to each other.

'I'll leave you guys to it,' Robert said. 'Just call on me if you want anything else.' He held eye contact with Glenn for a long, lingering moment before slowly drawing the curtain closed. Glenn heard his footsteps retreating back into the shop.

Glenn smiled, remarking at the sexual confidence a lot of young men seemed to possess these days. He was sure that he had not been so bold himself at that age. The boy, Robert, didn't seem to be much older than sixteen or seventeen.

There wasn't a lot of room in the changing stall. There was a wooden chair, a hook to hang the clothes on and a full-length mirror. Glenn undressed quickly and threw his own clothes over the back of the chair.

He was pleased with his choices. The top and trousers were a perfect fit and they were unlike anything else that he had in his wardrobe. He seemed to look different in them. The black top skimmed his chest and torso, skilfully caressing and accentuating the lean body underneath. His right bulky nipple swelled prominently beneath the smooth cotton.

Glenn smiled at his full reflection. He would wear these clothes tonight.

He called over to Matthew in the next stall. 'How are they? Do they fit you?'

'Great. Come and have a look.'

Glenn drew back the curtain and slipped through into Matthew's cubicle.

He looked stunning in his new clothes. The white shirt flared across his broad chest and tapered in perfectly to his narrow waist.

His bulky arms bulged out of the cut-off sleeves, showing off his muscles and his tattoo to magnificent effect.

'What do you think?' he asked, spreading his arms wide.

Glenn stepped into his embrace and kissed him. 'You look gorgeous.'

Matthew responded to his kisses, opening his mouth and thrusting his tongue forwards. Glenn's hand dropped to the front of his trousers to discern the rapidly hardening flesh there.

'Let's go home,' he whispered.

'Wait,' said Matthew, pulling back from Glenn's embrace. 'I've got something I want to show you. Close the curtain.'

Glenn stepped into the stall and drew the curtain along its rail behind him. Matthew was smiling. Glenn smiled too.

'What is it?'

Matthew unfastened his trousers slowly. He unzipped the fly. Glenn's pulse quickened. He could hear the voices of the two boys out on the shop floor. Matthew turned around and let go of the trousers. They dropped down to his ankles with a gentle gasp. Glenn knew that he wasn't wearing any underpants, but his buttocks were hidden beneath the tails of his shirt.

'What are you doing?' Glenn whispered. 'That boy could come back in here at any minute.'

'I wanted to show you this,' Matthew said softly.

He gathered up the shirt tails and raised them over his arse.

Glenn's eyes widened.

Between the creamy hemispheres of his buttocks protruded a flat piece of flesh-coloured rubber. It took a moment for him to realise what it was. Matthew had a butt plug inside him. What Glenn could see was its smooth base.

'What do you think?' Matthew said. 'I've had it in there all day.'

'Why?'

'So I would be ready for you.' Matthew grabbed a cheek in each hand and spread them apart. Glenn could see the lips of his swollen hole, bulging around the base of the fat rubber plug. Matthew contracted his anus back and forth, sucking the plug deeper into him like a baby with a dummy.

Glenn heard the sound of laugher out on the shop floor.

They had to be quick.

Matthew retrieved his wallet from his jacket and tossed Glenn a condom. Glenn unfastened his pants and shoved them all the way down to his feet. His leaking cock was hard and ready. He pulled the rubber out of its foil packet, stretched it over his fingertips, lowered it on to his head and quickly rolled it all the way down his shaft.

'Do you have any lube?' he whispered.

'No,' said Matthew, 'but it doesn't really matter. My arse is lubed up pretty well already. A bit of spit on your cock should do.'

Glenn grasped the soft rubber base of the butt plug. He eased it out of Matthew slowly. His arsehole was reluctant to release its prize. The moist pink lips widened over the thick round butt. Matthew had used a large plug – about six inches long and three inches thick. Glenn was careful. Finally he managed to release the widest point of its circumference from the tiny hole. The remainder of its length slipped out of him freely.

Glenn spat into his palm and fisted his saliva over the shaft of his cock. Matthew's arsehole was loose and relaxed. He pushed through the ring of muscle and buried his length all the way to the hilt. Matthew sighed. He leaned forwards and supported his weight on the back of the chair.

'Fuck me hard,' he hissed. 'I can take it.'

There was no time to savour the moment or sensation. They had to satisfy their hunger quickly. Glenn gripped his hips and picked up a fast rhythm. Matthew thrust back against him, match-ing him thrust for thrust. They fucked like animals, their heated coupling reflected in the full-length mirror. Glenn's breath hissed through his clenched teeth as he buried himself deep, hips thrusting hard. Matthew held himself rigid beneath him, lost in the carnality of such basic, feral sex. His legs were open, his feet spread as wide as his trousers would allow him.

Glenn's intent ears could hear the voices and laughter of the two assistants outside.

Suddenly he was coming. He held Matthew's hips and released all of his tension into him. His cock trembled and pulsated as it released its pleasure.

Matthew grunted. His cock erupted, sending a wide arch of

sperm into the air. It splattered against the full-length mirror, one rapid spurt after another.

Matthew rested his head against the back of the chair. They both laughed softly. Glenn withdrew his cock. He removed the condom and tied it off, wrapping it up in tissues from Matthew's jacket. He wiped off his cock, careful not to get any of his come on the clothes that he had not yet paid for.

Matthew inserted the plug back into his arse before changing back into his own clothes.

Robert smiled as they returned, red-faced, to the counter.

'Is everything all right?'

Glenn treated him to his best smile, hoping that it wasn't too obvious that he had just shot a terrific load up his male companion's arse.

'Everything's fine, thanks. We'll take all of these.'

Robert totalled up the bill while the other boy, called Reece, bagged up their clothes. Glenn handed over his credit card when Robert presented him with the final bill.

They walked back into the marketplace with their bags of shopping to catch a taxi home.

Matthew was in the shower. Through the open bathroom door, Glenn could hear him singing 'Drop the Boy'. Glenn smiled quietly to himself. He hadn't heard that song in years. It was half past six. Dean was expecting them in an hour. Glenn had already showered and was ready to get dressed. There was one thing he had to do first.

He took out the bulging black bag that he stashed away at the back of the wardrobe and emptied its contents on to the top of the bed. An assortment of sex toys spilled out across the duvet cover. The majority of the collection had been amassed during a five-month relationship he had once had with a man called Kyle. Kyle had been heavily into the 'playful' side of sex and had encouraged Glenn to experiment with toys and costumes in the brief time that they were together.

Despite his fondness for Kyle at the time, Glenn never really got into the whole sex-toy thing, preferring real flesh over rubber. Most of the toys had remained in the sack, unused since their break-up. Kyle had, however, been the inspiration for Glenn's porn pseudonym.

Matthew's stunt with the butt plug that afternoon and his amazing experience earlier in the week with Damien Marquez had reawakened a surprising, half-forgotten, interest in vibrators and dildos.

Glenn looked down at the assortment of rubber cocks and electrical toys spread across the bed. He wondered what the hell had possessed him to buy half of the stuff. He had never been aroused by Thai beads and yet there were three different varieties of them right there in front of him. The long, vibrating finger that Kyle had brought back from Amsterdam had always been more of a turn-off than an instrument of arousal.

Not all the playthings were completely useless. The various vibrators had provided him with a lot of pleasure when he was in the right frame of mind to use them. That was usually when he was on his own. If there was ever another man with him then he always favoured the real thing. But the dildos did have a use in his sex life. A big blunt object stuffed up his arse was perfect for giving that extra gush to his solo wank sessions. He loved to bare down hard on the counterfeit cock and just let his orgasm gush over his hands and stomach.

He had four different butt plugs. The smallest was about the size of his index finger and only marginally thicker. He had only used it once; its narrow girth had proved to be wholly unsatisfactory. He didn't dare walk around with it in in case it dropped right out of him.

He picked up the largest plug. It was the same size as the one that Matthew had wedged up his arse as he wandered around Durham city all day. That was the one that he would use. He put it to one side and stuffed all of the other toys back into the black bag and returned it to its home at the back of the wardrobe. He closed the door.

Matthew was still in the shower, warbling away to himself beneath the steaming jets.

Glenn flung himself down on top of the bed and picked up the butt plug. He reached over into the drawer and took out a tube of lubricant. He smeared the sticky gel all over the surface of the plug and then fingered some around the rim of his arse. His arsehole was tight and he had to shove another finger in there to loosen himself up. He pressed all the way in until his hand couldn't go any deeper. He slid his fingers backwards and forwards, stretching the taut ring.

He pulled out and rolled over on to his back. He raised his knees and thrust his arse forwards. He shoved the sticky butt plug down between his thighs, guiding it to his hole. The tip slid in easily. The shaft of the plug widened quickly. He breathed slowly through his nostrils, pressing the rubber deeper into him.

His arsehole stretched, widened. The shaft of the dildo thickened. It suddenly seemed impossible. There was no way this squat object was going to fit inside his tiny hole. He was right on the threshold of discomfort and pain. His hole felt as if it was about to split.

Suddenly he had broken through. The bulbous plug was right inside him and there was only the narrow stem for his sphincter to cope with. He relaxed, the pain diffusing. He lay still for a few moments, allowing his body to adjust to the intrusion to his bowel.

Matthew stepped out of the shower and came through into the bedroom, a damp towel wrapped around his slight waist. He smiled at Glenn, regarding his splayed thighs and crowded rectum.

'Are you all right, babe?'

Glenn rolled over and sat up on the edge of the bed. He sighed as the dildo was forced deeper into his rectum. He nodded.

'Are you going to wear that to the party?' Matthew asked. A heavy drop of water trickled down his naked chest.

Glenn nodded again, too dazed to find his voice.

'Do you want me to wear mine?'

'Yeah,' he said, his voice shaky. 'I want to see how long we can stand it until we have to sneak off and find a place to fuck.'

'That sounds nice,' Matthew said.

Glenn stood up slowly and took a couple of tentative steps. It was a bizarre sensation to walk around with a rectum crammed full of rubber. It took him several minutes to adjust. The ache had already begun in his balls. That sweet agony that would not be appeased until he tugged his cock and released his loins of their burden. He tried to ignore it, pulling on a pair of underpants.

He dressed slowly in his new clothes and found a way to walk and move without making it obvious that his arse was filled with a big, latex cock. He styled his hair and brushed his teeth. He watched Matthew through the open door as he lubed up his own arse and shoved in his plug. He wondered how long they would be able to keep their hands off each other. How long before the full sensation inside them became too much to bear.

Glenn was ready first. While he waited for Matthew to finish in the bathroom he splashed on some aftershave and went downstairs to find the videos that Dean had asked him for.

Matthew was ready by the time their taxi arrived. Glenn kissed him softly on the lips and caressed the lean curve of his buttocks, before he turned out the lights and went outside to the waiting car.

Twelve

Party Time

The house was built on old farmland two miles outside of Durham city. The original farmhouse had been demolished in the late 1980s and five new houses were built on the site between 1994 and 1996. Dean and Gary bought the last of the five properties to be completed. It was constructed in a small green valley a hundred yards away from the nearest house.

Though neither of the two men was a traditional country boy, they were immediately attracted to the seclusion and privacy that the farmland provided. After three years of living in the city, right on top of their neighbours, the seclusion offered by the house was paradise.

The house was large and well designed with five spacious bedrooms. There were two grand open gardens to the front and rear. At first they had toyed with the idea of building a swimming pool but finally decided against it. The shadows of the valley would mean that the water would always be cold. The mortgage was steep enough without the extra expense of heating a pool.

By nine o'clock almost all of the forty-five invited guests had arrived. It was a mild summer evening and the two hosts took advantage of the warm night air by throwing open the patio doors and setting up tables in the garden. There were a couple of long tables running down the side of the flower beds, piled high with food that had been prepared that afternoon. Carl, Gary's brother, stood over the barbecue cooking sausages and burgers. A free bar had been set up at the back of the house with a couple of drop-dead-gorgeous drag queens serving as waitresses.

Although a handful of men had gathered in the living room to watch the porn tapes that Dean had provided, the majority of the guests were outside in the garden. Gary had set up four speakers across the lawn to pipe out the music from his stereo system inside.

Dean had made a big fuss of Glenn when he first arrived with Matthew. As Gary took Matthew aside to get them something to drink, Dean took the opportunity to quiz Glenn about his date.

'He's fucking gorgeous!' he exclaimed. 'Where did you find him? You must move fast. What happened to the photographer you had the other day? I thought you were bringing him with you.'

'I never said that. I was only with Damien that one time.'

'That's a bit of a shame 'cause I was looking forward to meeting him. You'll have to introduce me another time. Anyway I've got enough on my plate tonight. You see those two men over there, the big blond guys? I met them in the Venue yesterday. They are so fucking horny, both of them. The one with the bleached hair is a copper. I invited them round to meet Gary. I'm looking forward to a *really* good time with them all later.'

Dean seemed to be pretty drunk for so early in the night. Glenn was convinced that he had also taken something. There was plenty of marijuana in evidence around the house, but Glenn knew that Dean also liked to dabble in harder drugs such as cocaine, speed and ecstasy. He wouldn't have put it past him to have taken a combination of any of those substances.

Glenn mingled casually through the crowd, introducing Matthew to many of his friends, most of whom tried to make a pass at either one or both of them. Although he smiled and made an effort to join in the conversations, Glenn was finding it increasingly difficult to concentrate on anything other than the big rubber plug up his arse. The tip of his dick was aching to spit out a wad of spunk.

He knew nearly all of the other guests. Joe Hart arrived on his own at ten o'clock with his camcorder. He was talking to Liam and Thomas, a couple in their late twenties from Spennymoor, over by the bar. Joe waved but Glenn hadn't had a chance to speak to him yet. Lee, the aspiring author from the supermarket, was also there with his boyfriend Eric.

'Hiya, sexy.'

Glenn jolted as a pair of firm hands fixed on his arse from behind, propelling the butt plug a fraction deeper into him.

Patrick Robins was an old boyfriend. Glenn turned and gazed into the dynamic blue eyes that had lost none of their power to hypnotise. Patrick had been his lover when he was twenty, the man who had taught him more about sex and sensuality than any of his previous boyfriends. Patrick was nearly forty now. His fair brown hair was starting to recede and the lines around his shiny blue eyes were etched a little deeper than when Glenn had last seen him. But he was still devilishly handsome. Even without his worldly good looks, the strength of his charismatic personality was enough to charm almost any man into a compromising situation.

Glenn introduced his old flame to his present lover. They shook hands, smiling, each showing an interest in the other.

'Are you here on your own?' Glenn asked.

'Kind of. Trevor and Stephen gave me a lift over but they're staying the night and I need to get home later.' His mouth widened into a broad wolfish grin. 'But I've got my eye on that little cutie over there. I'm thinking of taking him home with me.'

He pointed to a tall blond who was dressed in blue and sitting with a group of other guys whom Glenn did not recognise. He sat stiffly in his chair, seemingly unsure and uncomfortable in his surroundings, taking delicate sips from a glass of white wine.

Glenn laughed. 'He looks terrified.'

'He's called Adam. I asked Dean about him. He's an Oxford graduate.'

'You might scare him off.'

'I'll go easy on him,' Patrick sneered. 'At least to begin with.'

Glenn and Matthew left Patrick and went up to the bar to refill their glasses.

'Are you OK?' Glenn asked.

Matthew grinned. 'Yeah. Of course.'

'I know it's not easy when you don't really know anyone.'

'It's OK. I'm pretty sociable.'

'Will you wait here for me? I need to take a piss.'

'Only if you promise not to toss yourself off while you're in there.'

Glenn kissed him. 'It's hard to keep a promise like that but I'll try. I don't know about you but this dildo is driving me insane. It's torture. I feel like I've been right on the verge of coming for over an hour now. I don't think I can last much longer.'

Matthew brushed his fingers over the hardness in the front of Glenn's trousers. 'That's the point, hon. I promise you that when you do come your orgasm will be so sweet it'll bring you to tears.'

'The wait is more likely to bring on a nervous breakdown.'

'It'll be worth it.'

They kissed. Glenn left Matthew at the bar while he went inside. As he passed through the house on his way to the bathroom he heard moaning from the living room. He knew that it was more than just the soundtrack of a porno movie. He stuck his head around the door.

Three men were sitting on the sofa, cocks in hand. A fourth man was down on the floor in front of them taking it in turn to suck each of their cocks. He was naked from the waist down, stroking his own dick while he worked his way along the line. His face was drenched with saliva and sweat as he gobbled one hard cock at a time.

The sight heightened Glenn's own arousal. The temptation to unzip himself and offer his own cock to that wet, willing mouth was huge. He was already worked up into such a frenzy that it would not take him long. The warmth of a man's lips on his throbbing head would be enough to liberate the repressed forces within him. He would squirt come down that young guy's throat so hard and fast that he would choke.

Glenn groaned and turned away. He had promised himself to Matthew and he knew that his lover was right. His release would be all the more special for the wait and anguish he had to endure before he reached that final stage.

He locked himself in the bathroom. Pissing with a hard-on is never easy. It is even more arduous when the slightest touch of the cock is likely to bring on a gush of spurting cream. He withdrew his dick slowly, holding it at the root, carefully avoiding the ultrasensitive head. He had to lean forwards and direct his shaft down into the bowl. Deep breath. He gasped as the flow of urine began. The sensation of pissing alone was comparable to coming. His pisshole itched and burned with the flow. It seemed like it was never going to end.

At last the stream started to decrease. He contracted his urethra slowly, squeezing the last drops out of the pipe. He shook himself off very slowly from the root. It seemed as if his body was about to dissolve into a big, sloppy puddle of come.

He knew that he could not continue with this for much longer – an hour at the very most. Then he would have to take Matthew and lead him off to a bedroom or bathroom or a secluded stretch of hillside and fuck his arse until he drained his body of all this unbearable tension.

He flushed the toilet and zipped himself up. He washed his hands and went back downstairs. On his way back outside he ran into Dean in the kitchen. He was rolling a joint on the bench.

'What do you think?' Dean asked. 'Do you think it's going OK?'

'It's a great party,' Glenn said. 'They always are. I don't know why you worry so much.'

Dean licked the skin and sealed the joint. 'Have you seen what's going on in the living room?'

'Yeah. They're starting early. The cocksucking doesn't usually get going until midnight.'

'I was thinking of going in there and getting a bit of head myself.' He lit the joint and started puffing appreciatively on it. 'But the entertainment starts soon.'

Glenn accepted the joint from him and took a long draw. 'What entertainment?'

Dean snickered. 'It's another surprise. Two guys called Francisco and Greg. I saw them at a party in Blackpool last month and asked them if they would mind coming here tonight. They're upstairs right now getting ready.'

'What do they do?'

'You'll see. I don't want to spoil it for anyone. Gary wasn't with

145

me in Blackpool so he doesn't even know what kind of a show these fellas put on. Let's just say that it's bloody great entertainment.'

Matthew was still standing at the bar. He had been joined by Patrick, who was predictably hitting on him.

'What happened to the Oxford blond?' Glenn asked, taking his drink from Matthew.

Patrick shook his head. 'Turns out that he's not my type.'

'Or is it that you're not *his* type?' Glenn laughed.

Matthew slid his arm around Glenn's waist. 'Did you keep your promise?'

'It wasn't easy but I managed.'

'What promise is this?' Patrick asked.

'Private joke,' Glenn said.

'Suit yourself.'

Dean came out of the house on to the back lawn puffing on his joint. He winked at Glenn as he passed and then climbed up on top of a table. 'Can you all be quiet a minute,' he shouted, clapping his hands. 'Sssshhh! Quiet, please.'

Conversation across the lawn stopped and all eyes turned towards Dean. He was the centre of attention. A handful of men at the back of the garden gave him a spontaneous applause.

He bowed graciously and grinned. 'Thank you. Those of you who have been to parties here before will know that we usually just allow you all to get on and make your own entertainment. Well don't worry, guys, you'll get plenty of opportunity for that kind of thing later. Before you do, though, I've arranged a surprise for you all. I've brought along a couple of very nice boys who are going to do a bit of a show for you. Here they are, then: the gorgeous Francisco and the very fuckable Greg.'

A cheer went up across the crowd. Glenn and Matthew applauded. Dean climbed down off the table and came over to stand beside them.

The two performers came bounding out of the patio doors to the opening strains of 'Better the Devil You Know', Kylie rather than Steps. They were dressed in tight red shorts and heavy black boots. They had little devils' horns on top of their heads and their lithe young bodies were oiled up and shiny.

There was a dynamic contrast in the looks of the two young men. Greg was quite obviously the golden-skinned blond. He bounced across the lawn, thrusting and grinding. He was gorgeous: young, hard and smooth. He was the perfect image of a West Coast America beach bum. By comparison Francisco was a swarthy Latino hunk with milk-chocolate skin and spiky black hair. His dark body, chest, stomach and limbs, were all completely smooth but for two tiny tufts of jet-black hair underneath his arms. His face was lovely with a full, fleshy mouth and inky black eyes.

The two men danced together, gyrating against one another, caressing shoulders, nipples, buttocks. Their lips brushed. Their chemistry was palpable, their heat affecting every man in the garden. The crowd that had spread out around the periphery of the garden moved in for a closer look. Glenn and Matthew were right at the front with an unrestricted view. The pressure of the bodies behind them forced them nearer. Joe Hart pushed his way forwards, his camcorder raised to film the spectacle.

Francisco dropped to his knees in front of Greg and nuzzled his face into his groin. Greg smiled, rolling his eyes in an over-the-top, theatrical manner, expressing his pleasure for the benefit of the voyeuristic crowd. He gripped Francisco's head in both fists and ground his hips against his face, pretending to fuck his mouth. The Latino guy grasped Greg's golden thighs and wiggled his rump as part of the act.

Glenn watched the two performers, the profound state of his arousal heightening to a rarely glimpsed peak. He dared not move: the slightest motion of the plug inside him would tip the balance of power over the edge. Without any external stimulation his cock would tighten and release a wild spray of semen into his pants. He could sense that the exhibition was having just as potent an effect on Matthew. He could hear the deep, irregular rhythm of his lover's breath, perceive the weakening of his knees.

Francisco's fingers curled over the waistband of Greg's shorts. He ripped the flimsy attire down in one strong motion, revealing everything. Greg stepped out of the shorts and kicked them aside. He ground his hips, waggling his erect cock in front of his partner's face. Francisco's leaned closer and the blond smacked him in the face with the engorged organ. He repeated the manoeuvre, slapping the prone guy on either side of his upturned, smiling face. A long silvery trail of pre-come glistened on Francisco's delicious skin. Greg wiped the tip of his dick across his fleshy lips.

Francisco lay down on the grass. He lifted his legs into the air and, supporting his lower back with his hands, he raised himself up on to his shoulders. Greg removed the Latino guy's shorts, drawing them up over his outstretched legs and throwing them to the ground. There was a long, graceful curve to Francisco's cock: it arched out from his groin and curled over. The unsheathed tip touched the skin just below his navel.

Francisco rolled further back, bringing his legs down over his head. He bore all of his weight on his shoulders and brought his feet down just above his head, forming a tight arch with his body. The position caused his buttocks to spread, revealing all the hidden secrets of his body. The fine flesh of his cock and balls was a deeper colour than the creamy chocolate hue of his skin. His anus was several shades darker again. Thick brown grooves of flesh radiated from the tiny, central opening.

Glenn was astonished by the guy's beauty and graceful athleticism.

Greg sucked on his middle finger and gently pressed it to Francisco's clearly accessible gash. He traced a slow line around the rim.

'*Do it!*' somebody cried.

'*Finger him,*' called another voice.

The tip of Greg's finger disappeared into the brown hole. He pressed deeper, lazily past the first and second knuckle and then all the way in to the hilt. A spontaneous applause greeted the display. Francisco's face was flushed with the exertion of holding the upside-down position. Glenn could clearly make out the sheen of sweat across his brow and the heavier droplets that soaked his thick black hair.

Greg withdrew his finger. The pouting lips sucked at him like a mouth until the tip slid free. He gave Francisco's arsehole a little open-handed slap. The hole contracted.

Greg gave a casual hand signal to Dean.

Dean nodded and slipped away from the crowd and into the house.

'What's he doing?' Patrick whispered in Glenn's ear.

'I have no idea. He's been keeping this to himself.'

Dean returned a few seconds later, carrying something in both hands; it was some kind of parcel wrapped up in towels. The crowd was silent with anticipation and excitement.

No one knew what was going to happen next.

Dean placed the package down on the grass beside Francisco's arched body and stepped back.

'C'mon, Dean, what's going on?' Patrick asked him.

Dean winked. 'Wait and see,' he said. 'It's fucking awesome.'

Greg carefully unwrapped the towel, concealing its contents from the crowd. The entire audience held its breath at once. The knot of anticipation tightened in Glenn's stomach and his sphincter tightened on the butt plug. The heady smoke from Dean's joint wafted over him.

Greg removed the first item from the towel and held it up to the crowd, smiling. He had a clear, plastic funnel in his hand, with a wide rim and long, narrow spout.

'*Fuck!*' Glenn gasped.

'Jesus,' said Patrick. 'He's not gonna . . . *surely he's not*!

Dean laughed. '*He surely is!*'

Greg spread Francisco's arsehole with two fingers, opening him up. The Latino did not flinch from his difficult position when his partner inserted the tip of the six-inch spout into his anus.

Glenn was unsure of his own emotions. One part of him was disturbed by the scene they were acting out and the daunting uncertainty of exactly what these men were going to do next. A greater, more dominant part of him was compelled to keep watching. He could not avert his eyes from the open spectacle of Francisco's arse and the funnel that he flaunted in his hole.

Glenn, Matthew and Patrick gasped in unison when Greg reached down under the towel again and produced a can of beer.

'Fucking hell!' Patrick roared. 'He *can't* do that!'

'Don't be such a prude.' Dean chuckled. 'This is performance art, darling!'

Greg cracked open the can of beer. He held it high above Francisco's flared arse and carefully tilted the can. The contents spilled over in a long, direct stream straight into the well below.

The beer glugged and frothed around the wide basin of the funnel before gradually running down through the spout into the guy's arse. Greg tipped over the can until it was empty. He crushed the tin and tossed it aside.

He reached down again and produced another can. He snapped open the ring-pull and poured the entire contents of that into the funnel too.

'Wooahh!' Dean applauded. 'Fill him up.'

Greg did exactly that. He emptied a third can of beer into Francisco's butt and then, amazingly, a fourth.

'This is incredible,' Matthew said.

That was the last tin. Francisco now had four whole cans of beer inside him – two whole litres of gassy fluid. Greg spread his arms and took a bow. A cheer went up around the gathered crowd as the audience overcame their disbelief and applauded the magnificent achievement of the two performers.

'Fantastic,' Patrick cried.

'I told you they were great, didn't I?' said Dean.

'Just imagine what that little fucker will be like in bed with an arse as talented as that.'

Greg gently slapped Francisco's upturned rump.

The beer erupted from his rectum in a spectacular fountain. It shot out straight into the air in a spouting explosion, frothing and foaming as it teamed down over his body and the grass surrounding him. He opened his mouth to drink from his own manly geyser of beer. It spurted out of him like oil from a newly mined well, to rapturous applause. His entire body was dripping with the effervescent flood.

As the flow eventually ceased, he remained arched over in his strenuous position. Greg lowered his face into the wide cleft of his buttocks and drank the beer that lingered in the crevice. Francisco's arsehole was now concealed behind a layer of frothy white foam. Greg lapped it up with obvious enthusiasm, drinking deeply from the wide rim.

Dean lit up another joint and passed it round his friends. Glenn accepted it gratefully, drawing the thick smoke deep into his lungs. He held his breath for a moment before blowing out a long, lazy breath. He noticed how his hands were trembling. He couldn't go on with this any longer: he had to release the tension in his nuts and get this plug out of his arse before it drove him insane.

Greg had put on a condom and was introducing the tip of his dick into Francisco's spumescent hole. The Latino rolled over further, raising his hips. He gained another round of applause from the audience as they realised what he was about to do. He curled his pelvis over and took the head of his own cock into his mouth. It was incredible how much of the shaft he was able to swallow. He couldn't quiet manage to take himself all the way to the root but he succeeded in sliding a good four or five inches past his lips. Greg started to press back and forth into his arse.

Matthew suddenly turned to Glenn. 'I can't take any more of this,' he said, his voice ringing with desperation.

'Come on,' said Glenn. 'We'll go upstairs.'

No one took any notice of them as they slipped away: everyone else's attention was directed at the two men on the grass. The house was empty. Even the group in the living room had deserted their hard-core porn and mutual blow jobs in preference for the live show.

Glenn knew his way around the house. He also knew that whenever Dean had a party like this he set aside the two back rooms, for the benefit of any guests who wanted to fuck in privacy. It was rare that anyone did. The general ambience and erotic mood of the parties usually managed to overthrow any personal inhibitions. As the two men on the lawn had certified, sex in the present company did not have to be concealed behind closed doors.

Glenn did not want to share Matthew with the hungry eyes of a crowd. The secret of what they both had up their arses united them in a common bond. They shared the illicit confidence and they would share the pleasure in private.

Glenn took Matthew upstairs to the second bedroom on the first floor. The large double bed was made up ready and there was a huge bowl of condoms and lubricant at the side of it. Glenn wedged a chair under the door handle.

They did not have time to undress. Matthew unfastened his trousers and threw himself face down on the bed. Glenn quickly unzipped himself and pulled on one of the condoms provided. Matthew's arsehole squelched as Glenn pulled out the wide plug and replaced it with his cock. They fucked hard and fast; coming was the only consideration.

Glenn buried his cock inside Matthew and squeezed his own butt plug, tight, tight, tight.

'Oh fuck!' he gasped, surfing Matthew's arse on the hairline edge of pleasure.

Matthew tightened his rectum and pressed his hips back from the bed.

'Ah!' Glenn said, biting the shoulder of Matthew's shirt. 'Oh fuck. Oh shit! Fuck it. Fuck! Fuck! Fuck! *Fuuuccckk!*'

His urethra contracted as come surged up its length in long, body-shaking waves. He couldn't breathe, couldn't speak, couldn't think. His entire body trembled in paroxysms of pleasure. He gripped the butt plug in a vicelike grip as his prostate swelled and hardened against it. His buttocks still heaved, slamming his cock spasmodically into Matthew's arse, completely out of rhythm, reacting to a primeval instinct.

Matthew rolled out from under him, his cock sliding fluidly out of his arse in the dying moments of orgasm. He spun over on to his back, legs splayed, cock thrust forwards.

'*Make me come, you bastard!*'

Glenn grabbed his cock and fisted it madly. He shoved a couple of fingers right up his loose hole, finding his pleasure centre. He stroked the firm nub. Matthew groaned, a dark guttural sound from the depths of his chest. He arched his back from the bed, barely suppressing a scream. His body twisted, forcing his shirt up over his chest. He twisted both nipples.

His dick throbbed in Glenn's fist and squirted a huge load. The arch of creamy whiteness sailed straight into the air. A large gob splattered the bedclothes above his head. Another hit him right on the cheek. He mewed like a baby as Glenn fisted the last drops of come from his aching manhood.

He lay beneath him, straining for breath. His face was scarlet with exertion.

Glenn leaned forwards and licked the come from his cheek before falling down at his side to catch his own breath.

A loud, tumultuous cheer and the sound of enthusiastic applause drifted up from the garden below.

Thirteen

Seduced

The garden performance came to a spectacular conclusion when Greg pulled out of Francisco's arse. He pulled off the condom with deft fingers and jerked off to a splendid climax, spurting over his partner's arched body in long white bursts. His come dribbled down Francisco's brown thighs and tight ball sac. Their timing was perfect. As Greg showered the Latino with his sperm, Francisco blasted himself in the face with his own ejaculation. Thick, torpid fluid splattered his gorgeous features.

The rapturous applause was deafening. The crowd stomped and cheered and whistled, raising their hands high above their heads to applaud.

Francisco carefully eased his legs back over his head and Greg helped him to his feet. He wiped the spunk off his body with a towel and the two of them took a bow, basking in the adoration of the audience like chorus boys at the opening of a West End show. With a final wave, they picked up their costumes and towels and skipped back into the house.

Dean was ecstatic. The performance had surpassed all of his expectations. It was an even greater success than the show he had seen in Blackpool. His house guests flooded round, quick to congratulate him and voice their appreciation.

'Those guys were incredible!'

'Fucking awesome!'

'I've never seen anything like *that*!'

'Where did you find them?'

'It's the best thing I've ever seen.'

'The *horniest* thing I've ever seen!'

Gary slid his arm around Dean's tight waist and kissed him. 'Well done, darling. That was spectacular. I can't believe what I've just seen.'

'I wasn't sure if you'd like it,' Dean said, returning the kiss. 'I know you're not always keen on strip shows.'

'That was more than a strip show, Dean. It was a fucking extravaganza.'

'Thanks, Gary.' Dean slid his arm around his lover's shoulder. 'What did you think of your other surprise?'

'What? Carter and John?'

'What else?'

Gary grabbed Dean's wrist and piloted his hand down to his groin. He pressed his palm against the thick pulsatory life beneath his trousers. 'That's what I think of them. Fuckin' gorgeous.'

Dean squeezed his cock. 'I knew you'd be impressed. I had such a great time with those two yesterday that it seemed like a waste not to see them again.'

'I can't wait for the four of us to hit the bedroom. It's gonna be fantastic. I have to admit that I was dubious when you told me that John was a cop. Inviting him here didn't seem like the greatest idea, but he seems fine with it all.'

'I told you he'd be cool about it.'

'I'm gonna get back over to them. You coming?'

'I won't be long. I just want to have a word with Greg and Francisco. I'm gonna go up to thank them.'

Dean walked over the lawn towards the house, catching snatches of conversation along the way. Everyone was talking about the show. He felt justifiably pleased with himself.

He noticed that Glenn had disappeared along with his date. He couldn't really blame him. That guy Matthew was a very sexy little bastard with an incredibly humpy arse. Despite his passive inclinations he wouldn't mind screwing an arse like that himself.

Francisco and Greg were changing in Dean and Gary's bedroom. He told them to use it as it was the only room in the house that had an *en-suite* bathroom. Francisco was in the shower while Greg packed up their equipment. He paraded across the floor, completely naked but for his heavy black boots and devil's horns. His cock bounced softly against his golden thighs as he moved.

Dean stood in the open doorway and rapped lightly against the frame. 'Hi. Do you mind if I come in for a minute?' he said.

'Of course not,' Greg said, flashing his perfect white smile and making no attempt to cover up his nudity. 'It's your house.'

'I only came up to thank you. I thought you were great. Both of you.'

'Thanks, it's nice to be appreciated. You have some very nice friends too. They were a good group to perform for. Sometimes we have to work really hard to win over an audience. But tonight was great.'

'I wasn't sure if I'd be able to get you here. I'm so pleased that you came.'

'We are pretty busy,' Greg said, folding up a towel and packing it neatly into his huge leather hold-all. 'Next week we're going to Corfu. We're booked for the whole week at a private villa. We have to put on a different show every night.'

'Wow. How do you do it?'

'Oh, we have a few different routines. The four-can-trick is always the most popular, but we're working on a couple of variations on that.'

Dean sat down on the edge of the bed. 'Do you want to hang around for a while? The party will run for a long time yet. If you don't have to be somewhere else.'

'We wouldn't want to impose on you or your friends.'

'You wouldn't be. I'd love you to stay.'

'OK.' Gary sat down next to Dean and started to untie his boots. 'I'll just have a shower and get changed first. We'll be down to join you in about twenty minutes.'

Dean was thrilled. There was nothing more satisfying than a house filled with gorgeous men. He stood up.

'Do you want me to send anything up for you? Some drinks or something to eat?'

Greg pulled off his boots. 'A couple of cold beers would be nice.'

'I'll send someone up with them. See you soon.'

The summer sky had darkened considerably when he went back down to the garden but the grounds of the house were lit as brightly as day by the powerful lights mounted around the area.

Dean's man-hungry gaze was drawn immediately to the man standing at the bar.

Wow! Who the fuck is that?

The stranger was standing on his own, one elbow resting against the top of the bar. Dean didn't recognise him at all. He must have come along with one of the other guests, but even then Dean was sure that he knew just about everyone.

He was tall and lean, handsome in a rugged sort of way. He emitted a very palpable aura of danger and untamed sex. His mean gaze shifted around the bar and came into direct contact with Dean. Their eyes fastened on one another and held. The stranger's top lip curled upwards, half smiling, half sneering.

His tall frame was an amalgam of sharp angles. He was wearing a black, short-sleeve shirt, unfastened halfway down his chest. The shirt showed off the distinct line of his broad shoulders. The dark hair that dusted his lean torso could clearly be seen through the open V at the neck. His bare forearms were long and sinewy.

There was a severe countenance to his darkly handsome face. His narrow blue eyes, beneath thin, highly arched brows, gave his features a sly, almost evil cast. His nose was long and straight, in perfect conformity with the rigid line of his flawless jaw. His hair was dark and cut into a short crop that receded slightly from his high forehead. He had a slightly scruffy two or three days' growth of stubble.

Dean crossed over to the bar, feeling the stranger's hard, intimidating eyes on his body. He walked right up to him and stood defiantly at his side. He waved over Daniella, the six-foot transvestite waitress.

'Daniella, could you send a couple of beers upstairs for Greg and Francisco. They're both in my bedroom.'

Daniella nodded and carried out the order.

The stranger turned, leaning on one elbow, and looked directly into Dean's eyes. The half-smile continued to play over his thin lips.

'Hi,' Dean said.

'Hello.' His voice was deep and strangely emotionless.

Dean was completely entranced. He didn't think he had ever looked into a pair of eyes that were so brilliantly blue. So bright and dynamic and yet filled with an inexplicable darkness.

'I don't think I know you,' he said, his voice sounding as if it belonged to someone else.

'No.' The smile broadened into a wide grin. 'I don't think you do. I'm Anthony.'

His handshake was strong and dry. He held on to Dean's hand afterwards, declining to let go.

'I'm Dean. So who are you here with?'

The man ran his tongue slowly over the edge of his even, white teeth.

'Some friends,' he said at last.

Dean struggled to smile. The man was obviously bluffing. He wasn't here with anybody. He hadn't been invited. And yet he was so intriguing, so dangerously handsome, that Dean didn't want him to leave.

'What friends are they then? I know everyone here.'

Anthony leaned closer. His face, his eyes, were just inches away. Dean caught the sensuous odour of beer and cigarettes on his breath.

'Now you know me,' Anthony said slowly. '*We're* friends now, aren't we?'

Dean's mouth was dry. He couldn't tear his gaze away from that piercing blue stare.

'I suppose we are,' he said quietly.

'Sure we are. You like me. I can tell.'

'You're very sure of yourself, aren't you?'

His face was even closer now. 'I've got a good reason to be.'

Anthony thrust his hand into Dean's crotch, grabbing the thick swollen shaft. Dean gasped, blushing at the stranger's knowledge of his aroused state.

Anthony held his cock in a tight grip. His face came closer, his lips almost on top of Dean's.

'See what I mean?'

Upstairs, Glenn and Matthew lay together on top of the bed, in the warm girdle of each other's embrace. The first orgasm had not satisfied them. After so much prolonged anticipation and expectancy, their cocks had remained hard and unrepentant after the initial discharge of semen. They quickly shed the remainder of their clothes and, almost immediately, Glenn entered Matthew again. He moved inside him with long, slow strokes. Matthew melted beneath him, mewing and moaning until they gradually worked their bodies up to another peak.

The second orgasm was extensive and slow. They released themselves in long, undulating waves. As Glenn climaxed inside him, Matthew flooded their bellies with a whitewash of spunk.

Afterwards they lay still and content in exquisite silence.

Glenn held Matthew in his arms, enjoying the warmth of his flesh and the even pulse of his beating heart. Matthew's head rested against his chest and he breathed in the savoury scent of his damp hair.

'I can't believe it's only been four days,' Glenn said. 'I feel like I've known you for ever.'

'It's only four days since we met each other in the flesh,' Matthew said. 'But you've really known me for a lot longer than that.'

Glenn kissed the top of his head. 'It's as if there's never been anyone but you.'

Matthew gently caressed his cock and balls, playing with the soft organ. 'I didn't have you down as a romantic soul. I thought you were a sceptic when it comes to romance. I thought you'd shag anything with a pulse and then move on to the next willing receptacle.'

'I wouldn't have put it exactly like that, but you're not completely wrong. I've never really got beyond sex before. Not with anyone.'

'What are you trying to say?'

'I'm not sure. I'm not very good at this. I've had more than my share of disasters when it comes to relationships.' He inhaled slowly, searching for the right words to express what he was feeling. 'It just feels *nice*, that's all. Being with you. Whatever's happening between the two of us, I like it. I like having you around – it's nice to have someone that I can talk to as well as fuck. I think it would be nice if you were around for a lot longer.'

The words hung heavily in the air before Matthew eventually had to say, 'Glenn, you *know* I can't stay.'

'This afternoon you asked me if there had ever been anyone special in my life. If I had ever been in love.'

'You said no.'

'I lied. There is someone who I've been infatuated with for years. No other man, no amount of sex, has ever been able to replace him in my heart. Until now.' Glenn sighed. Speaking these words seemed to suddenly change every other sensation. It altered time. The sound of laughter and music from the party downstairs appeared to come from another world. 'When I'm with you, he doesn't matter to me at all.'

Matthew rolled over, lying across Glenn's chest, looking into his eyes. Glenn looked at his face, overwhelmed once again by the beauty and composure of his features. His face was as pure and as exquisite as an angel's. He ran a slow finger along the line of his brow, tracing the clear line down over his face and jaw. For one eternal moment they both felt crushed under the burden of sadness and inevitability.

'I suppose I'm just jinxed when it comes to relationships,' Glenn said, forcing a smile on to his face and a lightness into his voice.

'I don't know what to say to you,' Matthew said. 'Being here with you is perfect. It's like nothing else I've ever known. It's wonderful. But it can't last. I have no right to be here.'

'I know,' Glenn said. 'I know. Good things never last, do they?'

Matthew squeezed him tight. 'But I'm here now. Let's just enjoy this time together while it does last.'

'OK.'

They kissed. Matthew slipped his tongue into Glenn's mouth. They drew apart after a long, languorous moment.

'Are you hungry?' Glenn said. 'I'm starving.'

'Ravenous.'

'Let go back down. Dean will be sending out search parties for us soon.'

Dean had fallen under a very dark, sexual spell. It was disturbing and implausible and utterly exciting. There was something about Anthony's manner that frightened him and at the same time magnetised him. He couldn't get away from him even if he wanted to. But at that moment he didn't want to.

Anthony was licking his wolfish lips. He still held Dean's cock in a tight grip.

'That was a good show your friends put on earlier,' Anthony said. Dean could only murmur weakly. 'Everyone got off watching it.' His other hand was on the sweep of Dean's buttocks, pulling him closer. 'I can think of an even hotter act than that, though.'

'What?' Dean said.

'You, sucking my cock. Right here. Right now. In front of all your friends.'

In his mind, Dean tried to pull away, but his body did not move.

'I can't,' he stammered.

'You can. You *will*. I have the strongest intuition that sucking cock is one of the things that you do best.'

Anthony's hand moved up to the back of his neck, his tight fingers digging into the muscle. He shoved Dean down. He fell to his knees in front of the stranger, his face level with the swelling in his groin. Several groups of people nearby had perceived that something was going on and stopped to watch, their conversation faltering.

'Your audience has arrived.' Anthony sniggered. 'We can't disappoint anyone now. Let's get on with the show.'

There was something in the tone of Anthony's voice that compelled Dean to obey. He unbuckled his heavy leather belt, pulled down his zip and tugged his jeans and shorts down over his hairy thighs. Anthony's cock sprang up and swayed majestically in front of Dean's face. His eyes widened, devouring the wonderful sight.

It was a long, thick piece of meat, heavy, fleshy and roped with thick blue veins. The head was the size of a small apricot and several shades darker. It had slipped all the way out of its protective sheath of skin. Dean could smell the musky, slightly sweaty scent that the organ gave off. It hovered, less than an inch from his face.

'What are you waiting for?' There was a hard edge to Anthony's voice. '*Suck it.*'

Dean leaned forwards, skimming his tongue over the head of Anthony's cock, coating the crown in a thick wad of saliva. The flavour of Anthony's pre-come was just as pungent as a lot of guys' full load: very salty and strong. Dean hefted his hairy ball sac in his hand, impressed at the way it spilled over his palm. He skitted his tongue down the underside of the shaft, heading direct for his balls. He licked them, nuzzled them, rolled them around in his mouth. He nipped the hairy skin between his teeth.

Almost all of Dean's guests had now realised what was going on and had gathered round to watch their host suck cock. Dean saw Gary on the periphery of his vision, watching, smiling, his arms around Carter and John. Joe was closing in with his camera, committing the action to tape.

Dean nibbled his way back up to the head of the meaty shaft. When he reached the top he opened his mouth over the juicy apricot head and swallowed. He flexed his jaw and gobbled the shaft in its entirety. He could feel every vein and contour on the surface of his tongue as he swallowed it deeper, aiming for his gullet. He heard whispers and words of admiration as his lips closed around the root of Anthony's cock.

He pulled back, gasping for breath, and then went down for more. Opening wide, his lips swam down the cock, devouring its fleshy length. He buried the long shaft in his throat, burrowing his nose into the thick cluster of dark-brown pubes, breathing in the manliness of his bush. Dean's cheeks and throat were bloated with cock.

Anthony held Dean's head and started to pump his hips back and forth, fucking his face. He pushed deep into Dean's throat and groaned. Dean gagged. He pressed back against Anthony's thighs, regulating the speed and depth of his cocksucking. He bobbed back and forth, sucking, slurping, tightening his mouth and throat. Anthony gasped again. He whipped his cock out of Dean's mouth just as the first streams of spunk issued from the tip, splattering across his upturned face. His thigh muscles tightened as his load continued to pump out, hitting Dean on the cheek, on his closed eyes, on the mouth.

He reached down and helped him to rise to his feet. He kissed him all over the face, licking up the slowly dribbling come. He worked over his skin in long, careful strokes, ensuring that not a single drop of his precious load was wasted. Dean smiled as Anthony's tongue rasped over his skin. They kissed, sharing the sluggish taste of semen.

The crowd applauded.

Anthony raised a hand and hushed them.

'The show isn't over yet,' he grinned.

In less than a minute Dean was stripped and naked. Anthony had skinned his tight top over his head and quickly unfastened his trousers and dragged him out of them. Dean had protested weakly but his objections were no match for the determination of the other man.

Anthony spun him around and bent him over the edge of the bar. Dean rested his elbows on the surface as the other man manipulated him from behind. Anthony shoved a knee between Dean's thighs and spread his legs. He was exposed and vulnerable, every inch of his body unveiled to his friends. Anthony grabbed his arse and spread his chunky globes, revealing his honey-brown hole and the tuft of light-brown hair that surrounded it. Dean burned with humiliation.

'Come closer,' Anthony said to the crowd. 'Get a good look at this sweet little hole before I stuff it full of cock.'

Dean shut his eyes tight; he could hear their footsteps and their voices as they drew nearer. He could feel the intense heat of their lustful eyes as they feasted their vision on his spread ring.

Anthony held Dean's buttocks wide with one hand while he traced a finger around the furrowed rim. Dean's arse offered no resistance when he pressed his finger to the opening and shoved it inside.

Dean opened his eyes wide as Anthony wormed his finger into his tight hole. He groaned. Anthony found his prostate, pressed against it. He groaned again, louder this time.

'Oh fuck,' he gasped.

'That's right, 'Anthony said. 'You're gonna get fucked right here in front of all your friends. In front of your boyfriend.'

Dean grunted. There was another finger inside him now, stretching him, widening his hole.

Anthony crouched down in front of his arse, he spat into the hole. Dean felt the warm saliva trickling over his sensitive skin. Anthony spat again, pushing his spit right up inside him. He pulled out his fingers and shoved his tongue up there. Dean could feel it squirming into his chute like a small, wriggling cock. He pushed his hips back into Anthony's face.

Anthony stood up, 'Your arsehole tastes great,' he said, 'but it's gonna feel even better on the tip of my cock. Someone get me a rubber.'

Somebody came forward. Dean didn't look round to see who it was. He heard the tearing of a foil wrapper and then the snap of rubber as Anthony covered himself with the protective sheath.

Anthony wrapped an arm around his chest and pressed tightly against his back.

'Ready for this?'

'Yeah,' Dean gasped.

He reached behind him and took the primed cock in his hand, guiding it into the cleft of his buttocks. He positioned the head against his opening and pressed his hips back. His anus stretched over the bulbous crown and, with a sudden burst, Anthony's cock had pushed past his resistance and slid inside him.

Anthony started pumping his arse, giving him a few short strokes to get used to the intrusion and then moving up a few gears into a faster rhythm. Dean thrust back, meeting Anthony halfway on every stroke, tightening his sphincter around the fleshy log, moving his body to the same rhythm.

Anthony thrust in deeper, filling Dean's arsehole with his meat. Dean moaned. His knuckles were white as he gripped the surface of the bar. Anthony started to grind his hips, churning his cock around inside him. Dean groaned, louder. He turned his head, his mouth open for a kiss. Their mouths met; Anthony thrust his tongue into Dean's mouth as violently as he thrust his cock into his arse. They heaved and sweated as one.

Anthony pulled out of his arse and threw him down on to the floor. Dean rolled over on his back, the grass damp against his bare skin. Anthony kneeled down between his thighs, hoisted his ankles up on to his shoulders and rolled into him again.

Before going back down to rejoin the party, Glenn and Matthew crept along the hall to the bathroom. They were naked, their clothes bundled in front of them to conceal their modesty. Laughing like schoolboys, they skitted along the passage, darting from one doorway to the next until they slipped into the bathroom and locked the door.

They filled the sink up with hot water and took turns to wash themselves, cleaning their cocks and arseholes and washing the dry flakes of semen from their skin. They had to flatten down their sex-tangled hair with handfuls of water.

'What are you gonna do with your butt plug now?' Matthew asked, as he slipped a soapy hand up the crack of his arse.

Glenn was sitting on the edge of the bath, drying himself off. 'I don't know. I'm a bit too tired to go through all that again.'

They both laughed.

'I never thought I would ever say this,' Matthew said, 'but I think my butt has had enough excitement for one day.'

The two rubber plugs had been washed clean and were sitting on the toilet seat.

'Let's not bother putting them back in,' Glenn said.

'What are we gonna do with them? We can't just leave them there.'

Glenn thought for a moment as he put his clothes back on. It was a ridiculous predicament to be in.

'All right,' he said. 'I've got an idea. We'll hide them back in the bedroom until we're ready to go home.'

'What if someone finds them?'

'We'll just have to take that chance.'

When they were washed and dressed once more, the two men crept back along the passage to the bedroom, still sniggering like children. While Glenn scouted the room for a suitable place to conceal their toys, Matthew smoothed out the rumpled covers on the bed.

'Won't your friend mind that we fucked in his spare room?'

'No way. Don't worry, that bed will see plenty more fucking tonight. We might be the first to use it but we definitely won't be the last.'

Glenn hid the rubber phalluses at the back of the fitted wardrobe and closed the door. 'They should be safe enough in there for now. We'll just have to remember them when we go.'

He slid his arm around Matthew's waist and kissed his damp head. 'Come on, sexy, I think we should go back to the party. It sounds like they're having a hell of time down there. Listen to all that screaming.'

A crowd had gathered on the lawn, forming a circle around some kind of commotion on the grass. Everyone was cheering and shouting encouragement.

'Go on, let him have it!'

'Ride his arse!'

'Shaft the horny fucker!'

Glenn and Matthew exchanged quizzical glances. 'What is it? Another show?'

Glenn shrugged. 'I've no idea.'

They pushed their way into the huddle, shoving through to the front.

Glenn's jaw dropped at the sight of his best friend flat out on his back, his legs hoisted over the shoulders of a man he did not recognise and taking a severe pounding to his arse. Dean was bucking back against the man above him with a frenzied willingness to take him deeper. His arms flayed on the grass above his head as he twisted and groaned through gritted teeth. Whoever the stranger was he was really letting Dean have it rough. Their two bodies glistened with a thick coat of sweat.

Glenn laughed. 'My God, I've seen everything now.'

Matthew was rigid beside him. All the colour had drained away from his face; his pallor and his expression was ghastly.

'G-Glenn,' he gasped, his mouth so dry that he could hardly speak.

'Matthew, what is it?' Glenn put an arm around him. He was swaying and unsteady as if he was about to faint. 'Are you all right? You look ill. What's the matter?'

Matthew raised a hand, shaking badly, and pointed at the dark-haired man on the floor with Dean. 'That's Anthony,' he hissed, 'Anthony Pierce.'

'What?' Glenn stared incredulously at the man on the floor, his taut buttocks heaving as he slammed his dick violently in and out of Dean's arse.

'It's Anthony,' Matthew cried. 'Oh my God. *He's found me!*'

Fourteen

Running Scared

Matthew rushed back into the house. Glenn ran after him. His mind was racing but it still seemed a beat too slow to grasp what Matthew was saying.

What now? he thought. Another of his imaginary characters had supposedly crossed the boundary from fiction into the real world. He didn't know what to think or believe any longer. What the hell was he supposed to conclude from this?

'Matthew,' he shouted. 'Wait!'

He caught up with him in the front hallway. Matthew was shaking. He was obviously very frightened.

'We've got to get out of here,' he said, choking for breath. 'He's found me.'

'Wait a minute. Just calm down first.'

Glenn grabbed hold of him by both arms and forced him to stand still. His face was a mask of pure fear. His eyes darted back through the house towards the open patio doors and the scene beyond. He tried to pull away but Glenn held on to him tightly.

'Let go of me,' Matthew pleaded. 'I've got to get away from here before he sees me. Before he knows I'm here.'

'Just hold on a minute.' Glenn tried to remain calm, hoping that his own repose would have a quieting effect on Matthew. He kept

167

the tone of his voice moderate and composed. 'Are you absolutely certain that it's him? Are you sure that man out there is Anthony Pierce?'

'Of course I'm sure. I know him well enough, don't I? Glenn, please don't tell me that you still need convincing.'

'No. No, it's all right. I believe you.'

Matthew tried to pull away again. 'Then come on. Please, we've got to get away before he comes after me.'

'He's not going to do anything to you in front of all these people. You're safer here than anywhere else.'

'No. I want to leave. If you won't come with me then I'll go on my own.'

'We can't just run off like that. We're in the middle of the countryside here, miles from town. I'll have to ring for a taxi.'

'Then do it. Hurry up.'

'OK, come on.'

Glenn shepherded him through into the living room. The television was still on, playing to an empty audience. On screen four mid-European men were having sex on a creaky old bed. Glenn picked up the remote from the coffee table and muted the sound. He eased Matthew down into an armchair.

'Sit there. I'll phone for a taxi now. We'll be out of here as soon as it arrives. We shouldn't have to wait long at this time of night.'

Matthew sat uneasily on the edge of the chair, a bundle of nervous agitation. He twisted himself around to see through the open door, cagily watching for anyone coming into the house, while Glenn was on the telephone. He chewed anxiously on his cuticles.

Glenn hung up the phone. 'They're sending a car straight over.'

'How long will it take?'

Glenn raised his hands, placating him. 'Not long. Don't worry.'

'*How long?*'

'No more than ten minutes.'

'Ten minutes. Shit! We haven't got ten minutes.'

Glenn sat down on the arm of the chair and draped a protective arm over Matthew's shoulder. 'He's not going to find us in that time. He's out there fucking Dean right now. That's got to be

168

worth more than ten minutes of *anyone's* time. Try to calm down. I won't let him hurt you.'

Matthew shivered in his arms. 'The man is evil. You should know that better than anyone. If he wants to kill me, he will. No one will be able to stop him.'

They sat together waiting, Matthew leaning against Glenn's chest for comfort. With the silent images flickering across the television screen, they could hear cries and cheers of approval out on the back lawn. The sounds of real-life sex matched up remarkably well with the old porno tape. Whatever Anthony was doing to Dean, they were still hard at it.

'How long has it been?' Matthew asked. 'It should be here by now.'

'Only five minutes or so,' Glenn said, stroking the top of his head. 'It won't be long. Any time now. Sit tight, darling.'

Glenn glanced at the muted sex scene on the television. It seemed somewhat absurd to be watching a porno tape in a moment of crisis.

A tumultuous cheer and gleeful applause outside announced to the two of them that the sex act in the garden had reached a climax.

Matthew shot out of his seat. 'They've finished. He's gonna be in here any minute now.'

Glenn stood up. 'Maybe not. He hasn't seen you yet. We don't know for certain that he even knows that you're here.'

Matthew paced the floor, wringing his hands. 'Of course he knows I'm here. Why else would *he* be here?'

'He might just be looking for me.'

'He's bound to know that I'm with you. We have to get away from here quick.'

There were voices and laughter in the hall as people came into the house from the garden. Matthew stared through the open doorway with wide frightened eyes, expecting his greatest fear to manifest itself at any moment.

A car horn sounded out front. The taxi had arrived.

They both hurried through to the hall together, pushing past the shoulders of other men in their haste to reach the front door. Glenn fumbled with the lock. It clicked. The door swung open.

The taxi was waiting right in front of the house, the engine running.

Glenn heard Matthew's gasp behind him.

He spun round quickly.

Matthew was staring straight back down the hall to a figure standing in the open frame of the patio. Anthony Pierce stared directly back at him. He was completely naked, his skin still flushed with sex. His broad lips curled back from his teeth in a wide, lopsided sneer.

Glenn shuddered. There was no denying that the man at the other end of the hall was the physical embodiment of his fictional antihero. Both he and Matthew stared at him, transfixed.

Anthony took hold of his semihard cock. A long drool of come slithered from its tip. He held the shaft at the base and waved it in their direction.

Glenn's jaw dropped.

Matthew backed away, bumping into Glenn's chest. It broke the spell.

'Come on,' Glenn said, grabbing Matthew's arm and pulling him out towards the car. He glanced backwards over his shoulder.

Still holding his cock in his hand, Anthony threw back his head and laughed.

With his mocking tone ringing in their ears, the two men dived on to the back seat of the taxi.

'Get us out of here,' Glenn gasped. 'Just drive!'

Dean lay on his back on the lawn and tried to catch his breath. His entire body was burning up as the shock waves of orgasm slowly subsided. He lay in the exact same position that Anthony had left him in, his knees up and thighs spread, his freshly fucked arsehole gaping wide. His heart was thudding hard against his chest wall. He trembled.

He was *fucked*.

Thankfully, as Anthony pulled away and left him there, quivering on the floor, the crowd around him dispersed, giving him precious room to breathe. He sucked in great lungfuls of air through his open mouth. He was content just to lie there, happy never to move again. He lay perfectly still, savouring the indisputable sensation of complete and whole satisfaction.

This, he thought, is Heaven!

He sensed a presence above him. He opened his eyes slowly, reluctantly, to look up into Gary's proud, smiling eyes.

'I'm just checking that you're still alive.'

Dean gasped. 'I'm not a hundred per cent certain of that myself.'

Gary stretched down a hand. 'You can't lie there all night. Come on, I'll help you up.'

Aided by his lover, Dean struggled into a sitting position. He rubbed his eyes and shook his head, trying to clear the beautiful haze in his mind. Holding on to Gary's hand, he rose unsteadily to his feet. His clothes were strewn all over the grass around him.

'You look like you could do with a drink,' Gary said.

'Champagne,' he deadpanned. 'A fuck like that is well worth celebrating.'

Gary helped him to pick up his clothes.

'So who is that man?'

Dean shook his head. 'I have absolutely no idea. He says his name is Anthony, but that's as much as I know. Where did he go?'

'Into the house.'

Dean pulled on his trousers. His legs were unsteady and he had to support himself against the edge of the bar. He struggled into the rest of his clothes. Gary walked him slowly across to the table where Carter and John were waiting for them. He lowered himself carefully into a seat. His arsehole was wet and very loose.

'Can you sit down after that?' Carter mocked.

'Only just.'

Gary took out a joint, lit it and handed it over to Dean.

'Thanks, darlin',' he said, puffing appreciatively on the smoke. 'Is there any chance of that drink?'

'I'll get it for you,' John said, rising to his feet. 'We're all ready for a refill.' He picked up the empty bottles from the table and returned them to the bar.

Dean slouched back in his seat, '*Christ!*' he said. 'That was fucking incredible.'

'What on Earth got into you?' Gary asked, taking a hit on the joint himself. 'I've never known you to do anything like that before. Not in public.'

'I know, but I don't know what came over me. I just went over to find out who he was and the next thing I knew I was down on my knees sucking his cock.'

'Neither of you know who this guy is?' Carter asked, taking his turn to inhale.

'No.'

'Never seen him before in my life,' Dean said animatedly. 'You don't forget a good-looking bastard like than in a hurry. He's not your average casual piece of trade, is he?'

'So who invited him?' Carter asked.

'Not me,' said Gary.

'Nor me. He must have gate-crashed.'

'Cheeky cunt!'

The three of them laughed.

'I know one thing,' said Dean. 'I'm certainly not going to chuck him out now. Invited or not, he can stay as long as he likes.'

Matthew prised a gap in the blinds with two fingers and stared out into the dark night outside. He sat on the arm of a chair and sucked nervously at a cigarette. Since arriving home he had calmed down a little and was considerably less agitated.

Glenn came through from the kitchen with two mugs of hot coffee. He handed one to Matthew and tried to reassure him with a heartening smile.

'Are you all right now?'

Matthew's breath whistled through his teeth as he exhaled a tense cloud of smoke. He nodded and attempted to return the smile, but the conviction failed to register in his wide eyes.

Glenn leaned forwards and peered through the gap in the blinds. The estate was silent, there was no traffic, no barking dogs, not the slightest sign of life. None of the usual urban sounds to disturb the stillness of the clear night.

'Why don't you come away from the window?' Glenn asked softly. 'There's nobody out there.'

'There's nobody there yet,' Matthew sighed. 'But give him time. He'll be there.'

'The house is locked up. He can't get in.'

'That didn't stop me, did it? And Anthony is a hell of a lot more cunning than I am. If he wants to be in, a few locks won't keep him out.'

Glenn slumped down into the chair. He took a cigarette out of Matthew's packet on the coffee table and lit it. He had only just started to get used to the idea of Matthew coming into his life, he had not foreseen this latest surreal twist. The sight of Dean screwing on the lawn had been a big enough shock without the extra scare of finding out just exactly *who* he was screwing.

'So what are we going to do now?' Glenn asked

'I don't know. He's obviously intent on killing me and he's come here to see it through.'

'Are you sure about that? If he's so clever he could kill you any time he wanted to. We didn't know he was here. He could have taken you by surprise at any time. So why did he turn up tonight? Why give himself away?'

'Because he's fucking with me. He's playing games. Cat and mouse. It's what he does best. It's what he enjoys. He wanted me to know that he had found me. Fucking with my mind makes the game more interesting for him.'

The gentle click of the hands on the clock was like a ticking bomb in the heavy silence of the house. Matthew left his vigil at the window and began to slowly pace back and forth across the floor.

Glenn stared down into the dark depths of his coffee cup, searching for answers and solutions. Despite the turmoil and confusion of the night, his mood was unnaturally calm.

'What if we get to him first?' he said with composure.

Matthew stopped pacing. 'What?'

'What if we kill Anthony before he kills you.'

'How?'

'Hang on,' Glenn mused, thinking his idea through. 'I'm not sure if this will work or not, but considering how bizarre this whole situation has all been so far, I don't see why it wouldn't.'

'What is it?' Matthew implored. 'Come on, tell me.'

'If we think about this logically. You said that Anthony first

173

tried to hurt you after I began working on the new storyline for your characters. The version in which you were killed off.'

'Yeah, that's right.'

'If I wrote a new ending to that storyline and changed it so that it was *Anthony* who was killed rather than you, it should solve the problem.'

Matthew held his breath. 'Do you think it will work?'

'I don't know. You know more about the reality, or *non*reality, of all this than I do. Do *you* think it'll work?'

Matthew sank down on to the edge of the coffee table. Glenn could see the glimmer of hope beginning to shine through his tragic brown eyes. 'I – I'm not sure. If we were back in our own world, then yes, it would certainly change the way things were. But when we're both here I don't know how it will affect us.'

Glenn took Matthew's hand in his own. He was trembling.

'Can you think of any better ideas?'

'No.' Matthew's eyes were full of emotion and heavy with tears waiting to spill. 'But – but *killing* him? Are you sure we have to? After all, he's the killer, not me. I don't know if I could.'

Glenn faltered. He had been deliberately keeping something back from Matthew. A piece of information that put a new perspective on their situation. He didn't want to frighten Matthew any more than he already was, but he had a right to know the truth.

He held his hand tighter. 'Matthew, there's something else you should know. I don't now exactly what it means, but I think it's important. It can't be just a coincidence.'

'What is it?'

'Did you see who it was that Anthony was with in the garden tonight?'

'It was your friend,' Matthew answered. 'Dean, wasn't it?'

'Yes,' he replied, 'it was Dean.'

'So?'

'When I wrote *Everyday Hurts* I based a lot of my characters, or elements of their personality, on people that I knew. It's something I do in a lot of my writing.'

'What are you saying?'

'So . . .' Glenn struggled. 'When I created your character I had a definite role model in mind for you. It was Dean.' Matthew's jaw dropped open. 'It wasn't just a rough guide, either: I put a lot of Dean into you. I'm surprised you didn't notice tonight: the physical similarity between you is incredible.'

Matthew shook his head slowly as the relevance of the situation sank in.

'Anthony obviously realised the likeness between you as soon as he saw Dean,' Glenn continued. 'It's too much of a coincidence that he singled out the person that he did otherwise.'

'A cat-and-mouse game,' Matthew said. 'He fucked Dean as a message to me.'

'That's the way it would appear. Now can you think of any better ideas?'

The silence before he replied was lengthy.

'No,' he said at last.

'Then we'll try it this way,' Glenn said, drawing the last breath out of his cigarette. 'Go into the kitchen and make a huge pot of coffee. I'll go up and get started. It's going to be a long night.'

By a quarter to four in the morning it was all over. Glenn typed up the last sentence on to his computer screen and hit 'save', wiping out his previous story outline and replacing it with the new. He slouched back in his chair, his back and shoulders aching, and stared at the words in front of him.

It wasn't great; it certainly didn't read as a satisfactory follow-up to *Everyday Hurts*; but it served its purpose. The character of Anthony Pierce fell to his death from the top floor of a multistorey car park while trying to evade the police. Matthew survived to continue with his life, free from persecution. It was simple and clear-cut: the good guy wins, the bad guy loses.

He printed out one copy of the ten-page synopsis and switched off his computer.

There were a dozen or so cigarette stubs in the ashtray on top of his desk; the cafetière was empty. His eyes were tired and sore after staring at the screen for over two hours.

This was what he had wanted for months, to close the door on *Everyday Hurts* and absolve himself of all responsibility for it. Now that it was over, he felt strangely unsatisfied.

He collected the small stack of papers from the printer.

Matthew was in the bedroom, stretched out on top of the covers, facing the wall. He was still dressed in his party attire.

'I've finished,' Glenn said, lying down beside him on the bed.

'So what happens?' Matthew asked coldly, speaking to the wall.

'Don't you want to read it yourself?'

He lay still for a long moment, indecisive, before turning over slowly. Though his eyes were dry now, his face was red and swollen with the tears he had been crying.

Glenn handed him the manuscript. Neither of them spoke while he read through the words that spelled out the next era of his life. Glenn rested his head against the pillow and gazed at the ceiling, with hazy, tired eyes. He wanted to surrender himself to the oblivion of sleep so badly.

When he finished reading, Matthew put down the manuscript and turned his face to the wall again. For a long time silence prevailed.

'Do you think it will work?' he said at last.

'I don't know. It was worth a try.'

Glenn kicked off his shoes and rolled over. He was too tired to get up and undress himself. He crawled beneath the covers fully clothed.

'Glenn?'

'What?'

'I was wondering. If you based my character on Dean, was Anthony inspired by anyone you know?'

'Only a little,' Glenn replied. 'I used the physical features and a few characteristics of one man, but his evil nature was purely exaggerated.'

'So who was he?'

'Just an old boyfriend of mine,' he said. 'He was at the party tonight too. It was Patrick Robins.'

Fifteen

Patrick

It had been a great night for Patrick Robins. So what if he failed to cajole his way into the pants of the blond Oxford graduate? Patrick was not a man to wallow in his defeats. It was pretty obvious early in the evening that no amount of charm or charisma was going to get him what he wanted from the young beauty called Adam. The guy seemed to have an active discrimination against older men. So what? Patrick didn't have to waste his time on stuck-up little queens.

He had been pretty desperate to unload his balls, though. The fuckshow put on by the two hired performers had got him well and truly steamed up. The unexpected addition of Dean fucking for all the world to see as if his life depended on it only heightened his arousal.

Patrick didn't know who the stranger was who had given Dean's arse such an entertaining pounding, but he wouldn't have minded a bit of time with him himself. Of course Patrick didn't put his arse out for other men. He was one hundred per cent butch – a born top. He didn't take it up the hole under any circumstances.

This strange man, who liked to put on a show of sex, was a mean-looking bastard too. Patrick recognised the tough character-istics of another master. It was highly unlikely that he would bend over and offer up his arse for service, either. Pity. Patrick wasn't interested in sex without anal penetration. There was just no point in it. Wanking and blow jobs were good enough foreplay but they were no substitute for a horny fuck. It didn't matter how many times he came in a man's mouth, it didn't compare in the slightest degree to emptying his balls into a willing arse.

Patrick hated to get a man into bed, to get him all worked up and steamy, revved up to take it, only to discover that the other guy didn't 'do that'. *What is the fucking point?*

He enjoyed the extreme power of sex more than anything else – to mount another man and dominate him completely, making him grunt and beg for more. It was even better if the bottom was a little on the aggressive side – biting, twisting, slipping back and forth beneath him.

Dean was a good fuck. Patrick had had his arse quite a few times over the years. He loved the way that Dean reacted with a cock inside him; he loved it. He wasn't the kind of guy who was content to just lie back and take it. As a submissive he gave just as much as his dominant partner. There was always a lot of action when it came to fucking Dean.

Tonight Patrick had enjoyed a nice session with Lee and his boyfriend Eric in one of the spare bedrooms. Lee liked to think that he was butch – the bold little fucker had even tried to slip his cock into Patrick one time. But he was just like all other men when challenged by Patrick's mean confidence. He rolled over and spread his legs. Just as he had with Dean, Patrick had fucked the supermarket boy plenty over the years, but tonight was a first with Eric.

They were a cute couple, both the same age and similar in height and build. Lee was attractive in a hard, unconventional way; Eric was more traditionally handsome with bright blue eyes and a clear complexion. Very cute. His skin was so lucid and fair that Patrick wondered if he even had to shave more than once or twice a week.

Lee made the first move, asking if Patrick wanted to join them in the bedroom. He thought, what the hell! The Oxford blond would have given in eventually but it was too much like hard work, and here were two little cuties offering themselves to him on a plate.

The sex was better than he would have expected. They all stripped off and then he lay back on the bed while the two lovers sucked his cock, sharing him like a lollypop. They slobbered over his shiny head and took it in turns to alternate between his shaft and balls. Lee tried to jab a finger up his tight arsehole but he warned him off.

Patrick then fucked Lee really hard, teaching the cocky little shit a lesson. He forced him to stand over the end of the bed and rode him roughly from behind. He was unrelenting: he grabbed the young guy's hair and yanked his head back, hissing in his ear, 'Nothing like a tight chicken's arse for fucking. You were born to be screwed, mate. Get used to it.'

With each word he grunted, he rammed his cock in further. At first Lee tried to resist, to retain his dignity as a top and deny that he was enjoying the submissive role. But his basic human nature betrayed him, and very soon he was thrusting his hips back against Patrick, spearing himself on his cock, trying to take it deeper.

After Lee had spilled his seed all over the bedclothes, Patrick pulled out and forced him to watch while he gave his boyfriend the same treatment. With Eric there was no pretence, no martyrdom. He gasped and moaned and rocked his hips with enthusiastic delight the moment Patrick slipped his cock inside his ring.

When Eric was spent too, Patrick let go of himself and emptied his balls into him. Afterwards he pulled out and shoved Eric down on the bed beside his boyfriend. He climbed over them and tore off his condom, tipping the contents over their hard, sweaty bodies. He shook the last stream of cock juice from the tip of his dick and flicked it into Lee's face.

There was no doubt that he had enjoyed himself that night. The party had been great, and, though he would have preferred to experience some fresh meat, in the end he had been more than satisfied with Lee and Eric.

It had gone half past three. There were still a fair number of guests milling around the house. Things wouldn't really wind up until around six, and then the majority of those who were left would crash out on the floor until mid-afternoon, before rallying round to go home.

Patrick called a taxi. He went over to say goodnight to Dean and Gary, who were still smoking and drinking out in the garden with the couple from Newcastle.

'You're not going yet, are you?' Dean said.

''Fraid so. I've got to get home for the dogs.'

Patrick had two Rottweilers.

He bent over and kissed both of his hosts. 'Thanks, guys, I've had a great time.'

'Thanks for coming.'

'I'll call you one night through the week. Are you going out next weekend?'

Gary nodded. 'We were thinking of going down to Middlesbrough. Just for a change from the Newcastle scene. We'll pick you up if you want to come. Fancy something different?'

'Possibly. I'll think about it.'

He kissed them goodnight again and then went out the front to wait for his taxi to arrive.

There was a sharp chill to the air. The grass was wet with early-morning dew and the first streaks of dawn sunlight were starting to creep across the cloudless sky. Patrick breathed in deeply, the crisp air clearing the haze of smoke and alcohol from his head.

He wasn't really tired, but he wanted to get home. He'd had enough for one night and he didn't like to leave the dogs on their own for too long. He would have to walk them before he went to bed.

His eyes caught sight of movement on the other side of the dirt-track road. There was a figure in the shadows, hidden by the dark cover of the overhanging trees. He heard a groan. Patrick smiled.

Fucking in the bushes.

He glanced up the road, expecting to see the lights of his taxi coming over the hill at any minute.

He heard the groan from amid the trees once again. But this time he realised that something was wrong. It was not the sound of passion that he could hear but rather a cry of distress, of pain even.

He stared over the road, trying to see into the dense shadows between the trees. The illumination from the house behind him failed to reach the other side of the track and shed light on the darkness beyond the foliage.

The figure in the shadows let out a sharp gasp, a sudden cry of despair. Whoever was out there, it sounded like they were in trouble.

Patrick crossed the road. As he grew nearer he could see the pale contours of a pair of jeans, the long legs curled up on the ground, their possessor huddled into the root of the tree. His breath was heavy and laborious.

'Hey, mate, are you all right there?' The long, dewy grass shifted against Patrick's feet as he pushed his way into the undergrowth, straining to see more in the sombre darkness of the forest.

Now he could discern the shape of a loose black shirt and two bare arms protruding from the short sleeves. The man was holding his dark head in his hands, his gaze lowered to the damp ground beneath him.

Patrick stood over him and then dropped down to his haunches as he realised who the distressed figure was. It was the man who had fucked Dean for the benefit of all his voyeuristic friends.

'I didn't realise it was you,' Patrick said, putting a reassuring hand on the man's shoulder, impressed at the strong muscle he could discern there. 'What are you doing out here? Are you hurt? Have you been sick? Had a bit too much to drink, did you? Still, it won't do you any good sitting here on the wet grass.'

'*The bastards just tried to kill me,*' the man hissed, gripping his head in his hands.

'*What?* Who did? Have you been attacked?' It seemed unlikely out here. Patrick knew that Dean sometimes had trouble with travellers setting up campsites on the other side of the valley, but they were never violent. They would never attack anyone.

'Never mind,' the man said. 'I'll be all right in a few minutes. They think they can get me this way but they can't. They can't hurt me here.'

'Who are you talking about? Who tried to hurt you?' Patrick wondered if the man was hallucinating. There had been a multitude of different drugs being bandied about all night – he was probably having a bad trip.

'I said I'll be all right,' the man snapped.

181

'All right, mate, don't get lairy. I'm only trying to help. I won't bother next time.'

Frigging hell, talk about ungrateful. Last time I play the fucking Samaritan!

Patrick made a move to stand. The man's hand shot out and grabbed hold of his arm.

'Wait,' he said. 'Don't go. Just give me a minute to get my breath back.'

The stranger's pale face took on a luminous, almost supernatural incandescence in the dim light of the forest. He was a real handsome bastard, Patrick thought. A perfect package: great face, awesome body, beautiful cock. Pity that he seemed so fucked up in the head.

Still, he mused, it's not his head that I want to fuck.

'Let me help you up,' he said. 'It won't do you any good down here on the ground.'

He slid his arm around the man's tight waist and eased him up from the damp grass. The man put his arm around Patrick's shoulder and leaned against him. His feet were still a little shaky as he finally stood up.

'Who are you, anyway?' the man asked, leaning back against the trunk of a tree.

'My name's Patrick. I'm a friend of Dean's.'

The man looked up, alert with sudden interest. His hard eyes glistened like diamonds in the dull dawn light. He was hypnotic. Patrick was both compelled and perturbed by his intense gaze.

'Patrick who?'

'Robins.'

The man's moody face broke into an unexpected grin. He held out his hand. 'I'm Anthony,' he said. 'Thank you for helping me, Patrick. I didn't mean to snap just then. I was just a little shaky.' He eased his weight away from the tree and leaned into Patrick's chest. 'Actually, I recognise you now. I saw you earlier, at the party. You were watching me.'

Anthony's face was right in front of Patrick's, their eyes directly locked. Patrick was horrified to discover that his usual cocksure confidence had deserted him. He felt as nervous as a fifteen-year-old virgin. Not that he *had* been a virgin at fifteen.

'*Everyone* was watching you,' he said impotently, silently cursing his own timidity.

That handsome face and those lips were even closer now. 'But you were *really* watching me. I knew you liked me. Knew there could be some chemistry between us. I was going to come and talk to you but I lost sight of you after I finished with your friend. I was worried I'd missed my chance. But here you are. So maybe I haven't missed my chance after all.'

The mouth was upon him. Patrick opened to it, responding to the intensity of the kiss. Their tongues fought a battle, thrusting against one another, each trying to invade the other's mouth. Patrick felt his sexual confidence returning; his old aplomb had not let him down. He grabbed Anthony's hard arse and hauled his body tight against him, crushing their bulging cocks hard against each other. He dug his fingers into the firm muscle of his buttocks, determined that this arse would be his.

'Not here,' Anthony said, speaking through their kisses.

'Let's go back into the house.' Patrick grabbed the back of Anthony's head, gorging himself on his lips.

'No. I don't want to go back in there.'

'Where do you want to go?' Patrick suddenly found that he was sexually ravenous. The passion he had dissipated earlier with the two guys was ablaze again, only this time it raged even stronger. They had been easy conquests: he had topped Lee without effort. With Anthony it was different. He knew that getting his cock into this man's arsehole was no sure thing. He would have to work for it; he would have to fight.

'Let's go back to your place,' Anthony said. 'Then we'll have no interruptions.'

They continued kissing and groping, fumbling against one another until the taxi arrived moments later. On the back seat they struggled to restrain themselves. Their desire was intense. Anthony had aroused a hunger in him that he had seldom known before. It was as if he had been starved of sex for months, deprived even of masturbation. His balls were so full and ripe, ready to spill their load into this dangerously handsome stranger. The anticipation of sliding into that tight, forbidden hole was exquisite.

Patrick was already planning his manoeuvres. Gaining the upper hand over this stud wouldn't be easy. It was going to take cunning and skill. The reward for his efforts would be unique; glorious even. Just the anticipation of victory was a thrill. Patrick would plough Anthony's arse until he broke. He would ride him victoriously while he writhed beneath him, pleading like a whore for more of his dick.

Finally they were home. Patrick told Anthony to go straight upstairs and wait for him. He let the dogs out into the back garden – there was no way that he was going to take them for a walk now. They would have to content themselves on the lawn until their master was done.

A perverse thrill coursed through his veins as he locked the doors and climbed the stairs to the bedroom.

Anthony stood beside the bed in his mud-stained jeans. His shirt lay in a heap beside his feet. The grey light of dawn, gradually taking occupancy through the open curtains, gave his lean flesh the ashen appearance of stone.

Patrick closed the door behind him. They stood facing one another, squaring off. Patrick unbuttoned his shirt and cast it aside, just as proud of his own sculpted muscle as his opponent clearly was of his own.

'Why don't you come closer?' Anthony said, his arms open, an enticing invitation. There wasn't the slightest inch of surplus flesh on his taut torso. Every line and ridge and contour was precisely defined. The muscle flowed gracefully beneath his skin as he moved.

'I'd rather see you naked first,' Patrick replied. 'Strip.'

'After you.'

Patrick shook his head. 'You first.'

'Let's strip together, then.'

Anthony bent over, unfastened his boots and kicked them aside. Patrick slowly mirrored the action. Anthony undid his belt buckle and dragged the wide strip of leather through the loop holes of his jeans. Patrick reflected the manoeuvre. They unfastened their jeans together and shoved them down over their thighs. Two hard cocks slapped against two ridged stomachs in unison.

They stood before one another completely naked. In the shady, early-morning light they could easily have passed for twins, each resembled the other so much.

'Now,' said Anthony. 'Come here.'

Patrick approached him cautiously. It was apparent that they were both playing the same game for exactly the same prize. Only one of them would come out on top and Patrick had no intention of being anything other than victorious.

When he was two steps away from his open-armed opponent, Patrick suddenly lunged forward ramming the top of his head into Anthony's chest. Caught completely by surprise, Anthony lost his footing and collapsed under the weight of the assault, falling backwards on to the bed. Patrick followed through quickly, climbing on top of the prone man and pinning his body to the bed beneath him.

Anthony tried to roll free but Patrick had too much of an advantage, trapping his arms by the side of his body and locking his legs between his strong thighs.

Anthony twisted his head from side to side and Patrick kissed his face.

'Ha,' he said. 'That was much easier than I thought, mate. Guess you're not as good at this as you think you are. There's only ever one master in this game.' He locked his mouth over Anthony's and pressed down even harder, forcing his tongue between his lips. 'I win. Now when I tell you to, you're gonna open your legs and I'm gonna stick my cock all the way inside your tight little cunt.'

Patrick thought he had Anthony and that he had won. What he hadn't counted on was the sheer strength of the other man. He suddenly jerked his body beneath him, causing Patrick to lose a fraction of his hold. That fraction was all Anthony needed. Patrick lost his purchase on his wrists and suddenly he was free.

Anthony rolled out from under him. Patrick tried in vain to hold on, but he was too slow. Anthony grabbed him from behind, wrapping a strong arm around Patrick's neck. He tightened his grip. Patrick struggled to breathe, his throat caught in the bulging crock of Anthony's sinewy elbow.

Anthony reached over the side of the bed with his free hand, but his grip on Patrick's throat did not relax for a second. Patrick was on fire, his blood pounding in his temples. His eyes were glazed and his breath came in short gasps. He struggled in Anthony's grip but his efforts were futile. The other man was stronger and quicker.

Anthony whipped the thick strap of his belt around Patrick's elbows. In one swift motion he threaded the belt through the buckle and fastened it tight, securing his arms rigidly behind his back.

Patrick was suddenly afraid: he didn't like to be in such a vulnerable position. He was a prisoner. Completely and utterly helpless. He struggled and bucked but it was no good: the belt held. Anthony knew what he was doing and there was no way that he would be able to free himself on his own. The broad strap of leather cut into his muscle.

Anthony released his grip on Patrick's neck and shoved him forwards. He sprawled across the bed, his face pressed into the duvet.

'Let me go,' he spat, 'you cocksucking bastard. Loosen this fucking belt or I'll kill you.'

Anthony laughed. 'Big words from a man trussed up like a chicken. You might as well relax and get used to your new role. You're not going anywhere. I'm gonna spend some quality time with this peachy little arse of yours.'

'*Don't you fucking dare!*' he screamed.

'Or what?' Anthony taunted. He cracked his broad open palm against Patrick's bare buttocks.

Patrick groaned.

Anthony smacked him again. And again. His hand cracked loudly against the bare flesh. Patrick grunted into the bedclothes with each stroke. His arse started to redden and burn. His body glowed with perspiration. He shut his eyes, humiliated.

Anthony's breath quickened with the exertion of punishing him. After more than a minute of mercilessly stroking Patrick's buttocks, he stopped. He sat back on his haunches.

Patrick moaned. He opened his eyes. He tried to wipe his face on the bedclothes, his vision blurred with sweat and tears. He was frightened. He knew pretty much what to expect next. It was what he himself had done to other men, countless times. He lay still, trying not to show his fear, his dread of defeat. But Anthony knew. They both *knew*.

He felt Anthony's hand press into the cleft of his arse. Fear flickered afresh through his mind.

'What are you doing?' he asked, panicked.

'Frightened?' Anthony asked, spreading his crack with two fingers.

He didn't reply. He gritted his teeth and waited.

Anthony spat on to his hole. He opened his ring wide and Patrick felt the warm stream of salvia trickle into him. Anthony shoved a finger inside, pressing through the resistance of his arse. He tensed, tightening his sphincter. Fuck, that really hurt.

'You're only making it worse for yourself,' Anthony said teasingly. 'That's just a skinny little finger. How will you cope with a big fat cock, if you can't even bear a little finger up there?'

Patrick groaned.

Anthony laughed, pressing in further. He wriggled his finger. 'Come on, stud. Give it up a little. Let me have something to work with here.' He forced Patrick to rotate his arse in the most humiliating way. 'That's it. You're getting the hang of it now. It's too bad that some men have to fight their natural predilection to be a whore. You're a whore all right tonight, stud, with a nice pink arse just waiting for me to fuck it.'

Patrick grimaced as another finger wormed its way up his chute. It was unbearable. He gyrated his hips slowly, pushing back against Anthony's hand, praying for his rectum to relax.

He breathed a sigh of relief as Anthony took his fingers out of him. His ease was short-lived. Anthony unthreaded Patrick's own belt from the loops of his discarded jeans. *Crack!* The belt landed hard across his buttocks. He winced. Shit, it hurt. Anthony gave him another thrash and he couldn't stop himself from voicing his pain.

Crack! Crack! Crack! The leather cut through the air, biting into his tender skin. He grabbed a mouthful of the duvet and bit down hard. Anthony was really letting him have it rough. He writhed under the blows, unable to avoid them. *Crack!*

Finally he relented. Patrick spat out the duvet cover.

'Just one more thing,' Anthony whispered softly.

He grabbed hold of Patrick's waist and lifted his hips up, pulling him to his knees, his forehead still pressed into the bed. This was it. The inevitable.

Anthony entered him without any of the usual preliminary niceties. He fisted a gob of spit over the top of the shaft and shoved his long length all the way into Patrick's arse. Patrick screamed with pleasure.

Anthony swatted his arse with the flat of his hand. 'Shut up. That's my cock you can feel all the way inside your cunt. You better get used to it.' He gave a sharp jab of his hips to emphasise his point. 'Come on, slut, move your arse for me. I want you to work my cock with your hole. Push back.' He slapped his buttocks again.

Patrick did as he was told. He pressed his hips back against Anthony's rigid cock.

'Good boy. Now move along. I want you to take it all the way along and back. That's it. All the way to the top and back. Your hole feels really nice on my dick. Keep going like that, you little cock-slut.'

Somehow, despite his protests and his arrogant pride, Patrick began to surrender to what was happening. He worked Anthony's cock within the narrow walls of his arse, lifting his hips to meet his dominator thrust for thrust. The tension and fear had gone. He was seeing clearly for the first time. The clarity of mind was allowing him to experience something that he had not anticipated: pleasure. The kind of raw, unrestricted pleasure that he had never known before.

Anthony slid his hands beneath Patrick's ribs, and his fingers closed over his nipples. He twisted and squeezed. Patrick groaned; he arched his back and ground his hips back against Anthony even harder.

'That's the way, slut. Ride it like a whore!'

Anthony fucked him even harder, ramming his cock deep into his arse, jabbing it hard against his prostate. Patrick jerked. He was going to come. He was going to come with a great big dick wedged deep into his unused hole. He screamed. The pressure, the intensity, the surge within, it was all too much. Too much effort, too much cock, too much pleasure.

He erupted across the bed beneath him, squirting, shaking, trembling. It was an orgasm greater and more intense than any he had known. He was losing his mind as well as control. He screamed again, a long, continuous lament.

As the come drained from his balls all of his energy seemed to drain from his body. His knees buckled; his body weakened. His vision grew dim. He fell forwards across the bed, his consciousness slipping away.

He had only the vaguest perception of a flood inside as Anthony's cock filled his arse full of rich, creamy semen.

Then all he could feel was darkness.

Sixteen

Catching Up

Monday morning.

The alarm went off at seven, declaring with an irritating series of beeps that the weekend was over and it was time to go to work again. The clock was on Gary's side of the bed. He switched it off with a sigh of resignation and swung his legs straight over the side on to the floor. Dean protested with a sleepy growl and pulled the covers up over his head. Gary was always the first into the shower on a morning so Dean could afford to lie for another ten minutes or so in the warm nest of the bed.

If he wanted to, he could afford to lie there all day. It was summer – holiday time. There was no work and no kids to bother him right through until September. But, although he was reluctant to wake, Dean hated to waste his days in bed. There was too much he would miss if he idled his time beneath the covers. Even at this early hour the sunlight penetrated the heavy fabric of the curtains; it promised to be a glorious day, the warm sun filling it with countless possibilities. Ten more minutes, he promised himself, then I'll get up.

He dozed.

Gary turned on the radio. They were playing some big summer dance hit from last year, the name of which Dean couldn't remember – some one-hit wonder. Over the resonance of the music he heard Gary taking a very noisy piss, directing his flow straight into the watery depths of the toilet bowl. His own bladder was uncomfortably full, but it could wait – not time to get out of bed yet.

The sound of the shower running.

Dean relaxed, drawing the duvet around his broad shoulders. The alarm had rattled him out a vivid dream involving the dark-haired stranger from the party. He had been reliving the entire incident, once again lying down on the lawn, thighs spread, arsehole stuffed with cock. He murmured, smiling softly to himself. He closed his eyes tight, hoping the dream would return, but his longing went unfulfilled.

He hadn't seen the video footage of his little adventure yet. Joe had called on Sunday night to tell him how great it was and that he was going to run off a few copies that he would bring round later in the week. Dean couldn't wait to see it. He'd always enjoyed looking at photographs and videos of himself having sex.

The telephone rang down in the hall.

Gary had put his foot down and refused to have a phone in the bedroom. Dean had never really understood why but it wasn't worth an argument. Who the hell was calling at this time of day, anyway? He lay there waiting for the answering machine to take the call.

The phone rang and rang. Shit. They had forgotten to turn the damn machine on. *Ring-ring. Ring-ring.* Whoever it was wasn't going to give up without an answer.

Cursing, Dean tossed back the covers and jumped reluctantly out of bed. Not bothering with his dressing gown, he hurried along the passage and scooted, bare-arsed, down the stairs to answer the persistent phone.

'Hello?' He was out of breath when he picked up.

The caller on the other end did not answer straightaway.

'*Hello?*' Dean said again, unable to keep the irritation he felt at being dragged out of bed out of his tone. 'Is anyone there?'

The caller struggled to speak. 'D-Dean.'

He did not recognise the croaky voice. Whoever it was sounded ancient.

191

'Dean,' the caller said, his breath rattling down the receiver. 'It's Patrick.'

'Patrick!' Was this a joke? 'What's wrong with your voice? Are you all right?'

'I'm . . . no,' Patrick wheezed. 'I need to see you . . . Need to talk to you.'

'What's wrong? You sound terrible. Are you ill or something? Have you seen a doctor?'

'Will you come over? I . . . need help.'

'Of course I will.' Dean was concerned now – whatever was wrong with his friend sounded serious.

'Can you c–come now? P–please.'

Dean reassured him that he would be there as soon as he could. His car had been in the garage over the weekend for a service. He wasn't due to get it back until this afternoon. He'd have to ask Gary for a lift to Patrick's.

Dean went back upstairs. Gary was out of the shower and towelling himself off.

'Who was that?' he asked.

Dean told him while he took his robe from the hanger and pulled it on over his naked body.

'What's the matter with him?'

Dean shrugged. 'I've no idea. He wouldn't say. He sounded awful, though. If he hadn't told me who he was, I wouldn't have even recognised his voice.'

'He was fine when he left here on Saturday night,' Gary said.

'I know. He doesn't sound fine now, though. Whatever's happened to him has happened fast.' Dean turned on the shower again. 'I'll get ready now. Will you drop me off on your way to work?'

'Sure.'

Dean showered and dried himself off quickly. He didn't bother to shave. His mind was turning over possibilities. Patrick was a strong, healthy man: he couldn't imagine any illness that would reduce him to such a state in so short a time. He could have been attacked. Yes, that might explain it. He wouldn't be the first gay man to pick up a couple of guys for a casual threesome and find himself the victim of assault and robbery. It was one of the oldest tricks in the book. There were always dubious characters hanging round the Gardens if he had been cruising round there. It would also explain why Patrick was on his own and didn't want to notify his doctor or the police.

It must have happened sometime on Sunday.

Dean dressed quickly and went downstairs. Gary was finishing off his breakfast. Dean poured himself a glass of orange juice; he didn't bother with food. He shared his assault theory with Gary.

'You could be right,' Gary said, 'but it doesn't seem likely to me.'

'Why not?'

'Patrick's a big bloke. He's tough, too. He wouldn't be easy to overpower.'

'But if there was more than one attacker.'

'I don't think he's much into cruising, either, especially not down the Gardens. It's not really his style.'

'So what do you think has happened?'

Gary loaded his plates into the dishwasher. 'I don't think anything. I'd keep an open mind if I were you.'

'I'm just worried. You didn't hear his voice. There's something very wrong with him.'

Gary wrapped his arm around Dean, holding him in a tight, reassuring embrace. 'Come on,' he said. 'There's only one way you're gonna find out. Get your coat.'

Glenn lay in bed. Alone. Trying to rest, doze off if possible. Not sleeping. He hadn't really slept much all night. Half an hour here and there. Maybe two or three hours in total if he was lucky. He had lain still beside Matthew all through the night, each of them pretending to be asleep, knowing that the other was awake.

Matthew got up some time around six, inching silently out of bed, taking his robe from behind the bathroom door and creeping quietly downstairs. Glenn didn't go after him. They both needed time alone. Time to think about what they had done and consider the future.

At half past seven he finally decided that he could lie there no more. Rest, piece of mind, both were determined to elude him. He needed a piss. It was as good a reason as any to get his arse out of bed. He walked through to the bathroom with a heavy head. He had had a lot to drink the night before, in the hope that alcohol would help him to sleep. He had been wrong. It merely dried him out and gave him a headache. It afforded no comfort and little consolation.

He emptied his bladder and washed down two ibuprofen tablets with a handful of water. He should have taken only one, but he knew a single dose would be useless at remedying such a potent hangover.

He went downstairs reluctantly. Matthew had not spoken much since getting home from the party in the early hours of Sunday. He had been moody and introspective. They had kept out of each other's way.

He was sitting outside on the patio, in his blue towelling robe, his legs outstretched, his bare feet resting on the seat of another chair. He sat with his back to the house gazing out over the fields beyond the garden fence, a cigarette in one hand, a mug of coffee in the other.

Glenn went through into the kitchen first, pouring a cup of coffee for himself, filling it up with skimmed milk and sweetener. He lingered over the sink, rinsing off his teaspoon, delaying the moment when he would have to go out there and face Matthew. He sipped his coffee. It tasted disgusting – it always did when he had a hangover. He tipped it out and poured himself a glass of fruit juice instead.

He carried his drink outside.

A warm, clear morning had already established itself. Glenn sat at the table next to Matthew. Matthew continued to stare out over the garden – he couldn't or wouldn't meet Glenn's gaze. Glenn picked up the packet of cigarettes, lit one for himself. He inhaled, waited.

Nothing.

'You were up early,' he said at last, desperate to break the heavy silence.

Matthew shrugged. 'Couldn't sleep,' he said evenly.

'Me neither. Couldn't face getting up, though, so I just lay there, trying to rest. Have you been sitting here long?'

'Since I got up. It was a nice morning. I had to get out of the house.'

Glenn nodded, understanding.

A fat ginger-haired cat crept awkwardly along the top of the garden fence, traipsing a slow trail home after his night-time adventures. He paused for a moment, stopping to examine the two men sitting in the garden. He looked at them both directly, making eye contact with each. With an apparent lack of interest he continued on his journey back home and to bed.

'I think we should talk,' Glenn said.

'I don't have anything to say,' Matthew sighed. 'I've got so much going round and round in my head, I can't make sense of any of it.'

'That's why we should talk. You've hardly said a word to me since Saturday. I know you're upset. This isn't easy for me to cope with, either. It'll be a lot less difficult if we don't turn on each other.'

Matthew turned, looking at Glenn for the first time. His big brown eyes, ringed with deep shadows, shone with raw emotion. He looked innocent, tired, worried and vulnerable.

'We've killed a man,' he said choking on his own emotion.

After a pause Glenn answered. 'We had to. He was coming after you. It was the only thing to do.'

'Was it? We didn't really examine many other alternatives. We panicked and chose the harshest solution.'

Glenn didn't know what Matthew really wanted him to say. There were no easy answers to this problem. Nothing he could say could ease their guilt.

'I'm not sorry,' Matthew said. 'I'm not even angry. I don't feel anything at all. That's the problem. I feel empty inside. I don't think you understand. To you he was just another one of your characters. Someone in your head. You can't feel any remorse for killing him because he was never real to you. You didn't know him. Really know him. But he was real to me. Yeah, he was a complete bastard; he was dangerous. But I don't think he deserved to die.

'We were lovers,' he said. There were tears in his eyes. 'Not really lovers – that's probably the wrong vernacular. We didn't *love* each other. We had an affair. After the trial, after the events of your book. I knew what he was. I knew he was dangerous; I knew it was unsafe to get involved with him. But I had no choice. I was drawn to him so strongly. I couldn't resist him.'

'How long did you . . .?'

'Not long. A couple of months. If that. I knew he was just using me. He was destroying me. I left him. I didn't see him again after that. Until recently.'

'When I brought the two of you back together,' Glenn exclaimed slowly. 'In my story outline.'

Matthew nodded.

'I'm so sorry,' Glenn said.

'You couldn't have known. You're a writer. Your obligation was to your story and your readers. This is my fault. I had no right to come here and ask you to change the way that things were meant to be. It's your book, your story. No one else's.'

Glenn's cigarette had burned down to a stub, singeing his fingers. He crushed it out in the ashtray.

'What's going to happen now?' he asked.

Matthew shook his head. 'Nothing. It's all over. Anthony is dead. We just have to deal with that . . .'

'And move on?'

He nodded. 'Yes. We move on.'

Gary dropped Dean off at the end of the road.

'Do you want me to come in with you?' he asked.

'No,' Dean said, 'it'll be all right. Besides you'll be late for work.'

'Give me a ring later and tell me what it's all about.'

Dean kissed him. 'I will.'

Patrick lived in a three-bedroom semi on a modern housing estate. It was a very family-orientated place to live. Dean had often wondered what the hell attracted Patrick to the place. He hated kids.

As if to emphasise the point, Dean was halted in his tracks by a huge Range Rover that trundled down a driveway and over the path in front of him. The back of the vehicle was loaded up with kids, probably being ferried off to some school-holiday play group.

Dean tutted. What the hell did anyone living on a middle class suburban housing estate need with a huge, fuck-off Range Rover?

Dean taught mathematics to high-school and sixth-form kids. He abhorred the thought of teaching in a primary school. He would deal with the foul mouths and raging hormones of a bunch of teenagers any time rather than have to cope with the irrational tantrums and traumas of a bunch of younger kids. He didn't have the patience for it.

He caught a glimpse of movement through the windows of Patrick's house as he walked up the paved drive. He rang the bell.

He heard the unsteady shuffle of footsteps approaching the door. Three different locks were released.

Patrick wasn't usually so security-conscious. Not with two Rottweilers in the house, anyway.

The last key was turned in the lock and the door slowly opened inward.

Dean's eyes widened in shock.

Patrick Robins was almost unrecognisable. It was as if he had aged more than ten years in two days. He looked ghastly. His once handsome face was haggard and drawn. His usually brown skin was pallid and drab. His black robe hung listlessly over his ravished frame. Patrick had always been proud of his appearance, even vain, so it startled Dean to see him looking as ill and unkempt as he now did.

'*Jesus!*' he gasped. 'What the hell happened to you?'

Patrick held the door wider. 'Come in,' he said. His voice, too, was just a subdued remnant of its former self.

Dean followed him through into the living room. Patrick collapsed, as if exhausted, on to the sofa. He drew the folds of his robe over his frail-looking thighs. Dean stood over him. He couldn't believe the evidence of his own eyes. If had not seen Patrick just two days ago, he would have sworn that his friend had been wasting away in bed for months.

Patrick tried to light a cigarette. His hands were shaking and he didn't have the co-ordination to bring the flame to the tip of the cigarette. Dean took the lighter and lit it for him.

'You should see a doctor,' he said. 'You're obviously not well.'

'I don't need a doctor,' Patrick wheezed.

'Yes, you do. You look like you're at death's door. I don't know what it could be to send you into such a rapid decline, but you need seeing to. Who's your GP? I'm going to call them now and get someone out to see you.'

He picked up the phone.

'Dean, wait!' Patrick mustered as much force as he could manage into his voice. 'I asked you to come round here 'cause I need your help. I need you to tell me . . . tell me who that guy was on Saturday night. Anthony. Who is he? *What* is he?'

'Why? What's he got to do with anything?'

'I think he did this to me.'

'*What?*'

Patrick explained, slowly and with long and frequent pauses, what had happened to him at the weekend. He had to stop after each line of his narration to catch his breath. He told Dean about meeting Anthony after the party, about bringing him back home, of the struggle for sexual domination and his subsequent defeat.

'I was exhausted when he finished. Drained. I couldn't even open my eyes. I passed out immediately afterwards. He must have left me soon after that. I woke up last night, about nine o'clock, feeling like this: tired, sickly. I crawled down here to feed the dogs and then went straight back to bed. When I woke up this morning, I called you.'

'So what are you saying? You think Anthony did *this* to you?'

Patrick nodded. 'I'm sure he did. I could feel it happening. When he came inside me, I could feel him – drawing the life out of me. Like a vampire. I had no energy when he finished with me. Can you think of any other explanation for this?'

After a short delay Dean said, 'No. I can't think what could have done this to you.' He looked at his friend. What a sad, sorry state he had become. What he was saying didn't make any rational sense. It was the feverish talk of a madman. But, despite his own reasoning, Dean had a gut instinct about this whole story. He believed what Patrick was saying. He knew himself that there had been something extraordinary about Anthony. It was crazy, but he had felt as if he were under some kind of spell himself when he was with him. There was no way that he would have put on such a shameless sex show if he had been responsible for his own actions. Anthony had hypnotised him. He had cast a powerful spell.

'I'll make you something to eat,' Dean said. 'It'll build your strength up.'

'I don't think I could get anything down.'

'I think you should try.' Dean helped Patrick to his feet. 'If you won't see your doctor the least I can get you to do is eat. Even if it's just a slice of toast.'

Patrick clenched Dean's arm for support as they took one tiny step after another towards the kitchen. Dean was fearful that his friend would fall straight over on to the floor if he relaxed his grip just a fraction. Finally he managed to get him into the kitchen and sat him down at the table.

Dean pulled a joint out of his breast pocket. He lit it and handed it to Patrick.

'Here. It's the best medicine I know of.'

Patrick took a long pull and held the hash smoke in his lungs before it emerged again in a bilious wreath through his mouth and nostrils.

Dean filled the kettle with water and flicked the switch. He tossed a couple of bags into the waiting teapot.

'Do you know anything about Anthony?' Patrick asked, drawing comfort from the roach as an asthmatic would from an inhaler.

'No,' Dean sighed. 'Nobody seems to know who he is. He wasn't invited. He turned up on his own. Neither Gary nor I have ever seen him before.'

'Did anything happen to you? After he fucked you?'

He shook his head. 'No, I was fine. A little dazed but that's normal after such a hard fuck. I did feel odd beforehand, though.'

'Odd?' Patrick frowned.

'Mmm.' He took the joint from Patrick and toked thoughtfully. 'It was like . . . I wasn't in control of myself. You know me, Patrick: fucking in front of a crowd of friends isn't the sort of thing I would do. I couldn't stop myself, though. I got down and sucked his cock and got carried away from there. Part of me didn't want to do it and I *knew* that I shouldn't be doing it, but I couldn't stop. It was like being possessed by some cock-crazed demon.'

They both managed to laugh. The kettle came to the boil and

199

Dean made the tea. He stuck a couple of slices of white bread into the toaster.

Patrick struggled with the toast, but as he sipped his mug of tea a semblance of colour did start to seep back into his pallid face. Whatever it was that had happened to him, Dean didn't think that it was anything worse than exhaustion. He wasn't in any pain and he was showing no symptoms of anything more serious.

After half an hour Dean helped him back up the stairs to bed.

'Get your head down for a few hours. I think you need sleep more than anything. I'll ring work for you and tell them you won't be in for the rest of the week. I'll take the dogs out for a walk, too – they're probably desperate for the exercise.'

'You won't leave me, will you?' Patrick begged. 'I'm *frightened*.'

Dean stroked the back of his neck, soothing him. 'Don't worry. I'll take the dogs out and get you some shopping in, but I'll be here when you wake up.'

'I don't know what's happening to me.'

'Whatever it is I think you're over the worst of it. You look better already than when I first arrived. Try to get some sleep and don't worry.'

Patrick kissed him. There were tears in his eyes. 'Thanks, Dean. I owe you for this.'

'Ssshh,' Dean said holding him close. 'Just concentrate on getting better.'

The walls of the house seemed to be closing in and stifling Glenn. By the middle of the morning he had completed his yoga routine, showered and changed, cleaned up the kitchen and vacuumed through the downstairs rooms – anything to take his mind off the overwhelming burden of guilt he found himself subject to. The atmosphere with Matthew had not eased any. After going upstairs to shower and get dressed, Matthew had returned to his post on the patio and had remained there ever since. They had not spoken more than five words since breakfast.

Glenn was suffering from cabin fever. He had not ventured further than the back garden since Saturday night and now the self-imposed spell of incarceration was starting to put an intolerable pressure on his nerves. He had to get out.

He put the vacuum back in its home inside the kitchen cupboard and went outside to speak to his sullen partner.

Matthew glanced up as he came out and managed to force a weak excuse for a smile on to his troubled features.

'How are you?'

Matthew shrugged. 'OK.'

Glenn sat down beside him. After establishing such a close bond in the last week, the emotional distance that now intruded on their happiness was like a yawning chasm. Glenn had to overcome the doubt and darkness in their moods before it destroyed them.

'How do you feel about going into town for a few hours for a look about? Just to get away from the house for a while.'

Matthew seemed to brighten at the idea. 'OK. Where do you want to go?'

'We could go into Newcastle. I posed for some photographs last week. They're going to be used in a magazine along with an interview that I did. At some point this week I need to go in and give my approval of the shots before they go off to the publisher. We could go for a late lunch afterwards and maybe see a film.'

'All right. I'd like that.'

Satisfied that he had finally started to thaw the chill in Matthew's mood, Glenn went upstairs to change out of his casual jeans and T-shirt and into something more stylish. He wanted to make an effort, raising his own self-esteem by taking pride in his appearance.

His dressed carefully in a pair of cream, slim-fitting Dolce and Gabbana trousers that he had worn only once before. The narrow fit of the legs accentuated the long line of his limbs and sat high and tight on the curve of his buttocks. He pulled on a tight, V-necked sweater that hugged the fine contours of his chest and stomach and slipped his bare feet into a pair of white Louis Vuitton loafers.

Ordinarily Glenn didn't concern himself with high fashion and designer labels unless he had to. It was a necessary evil to turn out in the best gear for public functions, especially in London, but when he was at home he liked to slope around in clothes that made him feel comfortable – namely jeans and T-shirts. But today he felt like making an effort and he was glad that he had. The expensive clothes hung well on his highly toned body and caused him to carry himself with an extra degree of confidence.

It had turned out to be a hot summer day. Rather than take a taxi all the way into Newcastle, the two men got out at Durham and then took a train for the remainder of the journey. Glenn was glad of the change; all of the carriage windows were open and there was a refreshing breeze drifting down the length of the train.

It was almost midday and other travellers were relatively sparse. Glenn and Matthew sat side by side gazing out at the passing farmland and countryside. Matthew slid his hand over Glenn's thigh and joined it with his. Glenn turned away from the window. Matthew's eyes were smiling; the tight knots of tension that had clouded his face had almost vanished. Glenn squeezed his hand gently and returned the smile.

'How are you feeling now, darlin'?'

Matthew's smile was weary but shot through with a heartening ray of tranquillity. 'I'm all right. I'm starting to deal with it anyway.'

'That's good.' Glenn glanced down the railway carriage. There were a handful of other passengers scattered here and there, but no one was paying any attention to them. He leaned over in his seat and placed a daring kiss on Matthew's lips.

They both laughed, strengthening the bond between them.

They got off the train when it arrived at Central Station. Glenn decided to go to Damien's studio first and approve the photographs for *GAYZ*. Once that small work obligation was out of the way they would have the remainder of the day to do whatever they wanted.

The sun was assaulting the city with its fierce midday heat when they walked out of the protective shade of the railway station. Thankfully, the walk from the station to Damien's studio was a short one: less than five minutes. They were both sweltering when they reached the front door and pressed the intercom.

As with Glenn's inaugural visit the previous week, Jared answered the call and buzzed them inside. After the intense blaze out on the street, the shade of the old warehouse was blessedly cool. They slowly ascended the stairs to the photographic studio.

Jared, stripped down to a pair of half-length trousers and a pair of leather sandals, was waiting for them. He took them through to the waiting room.

'Damien's in the middle of a shoot,' he explained, indicating a screened-off wall on the far side of the studio. He handed Glenn a heavy manila envelope, a magnifying glass and a red pencil. 'These are your contact sheets. Have a look through them, cross out any that you don't like. Damien'll be out to see you soon.'

Jared disappeared behind the screen to assist his boss.

The photographs had exceeded all of Glenn's expectations. He regarded the sultry inch-square images on the contact sheet through the magnifying glass and marvelled at the results. In several of the shots he wouldn't have even recognised the model in the picture as himself.

Damien had created an image of pure sensuality and drop-dead beauty. The man in the photographs was otherworldly, unobtainable. Glenn had been obliged to pose for a lot of publicity pictures in the last few years, but none that had the visual impact of the contact sheets he held in his hand.

'Wow!' Matthew remarked. 'You look incredible.'

'Wow's right,' Glenn gasped. 'I can't believe that this is even me.'

A voice said, 'Believe it, babe, that's *all* you.'

Damien stood over them, grinning, a camera hoisted over his shoulder on a wide leather strap.

'No way,' Glenn said. 'What you've done with me here is inconceivable.'

'I haven't done much with you at all,' Damien said. 'If you remember, we hardly spent any time at all on your hair and make-up with you. What you see in those shots is Glenn Holden. Pure and simple.'

'Still –'

'Still nothing. Take a bit of credit where it's due, will you. All my camera did was capture what was in front of it.'

'Well, thank you.' Glenn blushed. 'I don't have a problem with any of these shots. You can use whatever ones you want to. They're all fantastic.'

It certainly was fantastic. The issue of *GAYZ* featuring his interview was due in less than a month. Glenn was already preparing himself for the personal panning he was going to receive in print from Freddie Brooks. But now, thanks to these photographs, the entire *GAYZ* débâcle was about to turn in his favour. Thanks to Damien Marquez, Glenn Holden was about to be reborn as a first-rate gay icon.

'Do you boys feel like a drink to celebrate?'

'No thanks. We can't stay long. I only dropped in to look at these.'

'And I thought you'd come to see me,' Damien said lasciviously. 'I thought you were gonna give me a call sometime.'

Glenn slipped his hand into Matthew's. 'I've been busy since I last saw you.'

Damien smiled, glancing appraisingly over Matthew. 'Are you going to introduce me to your friend?'

'Matthew, this is Damien. Damien, Matthew.'

Both men exchange interested smiles.

'I have to give you further credit, Glenn,' Damien mused. 'You have excellent taste. I met another one of your friends yesterday who was *very* nice. Very nice indeed.'

'Oh, yeah. Who was that.'

'He was called Anthony. I didn't get his surname.'

'What?' Matthew gasped.

'Anthony,' Damien said. 'A tall guy, dark hair. He said he knew you. He came round yesterday morning and asked me to take some pictures for him. Usually I would have told him to fuck off – I don't work Sundays and certainly not without an appointment. But this fella was *hot*. I would have done anything he asked me to.'

'Yesterday?' Glenn asked, his mind bewildered.

'Uh-huh. He gave me a real hard-on. I took the photos he wanted and then had trade with him. It was lovely.' Damien licked his lips. 'I even let him fuck me – and I don't do *that* for anyone.'

Matthew's hand had tightened in Glenn's grip. His knuckles blanching.

'Have you developed the shots yet? Could we have a look at them?'

'I shouldn't really. Client confidentiality and all that. But seeing as it's you.' He walked off behind his screen, returning moments later with another manila envelope. 'Just the contacts,' he said. 'I haven't blown up any of the shots yet.'

Glenn took the envelope from him and extracted two sheets. Even before looking through the clear lens of the magnifying glass he knew what he was going to see.

Anthony smiled up at him from the glossy colour image. Handsome, cunning and dangerous. He was naked in every shot, sporting a huge angry hard-on for the camera.

'He's pretty hot, isn't he?' Damien oozed.

Glenn's throat tightened. He tried to swallow before speaking. 'Y-yeah. He always was a horny bastard.'

Damien laughed. 'I don't need reminding. My arsehole is still recovering. I thought I was tough, but he is one mean little fuck.'

Glenn handed the contacts to Matthew across his lap, trying not to betray his trembling hands. He heard the sharp intake of Matthew's breath as he looked at the pictures.

'I haven't seen Anthony for a long time,' Glenn bluffed. 'Are you expecting him to come back?'

Damien shook his head. 'No. He asked me to deliver the pictures to his home address. It's a pity, though: I wouldn't mind seeing him some more.'

'Yeah.' Glenn forced his most convincing smile. 'Where is he living these days? I wouldn't mind seeing him myself. I might pay him a visit while I'm in town.'

'He's got a place up your way,' Damien said. 'In Durham. Give me a minute and I'll hunt out the address for you.' He walked away, over to his desk, out of earshot.

'*He's still alive!*' Matthew whispered. 'We didn't kill him.'

'We must have got it wrong,' gasped Glenn, overwhelmed by conflicting emotions of relief and fear. Although his conscience was now clear of any wrongdoing, the fact remained that Anthony Pierce was a very dangerous individual. Whatever Anthony hoped to achieve in tracking Glenn down to the party and turning up here at the photographer's studio, it was clear that he was working to some kind of personal agenda.

Damien returned with the address Anthony had left for him neatly copied out on to a piece of notepaper. Glenn glanced at the address. It was a place in Durham, less than fifteen minutes away from his own house. He folded up the note and stuffed it in his trouser pocket.

He thanked Damien, signed a consent form giving him permission to use any of the photographs that he wanted, and then quickly said goodbye.

Back out on the street, Matthew seemed to share his sense of relief and trepidation.

'What are we going to do?'

'Come on,' Glenn said, heading down the road towards the railway station. 'We're going back.'

'You're not planning to go after him, are you?'

'Yes,' Glenn said simply. 'This has gone far enough. We've put ourselves through hell this weekend all for nothing. The only way to resolve this now is to confront him. That's obviously what he wants, otherwise he wouldn't have come here. That's the only reason he came to Damien, to get this message to me.'

'But he's dangerous.'

'Maybe. That's why you're not coming with me.'

'What? You can't go after him alone.'

'I have to,' Glenn explained. 'You're the one he's after, or at least we think you are. I want you to go home and wait for me. Lock yourself in. I'll go to Anthony and find out what he wants.'

Matthew was nervous. 'I'm frightened.'

Glenn put his arms around him, pressing close. 'I'm scared too. But this is the only way. I'm not going to run away from him.' He wiped away the tears that were brimming over Matthew's lids.

'Go home,' he said. 'Wait for me.'

Seventeen

Face to Face

It was an ordinary-looking house on a very ordinary estate, built in the mid 1980s in a mock-Tudor style that had long since gone out of fashion with property developers. The house was detached. It stood on its own at the top of the road. Number one. Glenn predicated that it had most likely been the show house in the distant days when it was considered to be the height of suburban class. Now it was just a relic of the decade that had created it – dated, flashy and just a little bit sad.

An estate agent's sign was erected in the front garden. The house was up to let, fully furnished.

Although the path down the middle of the garden to the front door was little more than five or six yards, it might just as well have been a mile. It yawned before Glenn ominously. He felt like a prisoner on a pirate ship, about to walk the short plank over the side before plunging to his fate in shark-infested waters.

He concentrated, putting one foot in front of the other, searching the long, blank windows for signs of life within.

He saw the man inside, looking outwards. He had a can of beer in his hand, which he raised slowly to his lips and took a long draught. Through the vacant pane of glass Glenn could see the dark, dangerous glint in his eyes. He lowered the can and brushed a casual hand across his bare torso. All that he wore was a pair of tight black boxer shorts, riding low on his narrow waist and displaying the long, lean lines of his oblique muscles. He traced his fingers along the well-defined path, the Apollo's Belt, down over his stomach and into his groin. He smiled through the window, shifting his weight from one foot to the other, his body primed and waiting.

Glenn's heart started to pound wildly. He was afraid. He didn't trust Anthony and he didn't trust himself to be around him.

The front door opened before he knocked. The tight black fabric of Anthony's shorts hugged his tiny hips like a second skin, setting off the dynamic sculpture of his stomach and thigh muscles. He smiled, his cool eyes glistening like hard diamonds.

'Come in,' he said. He held the door open and walked away, leading Glenn into the house.

Glenn closed the door and followed him. A thousand conflicting emotions and thoughts seemed to be raging through his mind and yet he could concentrate on nothing but the animal-like grace of Anthony's back as he led him through into the living room.

The house was neat and tidy, just like a showroom. The walls were bright and the furniture was all modern, contrasting with the out-of-date exterior. It was all very bright and very bland, but what lay on the coffee table caught Glenn's attention. A pile of well-read, dog-eared paperbacks. He registered the titles, all of them familiar: *The First Time*, *Morning After*, *Everyday Hurts*, *Risk Addiction*. They were all his own novels.

Anthony picked up one of the books, glancing at the back-cover blurb. He smiled. 'I'm working my way through your back catalogue. It's not really my kind of thing, but pretty impressive just the same. I like to live life and experience it rather than read about it.'

He laughed softly and threw the book back down on top of the pile.

Glenn breathed deeply, fighting to overcome his fear. 'But this is *my* life, not yours.' He moved around the coffee table, closer to Anthony, determined to be strong. 'I got your message,' he said matter-of-factly.

Anthony's eyebrows shot up. 'Message? Oh, right. The photographer.' He started to laugh. 'Nice!'

'And Dean,' Glenn said softly. 'At the party.'

'Yeah. I like a good party. I like your friends, too.'

'Is that what this is all about?' Glenn asked calmly. '*This* life being preferable to your own.'

Anthony threw back his head, laughing. 'Hardly.'

'So come on, tell me. What do you want?'

'I guess you don't know your characters that well.'

'Tell me,' he said firmly.

Anthony smiled coolly. Without taking his eyes from Glenn's face he smoothed his hand slowly down the ridges of his stomach. Lower, brushing lightly over his groin and the long protuberance of his cock, bulging off to the left. His skin, with its light pelt of dark hair, shone like rich rose-gold. His eyes, beneath their long, arched brows, blazed with a blatant heat.

'How does it make you feel?' he said, slipping away from the question Glenn had given him. 'Seeing me like this. Seeing your words made flesh. I know I'm not your surrogate dream boy, like Matthew. Oh, by the way, I wanted to congratulate you on your excellent taste. Dean I mean. Very nice.'

'*What do you want?*' Glenn said firmly.

Anthony was closer now. 'I want to thank you. Patrick's a nice enough guy, but he's a bit on the rough side, isn't he? I think Dean translates pretty faithfully into Matthew but I'm so glad you had the good taste to refine Patrick's features. He's not really me at all, is he?'

He was close to him now. So close that Glenn could feel his breath on his face. Their eyes were riveted on each other – it was impossible to look away. Glenn could smell him, his deep masculine scent filling his nostrils. He could feel his heat. Anthony tilted his head, his eyes shining, his mouth just open. He was so close now, so warm, an embodiment of pure sexuality.

His hand suddenly shot forwards into Glenn's groin, grasping his cock and balls in one hand through the fabric of his trousers. He squeezed the hard shaft. Glenn burned red at the exposure of his arousal.

'Uh-huh,' Anthony said, his voice soft like velvet. 'Just as I thought.'

Then they were upon each other and there were no more words.

Glenn opened his arms and they attacked one another passionately. Anthony's hands were all over him as they kissed urgently, hurriedly. They were like animals: there was no tenderness just pure, unmitigated passion. They fought, thrusting, twisting against one another.

Anthony hurled Glenn against the wall. The breath was forced out of his lungs and into Anthony's kiss. He felt a surge of adrenalin and battled back, clutching, clawing, grabbing at Anthony's body. Anthony forced him back against the hard surface, crushing him with his powerful body. Their hard cocks throbbed against one another. Groaning, Glenn gasped for air.

He caressed Anthony's tiny hips, grasping the hard line of his pelvis. He slid his hands beneath the tight cotton shorts and scooped out his cock. He grabbed the throbbing organ tight, as though afraid of losing it. He jerked his wrist, sliding his hand back and forth over the engorged shaft, pulling at the skin, consumed with hunger.

Anthony's tongue was inside his mouth, pressing through his clenched teeth, exploring. Glenn responded by pushing back against him, forcing his own tongue in Anthony's mouth, tasting him.

Anthony shoved him brusquely down to his knees, driving his dripping cock into his open, willing mouth. He gagged as Anthony thrust his hips forwards, stuffing the oozing head all the way back into his throat. His hands were locked around the back of Glenn's head, thwarting any attempt to withdraw. Glenn had no other option but to accept the blunt intrusion and suck it.

He loosened the muscles at the back of his throat and extended his lower jaw, creating space for the big cock. Despite the discomfort and the humiliation of choking on it, he wanted this cock – wanted to suck it, kiss it, caress it. He wanted to milk it with his body, draining it of every last drop of masculine juice.

He abandoned the methodical approach to cocksucking that he had cultivated with years of practice and skill. Now he was like a novice, a virgin gaining his first taste of burning man flesh and simply hungering for more. He breathed heavily in and out through his nose while Anthony held his head in a tight grip and fucked his face, pounding him into submission. But he would not submit: he was as mean and aggressive in his role of cocksucker and bottom as Anthony was as his master. Regardless of position this was a battle for power and there was no confirmation of just *who* was in control.

Glenn grabbed Anthony's big balls while he sucked. He squeezed them in his tight grip and twisted. The dick, lying long against his tongue, swelled and leaped inside him.

Anthony grabbed a handful of hair and dragged his head backwards. A thick drool of pre-come and saliva dangled between Glenn's mouth and the fat tip of his cock. They were both breathless, smiling, flushed with the challenge that they each represented.

Anthony grabbed the base of his cock and beat it against Glenn's face, smearing the silvery trail across his cheeks. He dragged him back to his feet, lifting him by the hair. They kissed again, breathing hard against each other, their breath hot with emotion.

Anthony held him in his powerful grip. He picked Glenn up, spun him around and threw him down. He landed, half sprawling, over the back of the sofa. With the stealth and strength of a tiger, Anthony was upon him from behind. A hand on the back of Glenn's head shoved his face down into the cushions. He breathed in the nearly new scent of the sofa. He was bent almost double, draped down either side of the tall backrest. Anthony tore at his clothes from behind, yanking his trousers and his shorts down together. He shoved his tight trousers down around his knees, restricting the freedom of his legs.

Glenn tried to raise his head, but the hand on the back of his neck forced his face back down. His heart was beating wildly. He gasped, more from surprise than pain, as Anthony delivered a sharp, open-palmed crack to his bare arse. Then he slid his fingers into the crack, moving slowly, probing, rubbing, drawing closer to the hole. He touched the rim. Glenn flinched.

Anthony leaned over, shoving his fingers into Glenn's mouth.

'Suck these,' he said.

Glenn did, opening his mouth and working his tongue all over the proffered digits. He drooled over them, lubing them up, knowing exactly where they were going. When his hand was well soaked, Anthony pulled it out of Glenn's mouth and returned it to his arse.

Glenn fought to get his breathing under control. Anthony's fingers skittered over his arsehole, working round the rim in lazy, slippery circles. He stroked the narrow lips, seducing them, loosened them up. When he pressed the first finger inside, Glenn jumped. The finger slipped in all the way to the knuckle. Glenn groaned and rolled his hips slowly back, giving up his arse.

The passage relaxed further and Anthony followed through with another finger. His arselips fluttered. Anthony stretched his sphincter, widening it. A third finger wriggled in beside the other two. Glenn moaned, wiggling his arse, thrusting back against Anthony's hand, allowing him to enter him further. He pressed in deeper, harder, opening up his hole. It was a strain. Glenn bore down to take everything inside, determined that he would not be beaten. Anthony was an expert, applying just enough force to loosen up the narrow orifice.

Despite his resolve, Glenn moaned, loud and passionate, when Anthony stuck the fourth finger into him.

Shit. It was too much. *Too painful*. But he would not admit it. He sucked in air and waited for the pain to subside. It did, dulling down to a blunt, rather exquisite ache. Anthony rotated his wrist, turning his fingers slowly round inside him, opening the hole further.

He withdrew just as slowly. Before Glenn had a chance to relax, Anthony grabbed hold of his feet and lifted him over the backrest and down on to the sofa. He leaped over on top of him, back into his arms, kissing, clutching, grasping. They worked together, dragging the rest of Glenn's clothes from his body. They both rolled to the floor, naked, hard, wet.

Glenn rolled and twisted, managing to get on top of Anthony, head to toe, their mouths right on top of each other's cock. Glenn pressed home his advantage, forcing his dick into Anthony's mouth. He took it admirably, sucking the throbbing cock deep into his throat.

Glenn slipped his lips over the top of Anthony's dick again, tasting his slippery, salty flavour as pre-come oozed heavily from his tip. He slavered his tongue all around the leaky head, scooping up his thick sap and swallowing. Glenn pressed his hips down, forcing his own cock deep into the tight recesses of Anthony's throat. They both groaned and sucked one another furiously.

Though already hard, Anthony's cock hardened and lengthened further along Glenn's tongue. He tipped his head back, breathing through his nose as he took the organ deeper. Anthony was playing with his arsehole again while still sucking him off. He shoved a couple of fingers back into the slippery passage, quickly finding his prostate. He stroked the swollen nub, causing the flow of pre-come to increase significantly. Glenn shuddered as a spasm of pure pleasure racked his body.

They ground their hips against each other's face. Glenn breathed in the deep, musky scent of Anthony's balls past the blunt obstruction of his cock in his throat. The dark man's fingers slipped in and out of his greedy, grasping arsehole, smoothly stroking the sensitive nut within.

Glenn rolled off. He was close and didn't want to spoil the expectancy of sex by shooting off too soon. His cock popped noisily out of Anthony's wet mouth.

'Time to stop fooling around,' Anthony leered. 'I'm gonna fuck you.'

He produced the condoms from underneath one of the cushions. Glenn positioned himself on the floor, elbows resting on the edge of the sofa, as he waited for Anthony to sheath himself in latex. Glenn spread his knees wide, arse raised, poised and ready. The warm afternoon air caressed his creamy arsehole. He was ready.

Anthony kneeled behind him, both hands gripping his waist. He positioned his dick at the opening.

Glenn panted, expectation mounting. He felt the blunt head bearing hard against his waiting lips. He gasped as the man pressed into him, opening his sphincter wide. He was big – and hard. So fucking hard. His arsehole burned as it struggled to stretch wide enough. Anthony's pelvis pressed against his moist buttocks. He was in, all the way inside. The long underside of his cock throbbed against Glenn's prostate. He shuddered.

They started to fuck with hunger, rage and passion. Anthony

gripped Glenn's arse and rammed into him, his heavy balls bagging against the back of his thighs. His cock stroked his prostate with each thrust. Glenn was glowing, burning. He bore the weight of both their bodies on his elbows and thrust back, swallowing the cock with his arse before it could get away.

The house echoed to their grunts and gasps and the rhythmic fuck-slap of bare flesh against bare flesh. They both swore and cursed as they thrashed, twisted and heaved.

Glenn's body trembled as Anthony fucked him wild and hard. His cock jerked with each inward thrust and slapped against his belly. He refrained from touching himself, knowing that the tiniest stroke would bring on the flood.

As Anthony withdrew, Glenn pulled away from him, releasing his cock from his hungry hole. He rolled down on to the floor, over on to his back, knees raised to his chest. Anthony quickly took up position and shoved back into him. Glenn lifted his legs and rested his ankles on Anthony's broad shoulders. They resumed their wild, animal thrusts. The new position provided Glenn with a host of fresh sensations as the big cock penetrated him from a different angle, reaching deeper into him.

Glenn arched his back, twisting his head from side to side. 'Fuck me, you cunt! Fuck me!'

Oh, yes. He loved the feel of Anthony's full balls pressing against the base of his spine as he pumped his cock in and out of his arse. He squeezed his sphincter, gripping the thick rod. He heaved upwards, moving his body in rhythm with Anthony.

Anthony reached down, grabbing hold of his pierced tit, taking him by surprise. *Holy shit!* His tit was wired directly to the pleasure hot spot in his arse. He jolted, his legs twitching involuntarily, his ring tightening around the meat inside it. Anthony twisted the little steel bar.

'Oh, *fuuuccckk!*' he cried out. '*Aaaaaaggghhh!*'

It was a sensation like *nothing* else.

The big, sweet cock continued to pump away inside him.

Glenn wrapped his legs around Anthony's waist and they rolled again. Glenn was on top now, straddling his hips. It was his turn to control the pace. He rose and fell on the shaft, clamping it tight in his vice-hole, taking it deep. Anthony flexed inside him. Oh, shit! That was almost too much. He was so close now.

He flung himself forwards across Anthony's chest, burying his face into the hot crook of his shoulder. Anthony heaved against him, jerking his hips up from the floor, jabbing at the inner jewel. Glenn gasped. With a snarl he bit into the hard shoulder beneath him, tasting hot flesh and sweat. His heart was pounding even faster, his knees trembling with the excitement of such carnal pleasure.

He rocked his hips, his arsehole clutched. Anthony growled, almost there. Glenn pushed himself back, sitting high on his cock. He reared back, impaled, pounding. He arched his back, threw back his head, trembling. Without even touching it his long, hard dick erupted. Thick wads of come burst from his bulging piss slit, spitting high in the air in rupturing spurts. It arched high, splattering down Anthony's neck and his chest. A long stream struck him directly in the face, falling across his nose, his cheek and lips.

The tight spasms inside Glenn's arse at the moment of orgasm were too much. Anthony roared, jerked his hips. Glenn felt the hard turbulence along the sensitive inner lining. The big cock lengthened and swelled and then jerked in long rhythmic waves as Anthony filled him up.

Glenn pitched forwards, drained and drenched, enfolding Anthony in his warm embrace. Their bodies shivered with pleasure. Two hearts thumped wildly against one another.

Later they lay quietly next to each other. Anthony had pulled out and rid himself of the come-heavy rubber. Glenn's arsehole was completely wrecked, sore, but, fuck, he had enjoyed it. His head was on Anthony's chest, his face resting against the damp pelt of smooth hair.

'That was good,' Anthony said softly, without a trace of irony.

'Yeah,' Glenn sighed, savouring the warm looseness of his body.

'Bet you're sorry you tried to kill me now,' Anthony said.

'I didn't know . . .'

'Don't worry, it's not important any more. I just hope you realise now that I'm not here to hurt anyone.'

Glenn raised himself up on to one elbow, looking down into

215

Anthony's calm face and placid blue eyes. 'So what are you going to do?'

'I want to go back, get back to normal, get back to *my* life.'

'Can you do that?'

He looked straight into his eyes. 'If you help me I can.'

Glenn drew his finger along the firm line of his jaw, tracing the contours of his fleshy lips. 'What about Matthew?'

'I know you like him,' Anthony said mindfully. 'He's a nice guy. Whatever Matthew thinks of me, I like him too. And I know what he means to you. What Dean means to you. But it can't go on. You have to let him go. Matthew has no right to be here. Neither do I. It's your world and your life. Not ours. Matthew should never have come here.'

'He came because he was scared,' Glenn said. 'He was afraid of you.'

'I know, but it didn't used to be that way. At one time we were very close. After the court case . . .'

Glenn stroked his cheek softly. 'You had a relationship.'

'He told you.'

'Yes.' After a pause, he said, 'What are you trying to tell me here?'

'I think you know,' he answered simply.

'I can put everything right.'

'You're the only one who can. You'll have to start by overwriting your latest storyline. I can't go back to my life when I don't have a life.'

'And then what?'

'That's up to you,' Anthony whispered

Glenn looked into his earnest, clear, blue eyes and then started kissing him passionately.

Eighteen

The Last Kiss

He didn't get home until nearly ten.

Twilight had already claimed a major stake on the clear, summer-evening sky. The night was balmy and airless. The heat of the house almost overcame him as he let himself inside and closed the door behind him.

All the lights were out; he could just about see through the hallway in the grey tones of dusk. Music from upstairs drifted down to greet him. Groove Armarda and 'At the River'. Matthew was in the bedroom.

Glenn went straight up.

Matthew was lying on top of the bed, on his back, full-stretch, reading through a paperback copy of *Risk Addiction*. He was dressed in a plain black T-shirt and a pair of blue jeans. His feet were bare, his legs crossed at the ankle. The music played at medium volume on the metallic-coloured CD player next to the window. The bedroom curtains were still open to catch the dying minutes of the day. Two vanilla-scented candles burned slowly on the windowsill in narrow glass jars, and a third smouldered away on top of the bedside table.

Matthew marked his place in the book and put it down beside the bed.

He looked at Glenn with wide, resolute eyes.

'Are you OK?'

Glenn stared at him, expressionless. 'I'm fine,' he sighed. 'Are you?'

Matthew nodded slowly. 'Why don't you come and lie down with me for a little while?' He moved across the bed and gently patted the hollow he had left.

Glenn sat wearily. He took off his shoes and lay down in the warm space vacated by Matthew's body. He lay on his back, his gaze fixed on the ceiling and the flickering shadows created by the flames of the candles.

'It's over,' Matthew said at last, 'isn't it?'

The CD player was selecting tracks at random and 'At the River' was followed by the Aloof's 'One Night Stand'. Glenn smiled softly to himself, realising that he had last heard that track a week ago when he was in bed with Joe. The night he first saw Matthew. Had that really been only a week ago? He had promised Joe he would speak to him; other than a few words at Dean's party, he hadn't. Funny how he had forgotten.

'Yes,' he said finally answering Matthew's question. 'It's over. Nearly.'

'Nearly,' Matthew said, the word hanging heavy in the air. 'Was he angry?'

'No, he wasn't angry. I think he was hurt though, at the way things have turned out.'

'Did you have sex with him?'

'Yes,' Glenn said. There no point in lying.

'He's good,' Matthew murmured.

They lay still once again, neither of them speaking for a while, both lost in their individual thoughts. Both of them brooding on pretty much the *same* thoughts.

Matthew was first to break the silence.

'Glenn,' he said.

'Yes?'

'Did I do the wrong thing? In coming to you?'

Glenn rolled over on to his side, looking straight into Matthew's deep brown eyes. He stroked the side of his face, his stubble rasping

218

beneath his fingertips. 'No,' he said. 'You didn't do the wrong thing. I'm glad you came to me.'

A gentle smile broke across Matthew's troubled features. 'I'm glad I came here too. Whatever else has happened or shouldn't have happened, I'm glad I had the opportunity to meet you.'

Glenn caressed his cheek. 'I'm glad too,' he said.

'I know that I can't stay,' Matthew said softly. 'But it doesn't make leaving any easier.'

'No,' Glenn whispered sadly.

'Everything will be all right, won't it?'

'I promise. It'll all be fine for you.'

Matthew nodded. 'How about having a final drink together? One last glass of wine before I leave.'

'That would be nice,' Glenn said.

Matthew crawled over the top of him and climbed off the bed. 'I'll be right back.' His bare feet padded lightly down the stairs.

Glenn stretched on the bed. His body was aching, punishing him for forcing it into sexual positions that he was unused to. He sat up slowly, arching his back. His arsehole was still sticky and loose. He went through into the bathroom and filled the basin with cold water. He cupped the water in his hands and splashed it into his eyes.

The chill seemed to revive him a little.

He gazed at the reflection of his face. He looked tired. The emotional rollercoaster of the last week had left its marks in the lines and shadows beneath his eyes. The whites around his irises were streaked with tiny threadlike red lines.

It was not the face of a troubled man, more the face of a very tired man. In the last seven days he had lived through such vast extremes of emotion: passion, anger, joy, fear, ecstasy, love, hate. He had experienced every single one of them and each had left its mark on his spirit.

He sighed. He really needed a holiday, a little bit of time alone to clear his head and put his life into perspective. Time to sort himself out without the usual distractions that were integral to his life: sex, booze, work, smoking, dancing, clubbing, stress.

A few days alone on a quiet beach would be enough.

He emptied the sink and refilled it with warm water. He washed his face with a freshly scented scrub and dried himself off on a clean towel. There was a little bottle of eye drops in the cabinet. He hardly ever used them. After checking that the date on the bottle had not expired, he squeezed a couple of cool drops into each eye. The relief they gave him was almost instantaneous.

He heard Matthew come back into the bedroom.

He dried his face once more on the towel and went back through.

Matthew was sitting on the edge of the bed. 'Breathe' was on the CD player. Matthew had two glasses of white wine in his hands. The side of each glass was misted with condensation.

Glenn accepted the glass that was offered and sat down beside Matthew. They chinked their glasses.

'Cheers.'

'Cheers.'

It was a cool South Australian Chardonnay. His favourite. The fresh oaky flavour surged smoothly over his tongue and down his throat.

'Mmm,' he said.

Matthew rested his hand on his thigh. His touch was firm and warm. He squeezed the muscle gently.

'Glenn,' he said.

'Yes?'

'Kiss me.'

Glenn put down his glass and took him in his arms. Matthew's mouth was open, ready. Their tongues slowly slid against one another, mating, savouring the taste and warmth. Glenn's arm snaked around Matthew's waist, pulling him closer as their kisses deepened.

They undressed each other slowly, pulling aside one item of clothing at a time. Glenn deliberately prolonged the act, committing each line and contour of Matthew's body to memory as he gradually unwrapped it. When it was all over he didn't want to forget the tiniest detail.

In a while they were both naked, sitting on the edge of the bed, kissing, caressing, holding one another. Glenn's hands coursed delicately over the wide curves of flesh, committing the touch of his lover as well as the sight of him to memory. He dragged his fingers slowly through the thick forest of hair across his chest, wrapping the dark curls around his fingertips. He traced the sweep of muscle along his hard pecs, tenderly circling the hard brown points of his nipples.

All the while their lips brushed, their open mouths exchanging warmth, moisture and life.

Glenn reached into the bedside drawer and pulled out a wrapped condom. He placed the foil packet in Matthew's open palm.

'Put this on for me,' he said softly.

He leaned back, supporting his weight on his hands behind him. His cock stood up straight. Matthew tore the wrapper open with his teeth, he bent forward and placed a soft kiss on the ripe, swollen head before carefully rolling the condom down the engorged shaft. Glenn's cock throbbed at his touch. He caressed the cock with both hands, holding it, stroking, worshipping. Glenn closed his eyes and savoured the hands grazing his rubber-coated length.

He lowered himself back on to his elbows, gazing at Matthew through half-lidded eyes.

Matthew took a tube of lubricant out of the drawer and squeezed a huge blob of it into his palm. He rubbed his hands together, warming the sticky jelly. He started to kneed the cock between his hands again, rolling his palms from the root to the tip, getting it liberally coated in lube. Glenn sighed, savouring his slick caresses.

Matthew climbed on to the bed, on top of him. His knees pressing down on either side of his waist. He raised himself up and reached behind, taking Glenn's cock into his hand. He moved his hips in tight little circles. Glenn could feel the warm mouth of his arse brushing lightly over his throbbing head. He lowered his hips, the mouth pressing against his head, opening. It was tight. Glenn lay still, wanting this pleasure, this long anticipation, to last for ever. Matthew held him at the root and lowered his hips. The mouth of his arse stretched and widened and then suddenly it was open and his cock was inside. Matthew sank back, slowly impaling himself.

He stretched forward, lying down across Glenn's chest. Neither of them moved. Cock and arse were both still, one unit. They held each other, content to savour the sensation of their union. The reality that they were now one being.

For a long time they lay there, kissing, looking deep into each other's eyes. There was no need to speak. When they started to move they were hardly moving at all. They made love slowly, Matthew's hips scarcely stirring. His arsehole fluttered gently from within.

After an age Glenn rolled over on top of him, remaining inside, pushing him over on to his back and raising his legs around his waist. Even though he was on top he still made love to him slowly and tenderly, hardly moving inside him at all. He slid his hands beneath Matthew's arse, holding him, lifting him gently on to him, filling him.

Outside the window, the night sky turned black, creating long shadows in the room. Their silhouettes moved slowly against the wall, reflecting the gentle passion of their sexual union. In the soft light of a candle flame Glenn caught sight of the tears in Matthew's eyes.

When it seemed like they had made love for hours, they finally came together in long, gentle waves of pleasure. Matthew's cock throbbed and pulsed, sending out a steady stream of thick white semen. It spurted across their bellies, merging with the salty essence of sweat on their skin. Glenn broke inside him, his body trembling and pumping; his limbs quivered, his body racked with pleasure, pumping, spurting.

He collapsed against the wet body beneath him, holding it tightly in his arms. They lay trembling against each other, lost to the pleasure of each other's body in the warm, tender minutes of the night.

Glenn awoke around five. He did not know how long he had been asleep for. After the intensity of such profound sex, he had been exhausted and drained. The descent into sleep had been inescapable.

He woke up alone.

The bedclothes were tangled and damp, stained with the evidence of sex and still warm. But empty.

The house was silent and gloomy; all of the candles had burned out. Outside the window the grey fingers of morning were beginning to claw across the dark sky. Once the night eventually gave way, the day promised to be clear and bright.

Glenn rolled over in the gloom and switched on the bedside light. The two glasses of wine still stood beside the lamp, the contents barely touched. He propped himself up on one elbow and picked up his glass. The wine was warm and placid but it still managed to hit the right spot inside. He drained the glass.

With a sigh he swung his bare legs over the side of the bed.

Matthew was gone.

The house was empty and still.

He stood up and went into the bathroom. He took a piss without turning on the light. When he was finished he shook himself off and washed his hands. His tousled reflection stared back from the mirror above the basin. He almost didn't recognise himself in the shadowy light. He ran his wet hands through his hair, flattening down his sleepy spike.

So Matthew was gone. The adventure was over.

Nearly.

Despite the early hour the house was warm. Rather than pull on his robe, Glenn stepped into a clean pair of shorts and walked from the bedroom through into his study. He took Matthew's wineglass with him.

The curtains had been open all night. He opened the window wide, allowing the fresh morning breeze to clear the last cobwebs of sleep from his mind.

He turned towards his computer. In the dull light he could see that something was stuck to the screen. A Post-it note. He turned on the light and picked up the note. The writing flowed neatly across the small square of orange paper. It was from Matthew.

Happy endings work best!
love M.

Glenn smiled. He stuck the Post-it note down on top of his desk along with the glass of wine and switched on the computer. The hard drive began to purr and whirl as the machine slowly woke itself up.

Glenn sat down in his chair and waited.

He did not question what he was about to do. A more rational mind would have doubted its own sanity. Had the events of the past week been anything but a fantasy?

Had he not just woken up from the most vivid dream he had ever had?

Glenn did not have to ask.

The Windows icons had loaded on the screen before him. He selected the word-processor program and double-clicked the mouse. More purrs as the program opened. He scrolled down the file names, selected 'Story Outline' and double-clicked. When the document opened he deleted the entire contents.

Now he was faced with a blank screen. A blank page waiting to be filled with whatever he cared to imagine.

He picked up Matthew's wineglass and held it up to the empty screen.

'Here's to a happy ending,' he said.

He took a sip from the glass and put it back down. He took a deep breath, his fingers poised over the keyboard, and after a moment of fond contemplation he began to type.

IDOL NEW BOOKS

Information correct at time of printing. For up-to-date availability,
pleasse check www.idol-books.co.uk

MAESTRO
Published in May   Peter Slater

A young Spanish cello player, Ramon, journeys to the castle of master cellist Ernesto
Cavallo in the hope of masterclasses from the great musician. Ramon's own music is
technically perfect, but his playing lacks a certain essence – and so, Maestro Cavallo
arranges for Ramon to undergo a number of sexual trials in this darkly erotic, extremely
well-written novel.
£8.99/$10.95   ISBN 0 352 33511 4

FELLOWSHIP OF IRON
Published in July   Jack Stevens

Mike is a gym owner and a successful competitive bodybuilder. He lives the life of the
body beautiful and everything seems to be going swimmingly. So when his mentor and
former boyfriend Dave dies after using illegal steroids, Mike is determined to find out who
supplied his ex with drugs.
£8.99/$10.95   ISBN 0 352 33512 2

THE PHEROMONE BOMB
Published in September   Edward Ellis

A crack army unit – the Special Marine Corps, consisting of five British and five American
soldiers – are on a top-secret mission to investigate, and if necessary eliminate, an illegal
private army on a tropical island in the mid-Atlantic. What the tough, hard soldiers realise
when they investigate the island is that the enemy doesn't shoot them with bullets. The
enemy has discovered a powerful weapon: the pheromone bomb, which produces a gas –
and anyone on whom the gas settles is filled with irresistible homoerotic urges.
£8.99/$10.95   ISBN 0 352 33543 2

Also published:

DARK RIDER
Jack Gordon

While the rulers of a remote Scottish island play bizarre games of sexual dominance with
the Argentinian Angelo, his friend Robert – consumed with jealous longing for his coffee-
skinned companion – assuages his desires with the willing locals.
£6.99/$9.95   ISBN 0 352 33243 3

☐

VENETIAN TRADE
Richard Davis

From the deck of the ship that carries him into Venice, Rob Weaver catches his first glimpse of a beautiful but corrupt city where the dark alleys and misty canals hide debauchery and decadence. Here, he must learn to survive among men who would make him a plaything and a slave.

£6.99/$9.95

ISBN 0 352 33323 5

☐

THE LOVE OF OLD EGYPT
Philip Markham

It's 1925 and the deluxe cruiser carrying the young gigolo Jeremy Hessling has docked at Luxor. Jeremy dreams of being dominated by the Pharaohs of old, but quickly becomes involved with someone more accessible – Khalid, a young man of exceptional beauty.

£6.99/$9.95

ISBN 0 352 33354 5

☐

THE BLACK CHAMBER
Jack Gordon

Educated at the court of George II, Calum Monroe finds his native Scotland a dull, damp place. He relieves his boredom by donning a mask and holding up coaches in the guise of the Fox – a dashing highwayman. Chance throws him and neighbouring farmer Fergie McGregor together with Calum's sinister, perverse guardian, James Black.

£6.99/$9.95

ISBN 0 352 33373 1

☐

BOOTY BOYS
Jay Russell

Hard-bodied black British detective Alton Davies can't believe his eyes or his luck when he finds muscular African-American gangsta rapper Banji-B lounging in his office early one morning. Alton's disbelief – and his excitement – mounts as Banji-B asks him to track down a stolen videotape of a post-gig orgy.

£7.99/$10.95

ISBN 0 352 33446 0

☐

EASY MONEY
Bob Condron

One day an ad appears in the popular music press. Its aim: to enlist members for a new boyband. Young, working-class Mitch starts out as a raw recruit, but soon he becomes embroiled in the sexual tension that threatens to engulf the entire group. As the band soars meteorically to pop success, the atmosphere is quickly reaching fever pitch.

£7.99/$10.95

ISBN 0 352 33442 8

☐

SUREFORCE
Phil Votel

Not knowing what to do with his life once he's been thrown out of the army, Matt takes a job with the security firm Sureforce. Little does he know that the job is the ultimate mix of business and pleasure, and it's not long before Matt's hanging with the beefiest, meanest, hardest lads in town.

£7.99/$10.95

ISBN 0 352 33444 4

THE FAIR COP
Philip Markham

The Second World War is over and America is getting back to business as usual. In 1950s New York, that means dirty business. Hanson's a detective who's been dealt a lousy hand, but the Sullivan case is his big chance. How many junior detectives get handed blackmail, murder and perverted sex all in one day?

£7.99/$10.95 ISBN 0 352 33445 2

HOT ON THE TRAIL
Lukas Scott

The Midwest, 1849. *Hot on the Trail* is the story of the original American dream, where freedom is driven by wild passion. And when farmboy Brett skips town and encounters dangerous outlaw Luke Mitchell, sparks are bound to fly in this raunchy tale of hard cowboys, butch outlaws, dirty adventure and true grit.

£7.99/$10.95 ISBN 0 352 33461 4

STREET LIFE
Rupert Thomas

Ben is eighteen and tired of living in the suburbs. As there's little sexual adventure to be found there, he decides to run away from both A-levels and his comfortable home – to a new life in London. There, he's befriended by Lee, a homeless Scottish lad who offers him a friendly ear and the comfort of his sleeping bag.

£7.99/$10.95 ISBN 0 352 33374 X